Marked

Marked

LAURA WILLIAMS McCAFFREY

WITH ILLUSTRATIONS BY
Sally Cantirino

CLARION BOOKS
Houghton Mifflin Harcourt
Boston New York

Clarion Books

3 Park Avenue

New York, New York 10016

Copyright © 2016 by Laura Williams McCaffrey

Illustrations copyright © 2016 by Sally Cantirino

www.hmhco.com

The text was set in Adobe Caslon.

Library of Congress Cataloging-in-Publication Data
McCaffrey, Laura Williams.
Marked / Laura Williams McCaffrey.
pages cm
Summary: Sixteen-year-old Lyla lives in a bleak, controlling society where only the
brightest and most favored students succeed. When she is caught buying cheats in an
underground shadow market, she is tattooed — marked — as a criminal. Then she is offered
redemption and jumps at the chance, but it comes at a high cost, and doing what is
right means betraying the boy she has come to love. — Provided by publisher.
ISBN 978-0-547-23556-1 (hardback)
[1. Survival — Fiction. 2. Love — Fiction. 3. Criminals — Fiction. 4. Science fiction.]   I. Title.
PZ7.M122835Mar 2016
[Fic] — dc23
2015013604

Manufactured in the United States of America
DOC 10 9 8 7 6 5 4 3 2 1
4500577315

For Em and Will — tried and true

Marked

—CHAPTER ONE—

LYLA'S eyes opened. Darkness. Cold. The walls, too close, the ceiling, too low, crept toward her.

The room isn't squeezing shut. But she saw the walls press toward her and the ceiling sink. They closed her into a small, tight, airless cell, and then kept pressing in on her. She gripped the thin blanket, no protection at all.

Listen. She always forgot to listen. Coming through the dark was the sound of slow deep breaths drawing in, drifting out. Hope slept nearby, calm and quiet.

Lyla shut her eyes and listened hard. Matching her breath to Hope's, she took air in. Then, breath matching breath, she pushed air out.

In and out, with Hope. Their paired breaths sounded like one breath, one person. The walls and ceiling lifted away.

———

The second time Lyla woke, she gave up on sleep. Trying not to think of her airless, shut-in-the-cell night terrors, she lit a candle stub and climbed to the top of the farmhouse, into the small warm room she and Hope called the Aerie. She sat, careful not to let her feet brush over the piano keyboard painted on the floor near one wall. When Hope played the painted keys, she tilted her head as if she truly heard notes, and Lyla couldn't help treating the keys as though sound could rise from them.

The night terrors had started two weeks ago, not so long after Teacher Slate had invited her into her secondary school's Advanced Studies room, which kids mostly called the Bright. She'd finally earned scores good enough to win a seat in the Bright. Yet primary alchemyks was far more confusing than she'd thought it was going to be. It was like a strange language but also like a strange mathyk: a blend of numbers, symbols, letters, and words that you used to form equations. And she wasn't any good at learning them. But no primary alchemyks, no patron. No patron, no university. She'd be stuck grubbing for credit points the rest of her life. She wasn't going to let that happen.

Heat seeped through the floorboards and warmed the backs of her legs and heels. The sight of her Aerie wall floated her spirits up. Drawings she'd ripped from old paperzines and broadsheets, along with her one letter, covered the wall: a paneled zine strip of lanky Pirate Jackman in his old-fashioned black trousers and his wide-brimmed black hat; a zine panel of Lady Captain grinning from beneath her floppy brown hat; a glossy roof-leaper at night, the lacy glow of its nose, its undercarriage propellers, and its wings; the letter, with an ink drawing of an actual book, inviting her into the Bright; a large broadsheet of the university's tall, red brick library with its sign proclaiming AN OPEN DOOR FOR ALL WITH TALENT AND DILIGENCE.

There was also a lot to float up her spirits outside the Aerie's small window, down the dark hillside toward town. Though it was early, lights brighter and steadier than any candle's light already shone here and there: amber, blue, rose. Glittering, silent ice-ships skimmed the river ice, heading toward other towns downriver, or maybe even farther south, toward the cities. On the Hill, the steepest part of Hill's Ridge, where she lived, but nearer town, the many lights at the Project shone like a thick layer of red-orange coals. Trying to hold the shine of these lights within her, Lyla closed her eyes. She vowed for the millionth time to earn the scores she needed to keep her seat in the Bright. She vowed to become an inventor and construct clean, lovely machines. One day, she would be surrounded by sleek metal and light.

She heard Hope call from below, "Lyla?"

"Coming," she said, and climbed down from the Aerie.

In the dim candlelight of their bedroom, Hope was combing her smooth black curls. Even with sleep-droopy eyelids she was beautiful. "You couldn't sleep again?" she asked. "Have you been up for a while?"

"Not long."

Hope leaned over and kissed Lyla's temple. "Poor Ly."

"I'm all right."

Hope fetched hot water from the kitchen stove, and they sponged off. Then Lyla took her trousers from the well-sanded hooks Da had made for their bedroom in the fall, and she held them up in front of her. A patch in the backside was wearing thin. "I wish I could get new trousers. And boots."

"They've ripped through?" Hope asked.

"No—"

"We don't have the credit points, Ly."

"I know that, Hope. I said 'wish.'"

Hope's eyebrows rose in the way that meant, *Better not to wish after what you can't have.* But Hope only said, "I'll warm coffee. If we hurry we'll have time to walk by the university."

Why Hope couldn't simply say, "Me too," once in a while, Lyla didn't understand.

She quickly pulled on a sweater and trousers, and carried the candle down the dark hallway to the kitchen. "Coffee?" Hope lifted the percolator off the cookstove, poured poor-man's coffee into a mug, and handed it to Lyla.

Lyla raised the mug to her face. It smelled faintly of burned chicory roots. "Seems a little weak."

"I ran Ma and Da's grounds through again. The grounds were cold—Ma and Da must've left pretty early. Did you hear them?"

"No. I didn't hear them come home last night, either. They must be taking long shifts." Lyla's stomach growled; she wanted porridge, but she knew they were out. In the last few weeks, there'd been grain shortages in the shops. Words suddenly wrote themselves on the insides of her eyelids: *There'll be grain for sale at the next shadow market.* No, she couldn't risk going to another. Not ever again.

"You all right?" Hope asked. "You sound hungry."

"Yeah. I'm just eager to drink this."

Hope started to laugh. "Sure you are."

Lyla gulped it down. "Let's get on. So we can go by the university."

Lyla pulled on her coat and knit cap, and then she followed Hope outside. Together, they rushed over the packed-snow path through the clearing. They passed the barn, which leaned as though the north wind had reached out a hand and given it a shove. They passed the pines that didn't quite hide the remains of the old stream-driven tiller. The rust-red metal handles and tines poked up through the snow.

When the girls left their farm's path for the larger path, they went faster. The Hill was usually safe, but not always. Ever watchful, Hope walked with her back so straight, she seemed more than two inches taller and eighteen months older than Lyla. She had a graceful sway that made Lyla feel frizzy, bent, and short. Yet Lyla couldn't blame her sister for being so beautiful. The two slipped together over the ice-glazed snow and caught each other, holding tight and finding their balance.

Hope kept glancing at the horizon and the dawn orange. "I don't know if we'll have time."

"We left early enough," Lyla assured her.

Nearer town, they reached Project Road. Several banners hung from a rope strung between two trees: YOU'RE INVITED — 4TH MONTH 4 — THE PROJECT UNVEILED! and THE TOWN COUNCILOR'S PROJECT: PROTEAN POWER FOR EVERY HOME. Looking down that road, Lyla could see the fence and guards around the Project's long walls. The gabled towers at each corner stood far taller than the walls, their triangular windows illuminated pale yellow.

Lyla deliberately slowed, refusing to scurry across Project Road even though members of Red Fist might be lurking. A year or so ago, she'd stood before Town Councilor Hall with everyone else and she'd listened with a feeling fluttering inside her that she didn't have a name for. Surprise? Excitement? The town councilor announced that the prime councilor and senators had called for an era of charity among barons. Across Highland, town and city councilors, along with other barons, would build "Projects"—workshops where inventors would construct revolutionary machines that would make "clean Protean power affordable for all." None of the Projects had yet been unveiled, but since the councilor's announcement, the Projects all over Highland had become Red Fist targets, just like the one here in Hill's Ridge. So close to where Lyla walked, Red Fists had kept trying to break through the Project's fences. They knew that inside there'd be plenty of metal and other supplies to steal. Plenty to sell in their shadow markets.

The path leveled and curved, from trees to town. Just as Hope asked, "Do you smell that?" Lyla smelled something burning. A column of smoke rose from the center of town, the location of the university. Hope whispered, "Red Fist."

Lyla's feet drew her forward. "Wait," Hope said. "We shouldn't go that way."

"We'll be careful."

Hope shook her head, but she kept walking beside Lyla. On

Main Street they passed diggers who hauled shovels and pipes; two women bundled in the kind of brightly colored, thin wraps that merchants wore, whispering in short, sharp bursts. A huge digger walked ahead, a broad guy with a loping walk. Lyla leaned forward. Was it Gillis Waterhouse? No; when the guy turned to the left, that side of his face was unscarred.

"Look at that big guy's arm," murmured Hope. "Marked." Lyla glimpsed a dark line on his wrist, and she crossed with Hope, at the corner, to avoid him.

The smoke clogged Lyla's nose. In the narrow street, a blue peace officer snow-cruiser sped by, its rounded glass and metal body studded with lights like jewels. Its back tread circled, and its front skis bumped over the packed snow, taking it up the hill toward the smoke. Sirens called out a throaty undulating cry. More snow-cruisers careened past, so quickly, their treads and skis barely seemed to touch the ground.

Lyla sped up, pulling Hope along. They neared the prison, a flat-topped concrete building with windows like barred eyes looking down the hillside. Behind the windows were shifting forms. Inside the high barbed wire fence, guards stood in their blue caps and long blue overcoats. One at the fence's edge craned his head to peer up the slope in the direction of the university, and readjusted his rifle strap.

Hope slowed. "We should go back and take the Digger Street route instead."

"We'll just look," Lyla whispered.

"We have to keep out of the way."

They shouldn't get too close to a Red Fist attack or talk to Marked near an attack. These weren't official safety laws, but might as well have been. "We won't go close," Lyla said.

The officer with the rifle was looking at them. Lyla raised a hand in hello. He gave her a long, studying stare.

Hope whispered, "We should turn back."

"No. We'd look like we're trying to hide." Though going forward might make them look too interested in the attack. Sometimes there didn't seem to be any right thing to do.

As they passed the fence edge where the officer stood, he nodded at them. Then he turned away and studied the smoke.

"We aren't Red Fists. Or Marked," Lyla whispered to Hope, quickening her pace as they headed toward the smoke. "We should be able to walk where we want."

"No one says we can't."

But we're thinking we should turn away, Lyla wanted to point out. Instead of having the same old argument, she led Hope to the corner where Main Street met University Street. Hope said, "There still may be Red Fists nearby."

"If we have to, we'll bolt." Lyla grasped Hope's hand more tightly, a tense knot. They walked around the corner onto University Street.

Set back from the street, on the slope, the university's brick buildings still towered, whole and grand. Undulating lights still shone from the stained-glass windows. Some baron's roof-leaper— undercarriage propellers whirring, bright metal wings wide— soared from a peaked copper roof and glided through the sky.

The university was safe. Hope's mittened hand squeezed Lyla's, and Lyla squeezed back. Hope murmured, "It'll be all right."

Hope sounded more reassuring than certain. Across the way, on the far block, Lyla saw that a corner of the wrought-iron fence that surrounded the university was broken. Twisted chunks of its metal lay on the ground. Fire officers sprayed a burning guard tower with streams of water. Near them, peace officers spoke to a cluster of inventors, merchants, and diggers. One officer followed a hound that sniffed at the sidewalk, searching for a scent. "Red Fists broke the fence." Smoke stung the inside of Lyla's nose. "I can't believe they broke the university fence. How can they possibly think they could get in to steal anything that way?"

"Maybe they don't. Maybe they just broke it to show they can. To scare us." Hope was scanning the gathering crowd as if she thought someone near them might be a Red Fist crazy. "We should get on."

Lyla started quickly around a pair of merchants and then around tired-faced diggers covered in black mine dirt, pushing herself through the tangle.

"Wait," Hope called.

As Lyla shoved to the edge of the sidewalk, black and red swirls painted on the rim of a gutter grille caught her eye. They looked like an abstract pattern, but only to anyone who didn't know how to recognize shadow-market codes. Lyla stopped short and read the code hidden in the pattern: S 247. The location and date of the next Red Fist shadow market.

"What's wrong?" asked Hope, catching up to her.

"Nothing." She pulled Hope away from the code before an officer noticed it, and them standing near it. Lyla tried to scrape the message out of her mind, but it stayed emblazoned there: S 247. "Look. The other end of the university—it's perfectly fine."

She drew Hope away from the Red Fist attack and the Red Fist code, up two blocks, and across the street that ran past the university fence's many wrought-iron bars with wrought-iron flowers. The sirens quieted, and despite the drifting smoke, Lyla smelled food on a gust of wind: cooking meat and bread. Her almost-empty stomach threatened to collapse in on itself. Within the fence, at the end of a broad walkway, the library stood taller than the other buildings around it. Its older walls, built before the wars, were dark red. During the wars, spiritualists from the south, Gray Cloaks, fought barons because they thought Protean was an abomination. The walls that had been restored since the Gray Cloaks invaded and shattered them were lighter and pinker. One of the library's top corners was emblazoned with the number 7—the seventh university in Highland that barons completely repaired after the end of the wars. The top floor of the library was ringed with stained-glass windows. Names of inventors from the Great Invention Era shone blue, green, red, orange, and yellow in the pale winter light.

At the same time, as if sharing the same thought, Lyla and Hope turned the corner and walked toward the university's large gate. They stopped far from the two wrought-iron doors so that the guards in the brick towers wouldn't worry too much. They stood by the sign that proclaimed AN OPEN DOOR FOR ALL WITH TALENT AND DILIGENCE.

From across the street, a group of people walked toward the gate. They were university students, wearing long brown wool coats buttoned high against the cold. Their skin, no matter how fair or dark, was smooth and unchapped, likely protected by soft salves. They looked more serious, more studious, than the students who came to the club where Lyla worked with Hope, the Beacon. A few carried cups with tops—surely, thick real coffee with heavy cream and white sugar. The biggest guy wore a leather sack slung across his front. He hugged it, and his eyes scanned the street as if he expected someone to run up and try to grab it from him. The sack wasn't bulky, and its rounded shape didn't offer any clue as to what was in it. Lyla tried not to stare at him; she didn't want to look like a Red Fist thief.

One student, tall and thin, smiled at the others, though worry lines creased his forehead. "The officers will put out the fire, Mina," he said to a girl with many, long thick braids. "The fence can easily be fixed. Red Fist will have to slag off." He draped his arm around her.

She managed a smile. "For a skinny boy, you sure are heavy."

"Nah. You're just weak." He slumped against her, and she listed to the side.

"And since when have you had an earring?" Mina craned her neck to get a better look at his ear.

"Jimmy did it last night," he said. "What do you think, beloved?"

"I don't know if I like a boy in diamonds," said Mina. They all laughed, their graveness gone for a moment. Then they fell silent as one of them opened the gate with a key. After pulling the gate shut behind them, they headed in the direction of the library.

"Remember Mina?" Hope stared at the students. "She lived on Digger Street. A university inventor became her patron after she earned highest scores both her years in Advanced Studies."

Lyla peered through the bars at Mina. "I don't remember her. What class was she in?"

"Two years ahead of mine. She's been here more than a year."

"You earn high scores in Advanced Studies." Lyla couldn't say that she earned them too, because thus far she hadn't. "And I'm going to work harder." The dark, bold shadow-market code—S 247—filled her mind; if only she could remember Advanced Studies alchemyk symbols and words as easily. "I'm going to learn alchemyks really well. Better than anything else."

Mina and the rest climbed the library's granite steps. As they disappeared through the doorway, a couple of people on the library roof tossed a handful of small, bright metal things into the air. Lyla didn't know what the metal things were—a cloud of tiny Protean-powered machines?—but they were lovely. They glittered and circled like dozens of tiny fireflies.

"Let's get to Advanced Studies," said Hope.

Lyla stood at the wrought-iron gate a moment longer, not going. She stared at the granite steps, the paneled oak doors, the tall and spacious red-brick buildings, the window-shine, and the circling glitter beyond the bars.

PIRATE JACKMAN

THREATENED ALCHEMYKS

Threatened Alchemyks, episode 1

The *Great Northern Wars* continued. Gray Cloaks invaded and occupied more land.

The Cloak scourge destroyed all inventions. Far and wide, they preached the spiritualist superstition that Protean was created by "demons." They preached that inventors who built machines powered by Protean would break the world.

Their most recent law: The penalty for learning was death.

The Prime Councilor protected the few universities he could—and continued the fight.

The Cloaks tried to destroy every university in the land. The books they spared during attacks, they brought to their church in the capital and burned.

—CHAPTER TWO—

LYLA rolled the zine tightly and returned it to the pocket inside her coat. Leaving one of the school's cold, forgotten hallways, she smiled to herself. She was going to love this Pirate Jackman story, she could already tell. Usually, when Pirate Jackman and Lady Captain saved something, it was books or people or inventions that ended up in a big university in a big city. But *First Book of Alchemyk Equations* was important everywhere. Every university in Highland now had a copy, including the university in Hill's Ridge. She knew, all kids knew, that one of the things you had to do when you became a university student was memorize it.

As Lyla took a shortcut through a hallway where unused desks were stacked, she was filled with the silly, wild-hearted, little-girl wish she often had after reading *Pirate Jackman*—that she lived a hundred years ago and was a runner, fighting the Gray Cloaks, like the legendary Pirate Jackman and Lady Captain; that she ran supplies to the prime councilor's forces, saved refugees, and carried inventioneering books like *First Book of Alchemyk Equations,* which she'd rescued from destroyed universities, to the high plateaus where the free universities stood tall.

Instead she had to get to the Bright before she was late. Hope, of course, hadn't stopped in the hallway to read the *Jackman* in the zine they'd bought on the street. She'd gone straight to Advanced Studies, as she preferred to call the Bright. Lyla knew she should have gone too, but she couldn't help herself when it came to *Pirate Jackman.*

She neared a couple of Digger Street kids, who smelled like they hadn't washed in a week. Their sleeves hung partially over their hands, so she couldn't tell if they were Marked or not. She swerved to the opposite side of the hallway anyway. It was always best to stay away. She didn't want to end up like Jaime LaMer, who'd earned great scores in the Bright examinations last year but hadn't been recommended by his teachers to any patrons because he ran around with Marked. He hadn't been able to go to the university. As Lyla passed the Digger Street kids, she thought she heard one whisper, "S 247," the code for the next shadow market. Where there was food she couldn't afford to buy anywhere else: tender, juicy fruit, shipped from the southlands.

Trying to forget her empty stomach and food, Lyla walked quickly down the hallway. Even though she could see the white clouds of her own breath, she was suddenly overwarm, sweat beading at her hairline. Trips to the Bright always made her sweat. "In Advanced Studies, you learn only the simplest alchemyks, the basics of the language and the easiest equations," Teacher Slate had said to her on her second day. "If you can't learn these, there's no point in winning a patron. You won't be able to learn or to use higher alchemyks. There won't be any reason for you to continue to the university." *I'm trying to learn them,* Lyla had silently insisted. She was trying hard, yet she'd never before done so poorly in a class.

Entering the Bright was like entering a different school. The wood stove warmed the room without smoking. Sunlight shone through a large window. The air was clear. A broadsheet was tacked up in the corner by the window. Figures at the bottom wore ragged coats, like diggers and squatties. Above them stood farmers, with steam tillers, and officers in various uniforms. Above these stood merchants, some of whom reached down and handed sacks to the farmers and diggers, who gave them handfuls of paper slips — credit points. Other merchants reached toward the topmost figures, the barons. A couple of barons wore the black robes of senators, and one, the highest, stood at a podium that said PRIME COUNCILOR. Lyla often found herself staring at the broadsheet's dirt road, which wound from the picture's bottom corner to its top. A figure climbed the steep road, leaving the diggers and squatties behind and passing the merchants, heading upward toward the barons. Above the barons, in delicate black lettering: *Everyman Can Climb.* Lyla always wondered why it was "Everyman," like a name, instead of "Everybody" or "Every Man." She'd asked Teacher Slate, and he'd asked, "Why do you think?"

She didn't know, and this made her keep wondering, which was likely the reason Teacher Slate always answered questions with questions — to keep you thinking.

Lyla didn't head straight for her desk. Instead she walked

close to Teacher Slate's desk and the wrought-iron frame above it, which held the light—a large glass orb encircled by a shade of gauzy off-white paper. Within the orb, clear slender tubes connected at the glass's highest point to a thin foil wafer, and they spiraled downward through the orb. The tubes shone softly, as did the colored-glass moths that had been formed to perch on the spirals, their rose, yellow, and orange wings outstretched. Delicate glass and glow. If the inventor who built the orb sold it to another baron, she would likely earn more than Lyla's parents earned digging in the mines all winter.

Before Teacher Slate had invited Lyla into the Bright, the only orbs she'd seen up close were at work at the Beacon. This one was on loan to the Bright from an inventor who'd told Teacher Slate she hoped it would inspire students to study hard so they might one day construct their own startling Protean-powered inventions. The orb didn't actually look as though anything powered it, but Lyla knew somewhere within it—perhaps in the foil that connected to all the clear tubes—was a sliver of Protean. Protean in its solid state, Teacher Slate said, looked like golden pine pitch, and in its liquid state, like honey; its gaseous state, like sun-bathed fog; its light state, like a sunbeam. Occasionally Protean altered to a sound state and became like a whirring dragonfly wing in flight. It had taken hundreds of inventors over hundreds of years to develop alchemyks: the study of ways to fix Protean in a solid state and harness its raw, unpredictable power. A century ago, inventors had discovered how they might build machines that ran on Protean power. The machines built now were smaller and sleeker than those early ones, as well as vastly stronger. Lyla never longed to learn how to fix Da's smoking, steaming tiller, but staring into the Bright's light, she tried to notice every single detail. One day she'd construct her own large, dazzling orb, a glass moth of indigo shine.

"Northstrom?" Teacher Slate's voice, from behind her, was soft but commanding. "Are you planning to take your seat?"

Pulling her gaze away from the orb, Lyla turned toward Teacher Slate, who sat directly behind her in his wheeled chair. His massive hands tapped the wheels, as they frequently did when he wasn't rolling from desk to desk, lecturing, discussing, calling out questions. "Yes, of course, sir. Sorry."

"That's fine, Northstrom. But please go on. It's time to begin," he said, already starting to roll away from her.

She headed for her seat. From the corner of her eye, she saw Teacher crossing the room the way he sometimes did when impatient with them, spinning his wheels with short sharp pushes.

She hurried past Cornelia Millener and the guy whose name she always forgot; past Hope, who was already looking intently at a leaflet on her desk. Lyla sat at her own seat, her *own* desk of smooth, polished light-colored wood. A leaflet lay before her, still folded. She opened it and found the first page covered with many rows: strings of symbols. She couldn't remember the uses of a single one.

Teacher said in his clear, quick voice, "This is a practice test, to help you prepare for our upcoming examination. First years, these are all symbols we've learned in the last week or so. In the spaces beside them, write their names and at least two of their uses. Second years, yours include any equation you've learned since fall." Swinging his chair to face them, he looked directly at Lyla with his widely spaced, dark eyes. "You have no more than thirty clicks to complete your work. We have to pick up the pace."

Hope gave Lyla a glance, as if Lyla wouldn't otherwise realize that Teacher was talking directly to her, and she wanted to sink beneath her desk. She bent until her face was so near the test, she almost touched it with her nose. *No going drippy,* Lady Captain's voice said inside her. Lyla searched for at least one symbol she recognized.

"Northstrom."

Straightening with a quick jerk, she found she was looking directly at Teacher Slate. She fought an almost overwhelming urge to glance down at his too thin, too still legs; she stared at his very square, long forehead, and his deep-set eyes. "Yes, sir."

"Learning these is tough for you," he stated plainly.

"Yes, sir." She rushed on, before he could say, *So it'd be best for you to leave the Advanced Studies room.* "I'm studying harder. I'm learning it."

"Your computation skills are solid, Northstrom. It's the symbols you struggle with? They seem like meaningless shapes?"

"Yes, sir. I know I have to practice lots."

"Probably more than most, to receive passing scores and keep your seat," he said. Then to her surprise, he smiled a little sadly. "Life isn't always fair."

She struggled again to keep herself from looking at his legs, though maybe he was thinking of some other unfair thing in his life—that he was only a secondary-school teacher trained to teach primary alchemyks, instead of a full inventor. She smiled a little in return. "Yes, sir."

"So, do what you have to, Northstrom." He rapped his knuckles twice on her desk. Then he started to roll away, saying to the whole class, "I've been distracting Northstrom. So she'll have a chance to answer fully, I'm giving you five extra clicks."

A soft *woohoo* came from someone near the wood stove.

"Quiet," Teacher Slate said, turning his head in the direction of the sound, but Lyla thought she saw a fleeting smile before he faced forward again. He was pretty decent, for a teacher.

The clicks passed. Teacher rolled back and forth at the front of the room, a kind of pacing. Lyla tried to remember what she'd learned about the alchemyk symbols. In her lap, she squeezed one hand with the other.

Movement to the side caught her eye. It was the thin Digger Street guy who'd failed Teacher's last examination, Dane. He was in danger of losing his seat in the Bright. Dane looked from his practice test to a tiny piece of paper cupped in his hand. He read this paper, and then he added a note to those he already had on his test.

Lyla bent lower over her test. She wasn't sure whether or not Teacher expected them to squeal on one another; regardless, she'd rather not know enough about anyone else to be able to squeal.

She put her fingers next to two symbols. They looked similar, but they had very different uses in formulas and equations, like two words that sounded the same but meant very different things. She tried to recall which symbol meant what.

She could hear Dane writing. The small paper he held was likely an alchemyks cheat that he'd bought in the shadow market from a Red Fist. Lyla had never actually been close enough to cheats to read them, but they were supposed to have shortcuts and notes, secretly written by actual Advanced Studies teachers and university students in exchange for credit points. The notes made primary alchemyks easier to understand; everybody had heard of at least one kid who'd gotten high scores in Advanced Studies because of cheats. But everybody had also heard of kids who'd bought sham cheats—made-up words and symbols some Red Fist had written just to trick desperate Advanced Studies students into giving over credit points. Kids who used shams failed their examinations.

Lyla couldn't help wishing that Dane's cheat was a sham. Which wasn't nice. But if he did well, that might mean someone who struggled with primary alchemyks would have to choose— become a cheater who traded in the shadow market and keep a seat in the Bright, or stay honest but lose the seat and the chance to go to the university.

By the time Teacher told them to stop, Lyla's eyes were bleary and she still had a few blanks on her test. Dane rose and walked up the aisle to return his test to Teacher. He cradled it near his chest, so Lyla couldn't see what he'd written. She followed close behind him.

Dane held his test out to Teacher, and, taking it, Teacher gave it a brief top-to-bottom glance. Then he studied it more closely. He looked up at Dane. "Very thorough," he said in his quiet way. "Nice work."

Dane grinned. Lyla's Lady Captain voice silently spoke at his back: *Cheating slag.*

Then Lyla stood before Teacher and handed over her test. He scanned the cream paper and her ink writing. Her letters were messy, she suddenly realized, and she'd left a lot of answer spaces blank.

Teacher looked up at her. "Next session, you should study with him." Teacher gestured in the direction of Dane, who was still grinning as he scooped up his sack and coat. "Or your sister. You'll have to do much better than this on our upcoming examination."

Lyla felt her head nodding like a floppy doll's on its flimsy neck. She stopped. "Yes, sir. All right."

"Good." Teacher Slate tossed the test on his desk. "If you need more help than they give you, make an appointment with me. Before the examination."

"Yes, sir." She'd study with Hope and make an appointment only if she really had to, so he wouldn't think she'd given up on trying to do better on her own. "Sir . . ." She almost said Dane's name, but she hated squealing.

"Northstrom?"

"Never mind, sir." Ahead, Dane left the room, his smile still huge. "I'm sorry."

"You don't need to be sorry. Just work harder."

"Yes, sir. That's what I meant. I will."

"I look forward to seeing you do so. You should get along to your next class." Teacher tapped his fingers against the wheels of his chair. "Time's short."

Time's short, his tapping fingers seemed to repeat. *Time's short, time's short.*

S 247. At the shadow market, there would be cheats. There were always cheats. *I'm not a cheater.*

—CHAPTER THREE—

LYLA sat in the Aerie with her homework, weather observation sheets, on the floor by her crossed legs, and she stared out the window at the night sky. It was overcast, so there wasn't much weather to observe. She tried to think of alchemyk symbols and their uses. Instead: *S 247.*

Before she found out that Da regularly went to shadow markets, she hadn't understood why anyone would go. Then, several months ago, on one of the afternoons Hope had to practice piano for a school performance, Lyla was walking through town on her own. Ahead of her, on Digger Street, she spotted Da, though he'd told her that morning he had to work a double shift up at the mines. He stopped at the metalware shop door, and when she caught up with him, he acted very strange, insisting she leave him and go home. When she told Hope about Da, Hope's eyes became overbright. Hope said that Da sometimes went to shadow markets. How else did Lyla think Da brought home flour when there was so little to find anywhere, or chocolate flakes, or metal he needed to fix the steam scythe? How did he and Ma always have enough soothers to prevent Mine Cough? Stunned, Lyla had said, "But the mine owners give them soothers. And the rest—he goes to the shops. He buys them."

"You know that sometimes the mine owners don't have enough soothers to give out. Most diggers end up with Mine Cough now and again, but Da and Ma almost never do." Hope's voice shook. "Besides, think on what metalware costs. When something breaks and we're really low on credit points, how does Da buy so much? How can he possibly afford it all?"

Lyla hadn't answered. She had felt stupid.

According to Hope, Da had bought goods and soothers in the shadow markets their whole lives. Yet he didn't have any marks. Either peace officers hadn't caught him, or they'd caught him only before the Marks Law was passed five years ago. Back before Red Fist attacked the library in the capital, burning a section of the building and stealing a couple of books, and before the senate passed the safety laws, to stop Red Fist once and for all. Back when peace officers didn't mark anyone, so you didn't know who to cross the street to avoid, but you also didn't have to be afraid you'd get a blue prison-bar tattoo on your own right wrist. Somehow, it seemed worse to not only have a file at the prison the barons could read, but to also end up one of the Marked. *Everyone* could see a mark on you. People could shift seats to avoid you; they could insist on searching your bags before you entered school; they could tell your boss that only unmarked were allowed to serve their dinner or drinks. A lot of Marked weren't able to get jobs anywhere but the mines. Lyla's boss at the Beacon rarely hired Marked. Did someone really deserve to end up down a mine hole forever just because he got caught once at a shadow market?

Sometimes Lyla half hated barons, even though she wanted to be one. They didn't care if a law that was good for them wasn't so good for merchants or farmers or diggers. They didn't care if you needed something—*needed,* not just wanted—that the shops didn't have or that merchants charged more credit points for than you could afford. They thought if you could get what you needed only in the shadow market, you should do without. Once Lyla became an inventor, and earned enough gold for the prime councilor to name her a baron, she wouldn't forget what it was like to do without.

The first time Lyla snuck to the shadow market, she had gone because she had needed to. Hope had gotten a sliver while hauling wood, which she couldn't dig out, and the cut had filled with pus. None of the usual poultices worked. "It'll get better eventually," Hope said to her. "And you're not allowed to tell Ma and Da. They can't waste credit points on ointment. It's too costly." Hope washed the cut over and over, scrubbing it until her eyes watered.

Lyla hadn't wanted to break her promise to not tell Ma and Da, so she had decided to secretly search out the next shadow market. She discovered that her classmate Cornelia Millener knew about Red Fist codes. Cornelia said the codes and the ways you used them changed frequently so the peace officers wouldn't crack them. She often found them out, and she taught Lyla how to do it herself. She also said Lyla could always ask her for them.

So Lyla used the code, which was oddly fun. It was like solving a puzzle—a real puzzle, not just a computation puzzle some teacher wrote on a piece of paper so he could put an X next to it if you got it wrong. A hidden-away puzzle; Lyla solved it, and lots of other people didn't even know it existed.

Going, too, was more fun than it should have been. She felt scared and guilty, especially as she passed broadsheets that peace officers had hung on buildings: MARKS FOR YOUR PEACE OF MIND or MARKING CRIMINALS AT THE FIRST CRIME SO THERE WON'T BE A SECOND. Yet sneaking down streets, past peace officers and barons who didn't know where she was going, felt a lot like sneaking around through the woods with Gill Waterhouse when they were kids. She could see and hear every small thing around her. Her skin felt every small change in the direction of the wind.

She had to crouch near an abandoned warehouse until no one walked past on the street. Then she tiptoed down its stairs to its basement, where two huge Red Fists stood guard and asked her a lot of questions before they let her in. When they allowed her to pass them, she felt like giving a Lady Captain whoop.

The market was actually a lot like the summer outdoor markets that farms ran, with battered tables and people milling around. The vendors wore their collars buttoned high, hiding their tattoos of red fists dripping blood, so they looked more like the ragged squatties who lived in the abandoned warehouses by the river than the Red Fist guards. Many also were Marked, with blue bars tattooed on their wrists. One guy was selling hand-painted posters, and most of them gave Lyla the shivers: BREAK THE GATES and SCALE THE WALLS. A few of the posters, though, were kind of strange and silly: I EAT AT THE BEST TRASH CANS IN TOWN and DON'T DIG — DANCE. A woman was handing out bread for free. It didn't look moldy or burnt or anything, but Lyla walked past without taking any. There had to be a reason the woman was giving it away. Maybe she was trying to lure kids over to talk to her so she could convince them to join Red Fist. The rest of the vendors sold things found in shops, but for fewer credit points — dried peas, wool undertrousers, nails, and sheets of metal. The machines for sale were all steamers or smokers, but they were different from those most people were able to build for themselves. One was actually a small steamboat in a tub of water. The boat chugged from one end of the tub to the other. It even whistled. Lyla couldn't think what anyone would use it for, but she stood around the tub with everybody else and laughed when the boat gave its shrill *chir-eeeeep*.

Beside the tub was a table of medicines. She bought a bottle of ointment, so small that she knew Hope would believe she'd gotten it in a shop. She didn't like lying to Hope, but this was only a little lie, for Hope's own good.

After that, Lyla went to the market two other times. Once, she bought flour to slip in the almost-empty jar at home. Once, when the market was on Blue Plateau, she bought chocolate flakes. There was a guy with the woman at the free bread table, and he was giving away boxes of vegetables for free. His sign said GLEANINGS, which Lyla suspected actually meant "stolen from some baron's garden in the middle of the night." She walked quickly past their table and went to watch a four-wheeled steamer with a guy sitting on a low platform. He pulled a lever next to the steering bar and zoomed across the plateau. Laughing, Lyla suddenly realized that she'd gone back to the market because it was fun; she loved the odd sights, the sneaking, and the secret; she loved walking among the tables. But risking her chance to become a baron for a laugh? She vowed to never go again.

Also, there was last summer. Red Fists in the capital stole a bit of Protean and tried to build a machine with it so, the zines reported, they maybe could sell it to some not-so-law-respecting baron for gold. They messed up somehow, of course; they always messed up when they tried to build Protean-powered machines, because they didn't understand enough alchemyks to fix Protean in its safe solid state. So the volatile Protean had exploded and shattered everything: the machine, the Red Fists themselves, the sewer system where they had their lair, and the secondary school above the sewer, as well as all the students and teachers in the school. There were 572 dead, more than 400 hurt; and the dust from the explosion had sickened hundreds more.

The head of Red Fist, in the capital, wasn't hurt or dead, of course, just some of his crazies. No one in all of Highland could forgive Red Fist for the deaths of the 572. No one, in Hill's Ridge or anywhere else, should help Red Fist survive by shopping in its shadow markets.

Sitting in the Aerie, Lyla made herself think of the 572

instead of S 247, alchemyks cheats, and shadow markets. She recited all the alchemyk symbols and their uses that she could remember from the last Bright class. Then she climbed down into her bedroom and found Hope had fallen asleep with her clothes on. Lyla tucked blankets around her sister.

She heard the thudding sounds of Ma and Da coming home, but she couldn't hear them speaking to each other. Which might mean they were happy-quiet, smiling at some unspoken joke. Or angry-quiet, one leaving the room the other stood in. Though they likely were just weary-quiet, silently pulling off their dusty coats. In summer, they were different, louder. They took on very little mine work, and they stayed outside all day in the mild air and the sunshine, tending crops. Da tinkered with steam tillers and a boat-shaped steam buggy that he'd been building bit by bit for a few years. Da loved tinkering more than anything, but in winter, he rarely headed out to his workshop in the barn. In between his many mine shifts, he sat in his chair with his head tilted back, asleep. When he slept like that, Lyla avoided looking at him. At her age he'd earned a patron and a place at the University of Hill's Ridge, but then he'd gotten into some trouble he wouldn't tell her about and had lost his patron. He'd almost spent his whole life inventing clean, glowing, sleek Protean-powered machines, and now he was generally too tired to even build grimy steamers from old bent scraps.

If Lyla went out to say hello to Ma and Da, they'd probably ask how her studies in the Bright were going. She lay down on her bed. Then she got back up. She hadn't seen her parents in several days; she couldn't just avoid them.

In the glow of the kitchen's candlelight, Ma, long curls uncombed, was doing her usual whirl, putting away dishes while heating soup on the cookstove. She also scooped the debt basket off the table and flipped through several yellow slips of paper. Behind those were a few pink slips, third notices that had to be paid immediately or the debt hunters would come take things from the farm as payment. Just this fall, they'd lost the hand-crank clothes washer to debt hunters. Da sank into a chair. Although Ma and Da were both stringy-thin, they always seemed dense to Lyla, as if half formed from the rock they cleared away so inventors could siphon Protean rivulets from the mines. Ma kissed Lyla's cheek, and Lyla could smell smoke and sulfur.

As Ma straightened, Lyla was startled to see Ma's lips were tinged gray-blue, the way people's got when they had the Cough. But Ma and Da almost never had the Cough. "Are you tired, Ma?"

"Always." Ma smiled. "Do I look so terrible?" She gave her own cheeks a pinch; her lips lost the gray-blue tinge.

"You look good, MaryAnne," said Da. "You always look good."

"You're fine, Ma," Lyla said. Maybe her worrying over the Bright had made her see trouble that wasn't really there.

"And what about you?" Ma asked. "How was school?"

"All right."

"Just all right, Little Girl?" asked Da. "Where's Big Girl?"

"She's sleeping. Should I wake her?"

"I'll go in and give her a kiss in a bit. So, why was school just 'all right'?"

Ma asked, "Have you been drifting in class?"

"Ma, I pay attention."

"But school was just 'all right'?" Da asked again.

"Yeah. I could've done better in Advanced Studies today."

"Lyla, you didn't study?" Ma asked.

"Of course I did."

"You didn't study hard enough."

"I know, Ma. I know that. So I studied a lot tonight."

"Don't snip at me, Lyla. If you studied enough without my saying anything, I wouldn't have to."

Ma could be as irritating as Hope.

"You know, Little Girl, you're welcome to live with us forever," Da said plainly, as though he weren't teasing her. "Dig. Weed. Owe more credit points than you earn. University can't be better than that."

"Griff." Ma's tone was exasperated. "Why do you always have to make fun of our farm? It's not Digger Street."

"I'm not saying it is, MaryAnne. I'm just saying Little Girl's got somewhere to stay and plenty to do if she trips up and loses her seat in Advanced Studies."

"Da," Lyla said. "I'm not going to lose my seat."

"No?"

"No," she promised. "Absolutely not."

"That's my Little Girl," said Da. He gasped in an odd wheezing breath, but covered his mouth with his fist, like he did when he belched. "Scuse."

"Are you all right, Da?"

"I think the boar strip I ate earlier was cured bad. I don't trust that butcher down on Digger and Wares," Da said. Now his breathing sounded normal, but Ma's arms were crossed tightly around herself, the way she crossed them when she was trying to keep from spilling a secret.

"Get some sleep, Little Girl." Da rapped his belly with his knuckles. "If you need to use the crapper, you might want to go now. You don't want to have to use it after me."

"Ugh. Da. I'm pretending I didn't hear you say that." Lyla headed out of the kitchen, half convinced she'd imagined the beginnings of the Cough. But in the hallway, in the darkness, she stopped. She stood still and listened.

At first, a very long silence. Then Ma said something in a voice so hushed, Lyla couldn't hear what it was.

"We should just tell them, MaryAnne," Da said.

"Could you please keep your voice down?"

Da murmured something, and Lyla edged as close as she dared to the kitchen doorway. She heard Da say, "They're old enough to know where we get the extras from. They likely know already."

"They don't; they've never said a word about it," Ma said quietly. "They need to focus on those Advanced Studies examinations, not . . . anything else. You know how troubled Hope gets.

And Lyla, if she finds out, she'll think going to that place isn't so bad. It'd be better if you would stop. We can live with the Cough now and again."

"It wrecks your lungs."

"Only if you have it longer than two weeks," Ma said, but doubtfully.

"Barons are all slagging liars. And they think we're dim as posts. Even a kid wouldn't believe you can cough out bloody snot for two weeks and end up fine."

Lyla's stomach twisted, wringing out like a rag.

"They say they've studied it—"

"Probably so. They don't want the Cough to kill off diggers quickly. Then they might have to start digging rock themselves."

"Griff, why do you say these things? You don't really think barons are all terrible. If you did, you wouldn't want the girls to go to the university."

"I'm not saying they're terrible. I'm saying they watch their own backs. Like diggers; like anyone. Once the girls are inventors and barons, they'll have enough gold to watch their own backs well, and maybe yours and mine while they're at it."

"I'm too tired tonight to argue about barons."

"All right, my MaryAnne. No arguments. As long as you promise to keep taking soothers no matter where they come from."

"Well, they don't have to come from . . . anywhere else," Ma whispered. "Because the replacement doses arrive tomorrow, after morning shift."

"So that bastard of an overseer says. Settle down, Mary love. Settle down. I can't go 'anywhere else' anyway, because I'll be working a shift. If the fresh doses don't arrive tomorrow, we can use our cache. That should carry us till the next 'anywhere else' happens."

"The doses will come tomorrow."

Da laughed gently. "If you say so."

Lyla crept through her dark doorway and across the dark bedroom. She sank onto her bed. She could make out Hope's shoulder, its rise and fall as Hope breathed. Lyla's hands shook a little, and she interlaced her fingers to steady them.

She knew where Da's cache of extra soothers was, in a tin that sat inside a high cabinet in Da's workshop. It would be easy to place a few more of the tiny pills in the tin for Ma and Da. Lyla had enough credit points from working last week's shifts at the Beacon to buy several at the shadow market. There were always soothers at the shadow market.

She pressed her clasped hands to her forehead. But if she went to the shadow market one more time, she couldn't let herself go near the alchemyks cheats. She couldn't touch them. She couldn't even look at them.

Threatened Alchemyks, episode 2

—CHAPTER FOUR—

THE next day, as Lyla and Hope left school, Lyla kept thinking of the last *Pirate Jackman* and *First Book of Alchemyk Equations*. You could just make the book's title in the illustrations. She wondered if the copy at the University of Hill's Ridge looked anything like the copy in the zine. After finishing reading the strip, Lyla had gently, with two fingers, turned several pages of the newszine, so she could begin cracking the Red Fist S 247 code correctly. The *S* meant the second-day newszine and also meant the zine's second page. When she reached the second page, she read its headlines: "Projects Across Highland Progress," "Prime Councilor Releases Marks Law Statistics," "Red Fist Continues to Entice Youth," "How Close Are We to 'the Shift'?—Inventor Panel Speaks on Recent Attempts to Send and Receive Protean Through Air." The tricky part of the code was that she had to check each story with the 247, and either find the second word, the fourth word, and the seventh word; or the twenty-fourth word and the seventh word; or the second word and the forty-seventh word. She had counted words, and, after a while, she had thought she'd figured out the shadow-market location: Cheap Feet, third day, early dusk. As Lady Captain would say—*Cracked it!*

Today was the third day of the week. She had to get inside the shadow market—likely in the basement of the shoe store—without Hope noticing.

As they walked together, down the sloped, snow-packed path that led away from the school, Lyla schemed on how to keep Hope from staying right beside her all afternoon. She scanned ahead, up the hillside to where a spiral of red-orange lights shone: the Project. Nearer and lower on the hillside lay the town itself. The usual steam fog hung over the sections where diggers and merchants lived. Dirty gray haze. Nothing she saw gave her any ideas. At the corner of Pine Street and Main stood Masterson's Chronometer, the tall narrow brick tower. At its top, the chronometer's face shone, round and pale as the moon. Its swinging needle clicked around to each of its tiny glittering numbers. The needle had clicked for more than 120 years, and Teacher Slate had told them its Protean would power it for at least a thousand years. Wondrous; but this was no help.

Hope still at her side, Lyla started walking in the direction of Cheap Feet and the shadow market. Many peace officers patrolled the street—more than usual; they must have suspected.

The girls turned onto Digger. The street's oldest houses were poor, squat, crowded-too-close-together saltboxes half built into the side of Skullcap Hill. Before and during the wars, old-timers said, the diggers on Digger Street lived more like animals than people. Not so now. A few houses had two chimneys, one for smoke and another for steam; inside, steamer water-pumps or some other steam-powered machines churned. Broadsheets hung on a couple of yard fences: CHEAP PRICES = THIEVED GOODS: REPORT SHADOW MARKETS and PROTECT THE PROJECT! REPORT RED FIST! Lyla looked away.

Something moved ahead. Three ragged guys and a girl stood near the Cheap Feet sign. Lyla didn't recognize any of them, which meant they must have dropped out of school a long while ago. Their clothes were gray and worn, and they probably squatted in the old warehouses by the river. They were likely on their way into or out of the shadow market. Lyla slowed.

"Ly, don't stare. Just walk."

Head bent, Lyla looked at the guys and girl in glances. The guys didn't have coats or hats, only hooded sweatshirts. The girl's boots were wound with black cloth, as though to keep the soles on or to cover holes. Her trouser cuffs dragged.

A rare ache, always unexpected and startling, filled Lyla; she missed Gillis Waterhouse, whose size kept trouble away. Also, he always japed in the most terrible situations, which made them a lot less terrible. Trying to jape, Lyla murmured, "Those squatties can't be very good thieves. Look what they're wearing."

"Quit. They'll hear you," whispered Hope, barely seeming to move her mouth. "Don't give them a reason to stop us."

"Hey, hey," one called. He ran a hand over his hair, which was slicked back from his forehead. "Where you going?"

"Pretend you didn't hear," Hope whispered. Lyla kept her head down. She veered toward Cheap Feet.

"Anywhere, long as it's away from us," another of the squatties said, and then wiped his nose on his sleeve twice. On his wrist, two dark blue marks.

Hope tugged Lyla closer to Cheap Feet, farther from the squatties. The one with slicked-back hair didn't have mittens; he wore his sleeves tucked around his hands. Without mittens, his arms seemed to end in stumps.

He began to amble across the street, heading for them. "Come on. Come and play."

"Too good for us?" asked the girl, also starting for them.

Hope's stride lengthened.

"Pull up." The third guy took several leaping steps and stood before them, so they had to stop short at the mouth of an alley. His pupils were overlarge, and he gazed to the right and left of them, as if two other people stood there. He had to be flying on some pill or powder. Maybe he was even a dealer. "Two girls from Digger Street. Or maybe the Hill. I bet they're from the Hill, Spinner," he said in the direction of the girl, who wore several muddy-gray earrings in her ears and one in her nose. Then he stared past Hope's right shoulder. "Where you headed?"

"In there." Lyla pointed ahead to Cheap Feet.

"Someone's waiting for us," Hope lied. "We're late."

The guy edged closer to Lyla, his drifting eyes seeming to look all around her head. She straightened her cap, half expecting to feel her hidden thoughts spilling upward: no one was waiting for them, not at Cheap Feet or anywhere else.

"You work for barons?" asked the girl.

"Licking boots?" the guy with the slicked-back hair asked, so mild, as though he weren't actually insulting them. "Getting down on your knees and scrubbing out their crapper?"

"They don't call it a 'crapper,'" the girl mocked. "They call it a 'toy-lette.'" As the guy laughed, she said to Lyla and Hope, "You got some metal on you? Or chocolate flakes?"

"Turn out your pockets. Turn 'em out, turn 'em out," said the skinniest one in a singsong, wiping his nose on his sleeve again.

Hope and Lyla both turned out their coat and trouser pockets. Lyla thought of the credit points hidden in her boot. "We don't have anything," Hope said, quiet and calm but pressing her side against Lyla's. Lyla pressed back.

The girl leaned her grimy ale-smelling face close. "You shaky?" the girl asked. "Scared if we touch you, we might infest you—I mean, we'll infect you with . . . No, you're shaky 'cause you're hiding something good. In your boot? In your under-clothes?"

"No," Lyla and Hope said at the same time.

The squatties laughed. The one with slicked-back hair, who stood behind the rest, raised his handless arms. "They got something."

"Let's take a look. Unbutton!" shouted the one with the huge pupils. He grabbed Lyla's free arm.

Lyla yanked away, hitting the chainlink fence behind her, and shouted, "Don't!"

"Stop!" a loud voice called.

The squatties all jerked their heads to look. A peace officer pulling his stun club from his belt ran toward them. "Scatter," cried the squattie with the slicked-back hair.

The squatties took off, each heading in a separate direction. A second peace officer ran out of a narrow alley. She rushed up Digger Street after the girl.

"You all right?" The bulky peace officer stopped next to Lyla and Hope.

"Yeah, thanks," said Lyla.

"Fine, sir," Hope said. "Thank you."

"Those friends of yours?"

"No. Not at all, sir," Hope said. "We're so glad you came along." She smiled, her large black eyes luminous.

"That's . . . that's all right." Though the peace officer had to be several years older than they were, he opened his mouth, closed it, and opened it again, like a guy in his first year of secondary school, fumbling for words. "Someone told us about squatties making noise in the street. My pleasure."

They all stood for a moment. The peace officer stared at Hope as Lyla had seen so many guys do, blinking, sun-dazzled.

"Do you have more questions, sir?" Hope asked.

"You're set. You're good." He headed off in the direction of the alleys the squatties had run down.

Hope put her arm around Lyla's waist, holding tight. "You all right?"

"Yeah. Hey, he was smashed on you." Lyla held Hope's waist tight too. The squatties also had probably thought her beautiful; who knew what those guys would have done once they'd unbuttoned her clothes?

"Ly, that's not very funny. Are you about to tell me that I have something nasty hanging off my nose?"

"No. I'm not teasing you. I can't believe how dim you are." Lyla squeezed Hope. "You want to go into Cheap Feet for a moment? To catch our breath?" Lyla asked, but then felt bad for wanting to sneak to the shadow market right after that officer protected Hope. "Or we can get on home. We have a lot of homework and chores."

"I could use a moment around a bunch of people. And we could look at new boots. Sure, let's go in."

"None of the boots there are great," Lyla said as Hope walked toward Cheap Feet. "They're flimsy. With thin soles."

"You'd rather leave?" Hope stopped before the wooden door. She leaned and stared in the window. Lyla peered with her. The glass was so thick and uneven, everything inside appeared wavery. Figures moved through dim, blurry space, and light flickered. Lyla thought she heard a voice inside call, "Dane, how's the Bright?"

"Yeah, I do want to go in," she said to Hope.

"Silly. Why can't you make up your mind?"

"The officers and squatties shook me a little. That's all." Lyla couldn't quite look at Hope. "I'm steady now."

In Cheap Feet's stone cellar, the shadow market stretched before Lyla, full of flickering candlelight and swirling steam. The blanket lying nearest her was covered with plump purple southland fruits and little cups full of chocolate shavings. A thrill flickered in her like the candlelight.

Slipping away from Hope had been easier than she had expected. Upstairs, among the crooked rows of boxes and boots, she'd caught a glimpse of Dane. She'd told Hope that she had to ask him something about the Bright, which wasn't entirely a lie, and she'd left Hope looking at warm, ugly boots.

Lyla had trailed Dane through Cheap Feet, along a back hallway and down a stairway. A big guy, a Red Fist guard, stood at the cellar doorway. He had recognized Dane and let him in. Then the guard had stopped her and asked her a bunch of questions. Who was her family? Where did she live? What had she come here for? Her answers convinced him, apparently, to open the door, although he'd warned, in a very cold, very certain voice, "If I find out you're a squealer, I'll hunt you down."

"I'm no squealer," she'd promised.

And so here she was in the shadow market. *All right. Get in, get the soothers, get out. Quick.*

"Hey. Hey there, girl," called the vendor at the nearest blanket. He had the same taunting tone as the squatties on the street. "Want to see what's in my pocket?"

Lyla walked quickly past, ignoring his laughter. Across the cellar from her, Dane was heading toward the back wall. That must be where the cheats were; she wasn't going over there if she didn't have to. She scanned the blankets at her feet for medicine jars or bottles.

As she swerved by two filthy diggers, a merchant haggled over clusters of berries, bruised but plump. A tall woman rearranged the contents of her sack so the bag of nails she'd just bought was hidden deep within it. The free-bread woman was giving out bread. Next to her, the man with the posters had only a few: WREAK HAVOC and THE MINES = SLAVERY. Near the cellar's back corner and a door stood a thin fountain on a round base. Lyla crossed to the fountain. Its bottom was a basin; its top, a metal bird. Water arced out of the bird's metal beak and fell into the basin.

A woman with her hair in tiny spiky twists bent over and patted a leaping steamer shaped like a hare. The front of the woman's shirt read "Fight Morning Tyranny—Sleep In." Lyla was tempted to tell the woman the shirt was great. Then she spotted medicine bottles at the far side of the next blanket.

Walking over, Lyla pointed to a number of tins. She said to the vendor who crouched by them, "Soothers?"

"Fresh off the boat."

As Lyla dug her roll of credit points out of her boot and counted out ten for a small tin, Dane ambled by not far from her. He stopped at a blanket at the back of the cellar. On it sat a couple of rows of stacked rectangular papers. They were the perfect size to fit in the palm of a hand: cheats.

The vendor looked like a digger, his thin dusty trousers and coat freshly grimed as if from the mines. He and Dane exchanged *heys*, and Dane started to examine one of the rectangles of paper.

Tucking the newly bought tin of soothers into her pocket, Lyla edged to the corner of the blanket with the cheats. The vendor said, "Hey."

Dane looked up from the paper he studied. He squinted at her, as though he wasn't sure who she was. Then his face cleared, and he nodded. The sight of her didn't surprise him. Unlike Hope, Lyla was someone people expected to find at a shadow market, looking for cheats.

"Hey." He held out the cheat he'd been studying, his other hand already on the next.

Her hand extended. She took the cheat.

There were symbols she recognized from class the other day and, next to them, notes she didn't remember ever learning in the Bright. A long line of symbols she'd never seen before also covered the paper; a few looked like backwards sevens and zs.

It occurred to her that if the cheat wasn't a sham and she bought a number of real cheats over time, she could have her own stack, hidden in the Aerie. She could even string a needle with thread and sew them together; she'd make her own actual book.

She heard her voice ask, "How much?"

"Eight credit points," the seller said.

She cupped the cheat. "I only have slips for five."

"I'll take six."

"I said—"

"I could loan you a point," said Dane. "You get that, and

I'll get this one. We'll share." He held up the other slip, and he grinned. "Allies in theft."

"Pardon?"

"Like Pirate Jackman and Lady Captain."

"Pardon?" Lyla repeated. "Lady Captain doesn't steal."

"What do you mean? She steals all the time."

"She doesn't ever. She takes back books that Gray Cloaks stole."

Dane shrugged. "Same thing."

You're japing, right? Lyla's Lady Captain voice demanded. *It's not the same thing at all.*

"Could your sister get a cheat too? Then we'd have three."

"No. No way. I'd never bring her here."

"She's a straight-and-narrow? That's 'kay. You just get yours. You'll have to find a good hiding place she don't know about."

Lyla would. She'd have to hide the cheat. If she made her "book" of cheats, she'd have to hide that. She'd also have to lie to Hope about buying and using cheats. Over and over again, for always.

She couldn't lie to Hope every day, all day long. No matter what Dane or anyone else thought of her, she wasn't truly a cheat.

She placed the slip of paper back on the pile. "I have to think on it," she said so Dane would let her be.

"'Kaaay . . ." Dane said slowly, as if she'd confused him.

"See you at school."

Walking quickly toward the cellar's entrance, Lyla tried to

swerve around a huge guy who was setting a box on one of the blankets. Then he straightened. Lyla stared, startled. It was Gill Waterhouse. She hadn't seen him since he'd dropped out of school last year.

He still was taller than everyone else, and broader. He still wore his hair cropped close to his head. He still had long dark lashes and light eyes of no fixed color. They were blue today. They were winter sky, early-in-the-morning blue.

But then there was the rest of his face. The skin of his left cheek and most of the left side of his neck stretched tight or puckered into ridges and lopsided whirls. It looked like it had once partially melted.

Gill, noticing Lyla, looked down at her. His mouth drew up on one side. He gave her a sarcastic half smile. She flushed; when they were little and he lived at the farm near hers, she'd often seen him smile like that as people gawked at his scarred face. Scarred so badly, any gawker could guess, because his ma hadn't had enough credit points for a decent healer.

"Hey, Gill." Lyla kept her eyes away from the scar.

"Hey. You here alone?" he asked. He'd always talked to gawkers a lot too, so they had to stand there politely answering while they tried not to gawk.

"Hope's upstairs."

"And doesn't know you're down here."

"No." She wasn't going to explain all that to him. "How's your ma and Stan?"

He turned the bad side of his face a little away from her. The ruin was hidden except for rut edges carved away by the boiling water he'd accidentally pulled down on himself when he was small. "I saw Ma last week," he said, not seeming to notice the glance. "She's good."

"Wait. You don't live with them anymore?" she asked. "Where do you live?"

"There's an abandoned warehouse I stay in. Summer, I'll be able to take the boards off the windows. Look out at the river."

"Oh. Good to have your own place, I guess."

"Yeah. That's partly why I told my teachers and Stan they were slags and headed down the hill."

"You did what?"

"I'd said it in my head a million times. One day, I just said it out loud. Which felt good. They *are* slags."

It took Lyla a moment to comprehend that he'd ruined his life by saying things he simply could've kept inside like most people did. "You know, I should find Hope."

"Say hey to her for me. Maybe I'll see you before you leave. I'm almost done with my shift."

Not sure what he meant, Lyla asked, "Are you working in the mines?"

"No. My shift here." Gill gestured to the cellar, to the shadow market.

His sleeves were long, so she couldn't see if he was Marked. His collar was buttoned high, so she couldn't see if he had a Red Fist tattoo. "You work for Red Fist."

"I work for myself. I pick up all kinds of different jobs. Today

I been hauling a lot of stuff." He pointed to a door at the back of the cellar and another box sitting beside it. "Sometimes I look out; I mess with officers too close to the market. That's sort of fun. Leading them through the alleys and then disappearing. Friends took that job today. You probably saw them on the street."

"Friends?"

"Hard to believe, I know, but squatties do have friends." Gill's mouth drew up into the sarcastic half smile again.

Lyla stared into the winter-sky blue. "Three guys and a girl?"

"Yeah."

"I saw them. Peace officers came. They all ran," she told him. He was friends with guys who had wanted to force Hope to strip off her clothes.

"Officers won't catch them." He sounded untroubled. He ran one filthy hand over his close-cropped hair, like he used to when his thoughts wandered.

She used to want to know what he was thinking. "I got to go," she said. "See you."

"See you."

She walked toward the door that led to the stairway and Cheap Feet. Something was leaking out of her chest: the old Gill who'd lain next to her in the fields, head touching hers, and pointed out shapes in the stars. His hand above her, and the glimmering points of light—Bear, North Wind, Flying Heron—all leaking away.

The door ahead of her burst open. Peace officers in blue caps and coats ran into the cellar. Someone shouted, "Raid! Raid! Raid!"

As Lyla turned, people started scooping up blankets of goods. She ran for the cellar's back door. Ahead of her, Gill paused and looked toward the raiding officers. He gave them a big slag-off grin.

"Stop!" someone shouted as Gill disappeared through the back doorway.

A hand grabbed Lyla's arm, a peace officer's hand. Like in her night terrors, she was mute and breathless—still, cold ice.

—CHAPTER FIVE—

AFTER the officer took the tin of soothers from Lyla's pocket, he led her up the cellar steps and through Cheap Feet. Her skin felt ice-glazed.

Lyla looked down every aisle she passed, but she didn't see Hope. She also didn't see Hope on the street, among officers in their caps and long blue coats. And not among the diggers milling around, while the officers told them where to stand.

"This way," said the officer gripping Lyla's arm, and he gestured to a long metal trailer hitched to a snow-cruiser.

Her tongue was frozen. She nodded, really looking at his face for the first time. It was Junot Riverton, who'd been a couple of years ahead of Hope in school before he left for the officer trials. He'd grown taller and broader. His eyes were older, sort of watchful and sad.

As he led her up the metal steps to the trailer door, she glimpsed Hope near a lantern post. Hope turned, maybe to scan the street for Lyla. Lyla found herself edging behind Officer Riverton, so Hope wouldn't see her get hauled into the trailer.

The inside was like a big warehouse room, with metal walls, a metal table, and metal benches. A woman officer leaned against one of the walls, reading pages on a clipboard. Near her stood a stack of boxes. Lyla scanned everything for a glimpse of the pen that officers used to mark those guilty of violating safety laws. Like her.

She sat on a metal bench with her hands and wrists hidden under her thighs. She tried to attend to the questions Officer Riverton asked, rather than the whirl of her thoughts. "Northstrom," he said. "How did you find out where the shadow market was going to be?"

She forced her frozen tongue to move. "I overheard about the market in the halls at school, sir." This was a bit true; she'd spoken in the school hallway to Cornelia Millener about the market.

The woman officer jotted notes on her clipboard. Officer Riverton shook his head and said, "School," as if it was a useless kind of place. He drew Lyla's tin of soothers from his pocket, and he held it up. "You bought these in the market."

She didn't answer, as he didn't seem to be asking anything.

"Red Fist thieved it from one of the shipments sent from the capital. You've taken someone else's soothers." He shook his head a little again, as if, like school, she was kind of useless. "Just to avoid a few days of the Cough."

"My ma and da work in the mines, sir. Not me."

"They sent you?"

"No, no, sir! Not at all. They don't know I'm here. I came on my own, because they're getting ill."

"But if you brought home the soothers, they'd take them. Even though they'd guess you bought them in a market."

She couldn't tell him about Da's cache of soothers from the shadow market. "I thought I'd convince them, sir. Once I had the soothers there." Officer Riverton frowned. She didn't want him thinking too much on this, or deciding to question Ma and Da. "I also went to the market because I was having trouble in Advanced Studies, sir. I went to look at the cheats."

"That's a straight answer. I don't hear those much." He leaned back, his head tilting as he studied her. The woman officer raised her eyebrows. "I didn't find any cheats on you."

"I didn't buy one, sir."

"Why?"

"If I started cheating, I'd have to lie all the time to everyone, sir. Especially to Hope, Hope Northstrom, my sister."

"You hadn't thought of that before?" he asked.

To say "No, not until I was right in the market" would seem completely dimwitted. It *had* been dimwitted. "Advanced Studies is a tough class, sir. I got scared I was going to fail. I was stupid."

"Yeah. You were." His voice had gone flat, like Teacher Slate's when he was angry. "I trained in the capital last summer, when Red Fist's Protean accident killed the five hundred seventy-two. I helped look for survivors. None. No kids, no teachers. Not even any of the Red Fist that'd been in the sewer under the school. All dead."

Lyla was so cold, she had trouble nodding.

"For no good reason, just greed—Red Fist wanted to try to earn some gold. Mostly, Northstrom, in that rubble, there weren't bodies. Only pieces."

"I'm sorry," Lyla whispered, almost saying his name. "Sir."

"You should be. When you buy thieved goods or the steamers in the shadow market, you're giving Red Fist credit points. You're helping them thrive."

"I'm sorry," she whispered again.

"Northstrom," he said in the way he used to talk before becoming an officer, more soft and gentle. "I probably done you a favor, hauling you in. If you need these"—he picked up several small rectangular papers from the desk, a bunch of cheats—"you shouldn't be in Advanced Studies. Harnessing Protean is difficult. Don't you read the zines? Even university students make mistakes and—*bam!* We gotta go scrape bits of them off the walls."

Lyla's hands, still between the bottoms of her thighs and the metal bench, shook despite the press of all her weight. He was being a little bit nice; maybe he wouldn't mark her, maybe he'd just give her a warning. As politely as she could, she said, "Yes, sir."

"If you need cheats to pass Advanced Studies, you won't ever be any kind of inventor."

"Yes, sir."

"I'm glad you see what's so." Officer Riverton smiled at her, and Lyla smiled back.

Then he said, "Your right wrist, Northstorm."

"My—" She broke off.

Her arm rose. He asked her to roll up her sleeve, and she pulled back all her sleeves to her elbow. He grasped her arm and turned it underside up.

The woman officer handed him what looked like a metal rectangular pencil. Its end was a bunch of tiny needles. He jabbed the needles into Lyla's bare wrist. As the needles seared her skin, she cried out.

Officer Riverton released her. On her wrist, a dark blue vertical line. A tattoo like a prison bar.

"You can go. Northstrom, stay away from the market." He pointed at her wrist. "You don't want another," he said, as if another would matter, as if she hadn't already messed up her whole life.

———

The kitchen chair was hard beneath Lyla. She stared at the kitchen table, at the lit candle. The flickering candlelight made her eyes ache, but she kept looking at it, not down at her hands clutching each other in her lap, not at the door Ma and Da would soon come through, not at Hope kneeling in front of the wood stove. To Lyla's side, in the very edge of her vision, Hope moved; she rocked back and forth like a hurt animal. The candlelight stung Lyla's eyes, tiny sparks she blinked away.

Ma and Da came in, stomping snow from their boots. Their breathing was a little wheezy, but it wasn't terrible. "Girls," said Ma. "You're up so late."

Lyla looked at Hope, who looked at her. Hope's shoulders hunched.

"I have to tell you something," Lyla started. The story of the shadow market tumbled out, except she didn't say she'd gone to other markets, or that she'd eavesdropped and heard all they'd said about the Cough. By the doorway, Da stood completely still in his snowy coat and boots. Ma's mouth opened into a small, surprised O. Lyla explained about Officer Riverton. She meant to hold out the mark and show them, but her wrist pressed tightly against her side.

"I got marked," she said.

"What?" Ma asked.

Da looked away, out the door's window.

"I'm sorry. I'm sorry, I'm sorry."

"'Marked,'" Ma repeated. "You're Marked."

"I'm sorry," Lyla said one more time. Hope started to rock again, back and forth.

Ma stepped forward, and then stepped to the side. Her fingers slid into her hair. "What were you thinking?"

"I'm sorry."

"That's it, then. That's just it." Ma's hands dropped. Her voice was like a knife slicing against a chopping board—*click, click*. "You're done with school. You never liked it, anyway."

"I liked it all right."

"You could come up to the mine office tomorrow. Ask for a job."

"I—I . . ." Lyla faltered. "I still have my job at the Beacon."

"If Dulac keeps you on now that you're Marked. Will he give you more hours? No. That's an after-school job. Not real work."

"I'll tell Teacher Slate," Hope said softly.

"The officers will have sent a note. That's what they did when the Greenmont boy got himself in trouble last year. His ma told me he was expelled from Advanced Studies right after, the next morning. And the officers sent a notice to the baron he ran errands for, who fired him. That's how he ended up at the mines. He works down the hole most days."

Down the hole, in the dark, stony cold—which Da hated. Lyla saw Da studying his open hands, all the cracks in his skin. Mine dirt was ground so deeply into the cracks, he couldn't ever scrub it away: webs of blackened fissures through the heels of his hands, across his palms, up his fingers to the tips. He'd made Lyla promise more than once that she'd stay out of trouble and keep her hands pretty. She crossed her arms, burying her marked wrist in the folds of her sweater.

She noticed Da's face. A droplet of water ran down his cheek to his chin. Another droplet spilled from his eye down the side of his nose. She'd made Da cry.

She left the kitchen, as Ma said something she couldn't

make out. In her bedroom, on her bed, Lyla climbed under the covers, and curled into a ball.

The mark was sore and swollen. It itched like a spider bite. She wanted to dig her fingernails into the blue line. She longed to shred off her own skin.

Threatened Alchemyks, episode 3

—CHAPTER SIX—

IN the school bathroom's chill, Lyla leaned against the stall door. She wished there were more to read: Lady Cap outrunning Cloaks; Pirate Jackman tracking Lady Cap down. And *First Book of Alchemyk Equations*—how did they save it? Closing her eyes, Lyla hugged the zine to her chest. She pressed her chin against the thin, feathery pages.

At this exact moment, Hope was probably walking toward the warm, well-lit Bright and its orb, the glowing rose and yellow glass moths. Lyla pressed her fist against the metal stall's door hinges until her knuckles hurt.

Why had she even come to school? What was the point?

She had asked the same questions earlier, and Hope had told her what she already knew. "After you've finished school, you want to work for a merchant in a shop instead of down in the mines, so you need decent references." Hope had pointed at Lyla's newly marked wrist. "Do you think any teacher will give you a good reference today?"

She hadn't bothered to answer.

In the bathroom stall, she scraped her knuckles against the door hinges. She had to go to the second civics class that she now had to take because she was expelled from the Bright. She pushed off from the metal wall.

Outside the bathroom, she started down the hallway. A couple of seventh years walking in her direction swerved, keeping their distance. One openly stared at her wrist, though she had her sleeve pulled so far down over it that her hand was almost entirely covered. People must be whispering about her and the other kid who'd gotten himself marked, though not Dane. Dane had managed to escape. As the seventh years passed her, one said something, and the other laughed. Lyla stared straight ahead, freezing her face into an I-don't-care-what-you-slagging-think-of-me mask.

She wished she could rip down the hallway broadsheets: AIM HIGH!—HEAD FOR THE BRIGHT!; YOU COULD INVENT THE FUTURE; KEEP YOUR WRISTS CLEAN. She turned down the next hallway and immediately stopped. She'd accidentally walked toward the Bright, and ahead of her, rolling away from her, was Teacher Slate. His large arms and hands spun his wheels steadily. Lyla's eyes suddenly stung. She backed up.

The day was terrible all the way through. Teachers lectured her on needing to work hard for good recommendations, their voices scolding or weary. One, on hearing the crackle of the zine under her coat, demanded she hand it to him, and then he tossed it in a junk barrel. The zine, with its *Pirate Jackman*, fell over crumpled waxy papers, instantly getting speckled with yellow translucent grease. It lay crooked, its grease-speckled wings splayed.

On the way home, Hope barely spoke to her. Lyla slogged through her chores, hauling kindling and warming water. Hope started homework.

Lyla curled up on her bed, her back to Hope, her marked wrist pressed against the pillow so she didn't have to look at it. She was a slagging stupid idiot. A knock startled her.

Hope asked, "What is that?"

"The front door?" As Lyla pushed herself up, Hope headed for the kitchen. Lyla heard the door open, and then voices murmured.

"Lyla? It's for you."

Perplexed, she rose and shambled into the kitchen. A tall, wiry messenger stood in the doorway, his trousers, coat, and hat encrusted with ice crystals. He held out a piece of paper. "Lyla Northstrom. From Officer Riverton. He wants a reply."

Lyla looked at Hope, whose eyes were wide. They both shrugged at the same time. Lyla swallowed a nervous laugh. She took the message and unfolded it.

The blocky words asked her to meet with Officer Riverton in the morning. THERE MIGHT BE A WAY YOU CAN GET THE MARK SCRAPED OFF.

She read the line again, to make certain she hadn't dreamed it up. THERE MIGHT BE A WAY YOU CAN GET THE MARK SCRAPED OFF.

Lyla walked toward the flat-topped concrete prison. She wished Hope were walking next to her, bossing her about tidying her hair and about what to say to Officer Riverton. Today was another Bright-room day, but earlier this morning, Hope had actually, for a moment, considered telling the school she was ill so she could go along to the meeting, too.

"Quit being dimwitted," Lyla had said.

"I just—There's some hairpins around here somewhere." Hope had moved things around on their shelves. "I could pin back your hair."

"Would you stop about my hair? You're making me more jittery. If you don't head out to school soon, aren't you going to be late?"

"All right. All right." Hope turned to Lyla. "I wish I didn't have to tell the school you've got to meet an officer at the prison. They'll assume you're in trouble again."

"The message says that's what I should tell people. If I have to tell them anything." Lyla paused, suddenly realizing something. "Do you think he meant you, too? I shouldn't tell you anything?"

"Oh. I guess. Maybe. It's okay, though," Hope assured her. "I won't tell anybody that he mentioned scraping your marks. And Ma and Da don't know. But if he actually wants you to keep secrets from your whole family—that would be odd."

Hope's face shifted: troubled, wary. Lyla felt ill. Every so often, there were whispers that an officer promised girls, or sometimes guys, that he'd scrape their marks if they let him grope them, or worse.

"At school, Junot Riverton was a decent guy," Hope told her. "Quiet. Sort of sweet. And upright. He can't have changed that much."

"So what does he want?" Lyla asked.

Hope shrugged. Then she cupped Lyla's face with both her hands. Her palms warmed Lyla's cheeks. "You'll be all right."

"Yeah. And I won't mess up," Lyla promised.

I won't mess up, Lyla silently vowed again as she reached the prison fence's gate. A peace officer guard waited, two hounds flanking him, watching her. She steadily said her name, and he checked a clipboard. He nodded, opened the fence, and let her into the prison yard.

Lyla tightened her hands into fists so they'd quit trembling. Up the gray slate path, through the huge metal door, into a concrete room with barred windows. Small oval orbs in the ceiling corners shone a pale white-yellow. At a desk sat another officer with a clipboard, whose braid was bound with a red ribbon. Lyla kept looking at that red ribbon as she told the woman her name.

The officer let Lyla into another chilly concrete room. It had one bench and a table with papers spread out on it. Officer Riverton stood across the table from her, his hands in his pockets. He studied her. She stood as upright as she could.

"Northstrom." He gestured to the bench.

She sat. "Sir."

"You're all right?"

She pulled her sleeve far over the mark, almost all the way over her hand. "Yes, sir. Fine."

He nodded, still studying. She sat straighter. He asked, "Not such a disappointment? The mark?"

"It is, sir. A big disappointment."

"Did you tell your ma and da?"

Lyla's mouth stuck closed. She nodded.

"They were upset?"

She nodded again. Then she was able to say, "They were, sir."

"All right." He jotted a note on a paper. "After Teacher Slate got our notice about you, he came right to see me. He said you're a decent student."

"He did? I mean, sir, I haven't done as good in the Bright as I aimed to."

"He said that primary alchemyks is tough for you. But you work hard. And you don't get the same thing wrong twice. Also, how did he say it?" Officer Riverton looked through the papers on the desk. "He called you 'intellectually curious.' You ask questions and want to know how things work. He said you had 'great potential.'"

"He was angry you'd gone to buy cheats. He thought you could've studied hard enough to pass your examinations."

Lyla whispered, "I didn't know he thought that, sir."

The officer said, "Pardon?"

She said it louder.

"All right." He jotted again on a paper. She had the strange thought that he was computing: Disappointed family + disappointed teacher = ?

He added, "And when I questioned you, you could've just talked about the soothers, maybe even tried to cast blame on your ma and da, but you confessed you were tempted by the cheats." He shifted the papers, first one way, then the other, then the first way again. He stuck his hands back in his pockets.

"'Kay." His eyes searched her, but she couldn't tell for what. "After you left, I noticed the address you gave. The Waterhouses used to own the farm next to your ma and da's place?"

"Y-yes, s-sir," Lyla stammered.

"Were you and Gillis Waterhouse friends?"

"Yes, sir."

"Good friends?"

"When we were little, sir. They moved to Digger Street when we were eleven. We haven't been close friends in a long while."

"So you haven't talked much to him in the last few years."

"No, sir."

"Great. That's great. So could you start running around together again if you wanted to?" Officer Riverton asked in a rush.

"I don't understand, sir," Lyla said, though she suspected she did.

"We've caught Waterhouse twice running errands for Red Fist. He doesn't have the fist tattoo yet, but he will soon."

"Sir, Gill wouldn't—"

"I know this is hard for you to accept. You gotta understand that Red Fist is good at stirring up anger. It makes angry young guys who've messed up blame everybody else for their failures. It convinces them they're not really stealing or wrecking things—they're getting revenge."

Lyla had seen Gill working for Red Fist with her own eyes, Gill and his terrible squattie friends.

"Maybe Waterhouse doesn't think he'll get himself tattooed. But I've seen this pattern," Officer Riverton told her. "I know what he's gonna do better than he knows himself."

"You want me to run around with Gill so I can spy on . . ." *Him.* "Red Fist?"

"Yeah. You'll have to be careful. Waterhouse might try to convince you he's been wronged somehow. That what he's doing isn't his fault, that he has no choice. He probably believes his own lies. You'll have to be tough and not listen to his crap. Just run around with him, and then tell me what you see, who you meet, what you do. And especially"—his voice lowered—"Red Fist maybe has this big attack they're scheming on the Project. And maybe Red Fist here is planning something with Red Fist in other towns or the capital. If you hear anything about that, even something little, you tell me right off."

"But—"

"You can tell *only* me," he said. "Not any of the brothers." He gestured to the door. "Most are decent, but maybe one or two aren't. They might squeal to Red Fist for credit points. So none of them can find out about you."

"I'll get hauled in over and over, sir. I'll get covered in marks."

"If you're caught by officers other than me, yeah. Otherwise Waterhouse and the rest will suspect you're squealing to us. But once you've done your tour of service, all of the marks will get scraped."

Lyla put her marked arm behind her back. "I've seen guys who've paid to have their marks cut off. They've got these bad scars." Terrible scars, almost as easy to spot as marks.

"Yeah, those are so ugly, we don't even bother to re-mark them. But we scrape marks off different. We pay for a great healer, and you can barely see the scar. Your wrist is clean."

Lyla felt herself nodding.

"The tour will be a year. If you do well, especially if you help me uncover this big Red Fist scheme, you'll impress my captain. We both will," he said forcefully, as if maybe he hadn't impressed his captain yet and badly wanted to. "I'll earn a promotion. And you'll get your marks scraped."

"You'll have to earn the promotion for me to get my marks scraped, sir?"

"Yeah, you're gonna have to really work to get scraped—that's what my captain said. You gotta find out something really important. Then we'll both get what we want. I'll have Teacher Slate tutor you one-to-one, so you'll learn primary alchemyks the way barons' kids do. And I'll show my reports on your tour to a number of prospective patrons, ones who've sent kids to our university before."

"'Prospective patrons'?" Lyla repeated.

"I think this offer could be the start of a whole new way for kids to turn their lives around," said Officer Riverton. "Kids who mess up, but aren't bad or troubled. They've just made a wrong choice. So, they can do a tour of service, and earn a second chance. Look, this could be a real triumph." Officer Riverton actually smiled, a sweet little-boy smile. "We could save people."

Lyla opened her mouth, not sure what she was going to say. Then she told him, "All right, sir. I will."

What choice did she have?

—CHAPTER SEVEN—

SITTING in the Aerie, Lyla thought of Officer Riverton's lists of *do*s and *don't*s, of the way to contact him, and all the rest. She decided that the easiest way to find Gill would be to go to the next shadow market. Here was the problem—Gill knew her; he knew she'd never in a million years want to start running around with squatties and Red Fist. But becoming Marked changed everything. He must know that, too. She had to convince him that getting a mark had changed her.

She couldn't help thinking that when Gill eventually found out she had squealed on him and Red Fist, he would hate her forever.

He's the one who decided to run around with Red Fist. That's not your fault.

"Lyla?" Hope's voice came from below.

Lyla didn't answer. Officer Riverton had said she couldn't talk to anyone about her tour. Not her parents, whom he was speaking with right now in town, though he wasn't telling them any details, just making sure they didn't get in her way. And not Hope. In the past, she certainly had kept secrets from Hope, but they tended to be small, and Lyla told parts or all of them eventually. She'd never before *had* to keep a big secret from Hope.

Apparently she wasn't good at it. She'd already let slip that the meeting with Riverton had to do with Gill. Hope had guessed she was supposed to report on Gill somehow.

Hope climbed up the ladder and into the Aerie, saying, "I knew you were here." She set down her candle near the painted-on-the-floor piano and sat cross-legged nearby. She gave a thin-lipped smile. "I won't ask any questions. I promise."

"I'd tell you more if I could."

"I know." Hope tapped one of the piano's white keys. "What do you think Officer Riverton's saying to Ma and Da?"

Lyla shook her head. "I don't know. He's . . . enthusiastic. That'll reassure Ma."

"Or worry her." Hope played a chord. "Look. I won't ask more about it. Just. If Gill finds out you're squealing on him, he'll be really mad and upset."

Lyla looked at the Aerie wall and Lady Captain grinning wide. "So, I gotta make sure"—she almost said "they," as in Red Fist—"Gill doesn't find out I'm squealing."

"This isn't a zine strip."

"I know that, Hope, but there were real runners during the wars, like Lady Captain. The Gray Cloaks were real. Lady Captain spied on them. People do lots of tough things when they have to."

"I'm not saying they don't. I'm saying life isn't a zine strip.

Lady Captain is going to be all right by the last page of every single story. Real runners got badly hurt all the time."

"I know, Hope. I'm not dumb. Would you rather I stay Marked? You'll be the clean sister; I'll be the Marked sister. From now on."

"That's not what I'm saying either."

"When people make a mistake" — *which you don't, but everyone else does* — "they gotta fix it. So, I am."

Hope pressed the heels of her hands to her eyes. "I know." Her shoulders rose and fell. Then she dropped her hands and sat upright in a way that made Lyla think of old-fashioned dress cinches, laces pulled tight, bone-stays rigid. "All I'm saying is, when you're running around with Gill, don't start thinking you're only playing some game off in the woods."

"We won't be in the woods."

"You know what I mean."

"I can tell when I'm playing a game and when I'm not, Hope."

"But the two of you always used to— You'd forget everything else while you were out on your 'adventures.' Remember that time you got home late, and you didn't even realize how dark and cold it was? Your ears were frostbit."

"I'm not eight anymore." Lyla touched her earlobes. "And my ears were only frostbit a little. They ended up fine."

Before Hope could start in again, Lyla said, "You're not helping. You're making me jittery."

"Sorry."

Hope rested her hands on the piano keys. She played several chords, tilting her head as if she heard their song.

"Anyway," Lyla said. "Gill's different now. He's a squattie. He works for Red Fist. The old Gill never would've."

"Maybe not. He *was* sweet. He always loved trouble, though. So sad. He's smart enough to earn a seat in the Bright."

"He's smarter than Dane and some of the other kids already in there."

"But they want to be there, and he doesn't. That's the difference." Hope tapped a black key. "You can't make someone want something he doesn't."

Lyla kept silent, so Hope would stop going on and on about Gill.

A loud slam downstairs made them both start. Hope said, "Ma and Da are home."

"Sounds like Ma is, at least," Lyla said, with a laugh.

Hope gave a brief smile, and she crawled to the ladder.

Lyla followed, trying to hear any hint of what had happened with Officer Riverton. As she and Hope crossed their bedroom, a second door slammed; it sounded like Ma and Da's bedroom door, toward the back of the house.

"Ma's upset," murmured Hope, stopping in the hallway as if she wasn't quite sure what direction to head in. "I'll check on her."

Lyla went alone to the kitchen. Da looked up from unlacing his boots. He straightened. "Well, Little Girl. Riverton's offering you the chance to pull your fat out of the fire. You want to do it?"

"Yeah, Da."

He smiled for the first time since she became Marked. "You've got some guts, that's sure." His smile dropped away. "I don't know what his offer is, but I can tell it isn't safe."

"I know."

"Look, you don't have to tell him yes. There's no shame in working for a merchant," Da stated, his tone flat, not urging. "If you stay straight, you can earn decent references before you finish school. You can work in a shop."

"Da—"

"Plus we'll always need you here on the farm in the summers. It isn't a terrible life." He rose very slowly, wincing, a hand on his back.

"Right. No. I mean. Riverton said I can't tell you a lot. But he's really giving me a good chance. I promise."

"The best of two bad choices?" Da shook his head. "If it gets too tough, you tell me. Right off."

"I will." But she wasn't going to beg help that way.

Da began to pinch at a fissure in one of his thumbs as though he was trying to work out a sliver. "I'd let your ma be for a while. She's pretty worried. And disappointed in you."

Lyla wanted to say, "I'll fix it, I promise," but words wouldn't change a thing. She had to go out, and she had to actually fix what she'd wrecked. The sooner, the better.

In the morning, Lyla went to school with Hope and tried to attend to civics and computation. Instead, she kept wishing she'd hear something about the next shadow market so she could get to it and find Gill.

At midday, she went to thank Teacher Slate for helping her get a second chance. As she started down the long hallway to the Bright, kids kept glancing toward her wrist. She pulled her sleeve low.

The door to the Bright was unlatched. At her knock, it swung away from her. "Teacher Slate?"

Lyla slipped through the opening into sunshine, light, and steady warmth. Teacher Slate wasn't in the room, but leaflets lay scattered across his desk. The orb shone, its glass moths bright yellow, orange, and rose.

At the back of the room, the closet door was open. "Sir?" No answer.

She walked around the room's edge, past shelves labeled with symbols she didn't recognize, spirals with dots. In the corner nearest the closet door sat a row of small, labeled boxes: "Scales," "Metals (Various)." These had to be for the Bright room students who passed all their examinations and won patrons, the ones who would spend their last few months in the Bright learning to use the least volatile chemyks and metals. Her hand drifted out of her pocket to rest before the boxes.

Beside the small boxes sat a large metal box without a label. A combination padlock hung from its handle. She bet it held the chemyks.

From the closet doorway came a clicking sound. Lyla stepped

back from the padlocked metal box, almost knocking into a chair. "Sir?"

"Is someone there?"

"Teacher Slate? It's Lyla Northstrom."

"I'll be right out."

She quickly returned to his desk and the wood stove. So he wouldn't think she was peering at the leaflets on his desk, she stared up at the orb. The smooth oval glowed yellow. The delicate moths perched on their slender glass spirals. Lyla wished that she sketched so she could draw the orb and keep it with her all the many weeks and months she wouldn't see it.

She heard the sound of wheels. Teacher Slate rolled out of the closet with two boxes stacked on his lap. At the sight of her, his wide forehead creased. "Northstrom."

She'd intended to say her *thank you* right off, but he rolled to her with short, impatient pushes. "You probably want the door closed." After setting the boxes on his desk, he passed her and shut the door.

"Yes, sir. Right."

He rolled back to face her. She began again. "Thank you so much."

He drummed his wheels with the flats of his palms. "What did Riverton offer you, exactly?"

"Pardon? Oh. Sir, I can't really tell you."

"And he wouldn't tell me either," Teacher Slate said slowly. "Which means you aren't on a cleaning crew or something."

"Cleaning crew, sir?"

Teacher Slate rubbed his forehead with his fingers. "When I went to him, I thought he'd simply assign you to do grunt work. But that's not what he's requiring of you, is it?"

"No, sir."

"He wants you to spy or something."

"Sir, I can't. I'm sorry." Lyla went on quickly, "He did tell me that if I serve my tour and get scraped, you'll teach me one-to-one. Is that so, sir?"

"I'll teach you," he said. "But I suspect you have a lot ahead of you before you start studying alchemyks again." He winced. "Look, Northstrom. I've known Riverton's family since he was small. I tried to convince him to take a seat in Advanced Studies, but he was determined to become an officer. He's exceptionally dedicated. He wanted to serve under this captain who's set on smashing Red Fist in Hill's Ridge, to prove it can be done here. Which means it could be done in other towns, maybe even the capital, where Red Fist is strongest." Teacher pushed his wheels a little forward and drew them a little back. "I'm not explaining myself very well. What I'm trying to say, Northstorm, is that Riverton'll take care of you, in his way, but the stark truth is that you're less important to him than his mission. Do you understand what I'm getting at?"

She realized she'd already had this suspicion, hazily; hearing Teacher say it made it clear. "You mean if helping me might ruin his chances to smash Red Fist, he won't help me."

"Yes. You'll be on your own, Northstrom."

"I can't trust him."

"I suppose that's a fair way to put it. I'm sorry. Have I upset you?"

"No. Well, a little," she admitted.

"If you need help, you can come to me, Northstrom. I'll do what I can."

"Thank you, sir. But I won't mess up, I promise."

"You can't promise that." Teacher smiled sadly. "We all make errors in judgment."

He rested his hands on his spindly legs. His baggy trousers hung in folds over his knees, which pointed off to the side.

Lyla looked quickly to his face. He raised his eyebrows—a kind of *Well?* Maybe she could ask what had happened. Did she really want to know?

"I have to get to my next class." She turned away from him, but then turned back. "I probably won't quit messing up, sir. But I'm going to try."

He laughed a little. "Northstrom, I'll hold you to it."

Threatened Alchemyks, episode 4

—CHAPTER EIGHT—

WALKING to town with Hope, Lyla tried to wonder only about Pirate Jackman's search for Lady Captain, but she also kept wondering about the next shadow market. According to the new Red Fist code, the next market was a couple of days off, at the Spice Shack. A couple of days had never seemed so long before. Lyla would have to drag through school, and survive her first night at her job, at the Beacon, as one of the Marked. The owner let Marked only scrub, so she was going to have to stop checking coats and start scrubbing floors. It was gritty, filthy work, which everyone would know she now had to do because she'd been an idiot.

As she and Hope headed through town toward the nightclub, Lyla noticed more peace officers on the streets than usual. Several hung broadsheets with a spectograph of a dirty girl, her cheeks thin, her eyes glaring. It read UNIVERSITY BOMBER. DO NOT AP-PROACH. REPORT ANY SIGHTINGS IMMEDIATELY. Gill might know that girl; Lyla's stomach crumpled. She wanted the wait to be over. She wanted to start on this "tour of service" for real.

Lyla followed Hope onto Center Street and into the most dazzling part of town, the Lift. She peered down a side street toward the Lift's stone and glass tower, and she vowed she was going to earn this mark off. She would go to the University of Hill's Ridge, and, eventually, she would earn gold for her inventions. Then she'd come often to the tower for rides. She'd sit in a glass and metal bauble as cables drew it over many copper roofs toward the riverside tower; below her, the entire town, the frozen river and its ice-ships, the Project with its ember glow. Even the mine, which she imagined must be a vast whirlpool of darkness and light speckles.

Dusk made the Lift's oval baubles, traveling through the air, shine pearlescent. Lyla and Hope passed below. Sleek snow-cruisers slid by in the street, one gold and one deep blue. Ahead stood the Beacon's polished oak door. The doorkeep gave them a *hey* as they entered the Beacon's wondrous stairway. Along the high ceiling, river-stone-size orbs gleamed. Veins of gold glinted in the walls. From the club above, music sang out loudly, and a fast drumbeat shook the wooden landing beneath Lyla's feet as she and Hope climbed the stairs two at a time.

Ahead was the doorway opening, a dragon's mouth. Stone teeth jutted down from the top edge and up from the floor. Hope bent low to avoid them. Lyla followed. As she stepped through the door, she reached up to brush one of the sharp tooth points.

All along the high ceiling, red-orange orbs shone like gems. Washed red by their glow, the owner stood near the doorway. His stare pinned Lyla where she stood.

"Northstrom." He had never before said her name that way, as if she were a hound that had crapped on his floor.

"Sir."

"And Northstrom." He smiled at Hope.

She smiled back, brightening. "Yes, sir."

As he looked at Lyla, his smile dropped. "I received the peace officer's notification." He didn't bother to lower his voice; a few barons with diamonds in their hair glanced over. This apparently was part of the punishment: he was going to make sure everyone knew she was Marked. The owner said, "Marked don't work my coat check."

"Yes, sir. I know."

"I considered firing you. But you aren't a shirker. Just, apparently, dim."

Someone laughed, a university student in a gauzy shirt. It seemed as if he was laughing at her, though he wasn't looking at her. A group of them stood at the edge of the crowded dance floor, watching the owner with expectant grins. Lyla couldn't bring herself to say, for all of them to hear, "Yes, sir."

"Northstrom, are you attending to me?"

"Yes, sir," she whispered.

"My new girl can't start tonight, so you'll work the check. Next week, you'll be scrubbing."

"Yes, sir."

"What's that grim face for, Northstrom? You're too good to scrub?"

"No, sir," she said quickly, trying to smooth her face.

"There are plenty of Marked who'd vastly prefer working here to heading down the hole. If you'd prefer the hole, you should go."

Lyla looked steadily at the owner. "I don't prefer the hole."

"She'll keep working hard, sir." Hope stepped up to stand at Lyla's elbow. "I'll make certain."

The owner gave Hope another of his thin smiles. "I know you will, Northstrom. I appreciate your sense of duty."

"Yes, sir."

He looked away, his smile gone. "You two need to go."

As Hope and Lyla walked past the university students, one said, "Let's see the mark." The others called, "Yeah, girl, let's see it." "Bare the mark, Scrub."

"Don't listen," murmured Hope.

"I'm not." Lyla forced herself to walk on as their laughter trailed her.

"I should go change." Hope gave Lyla's cheek a swift, firm kiss, leaving a little greasy lip salve behind. "Sorry," she said, rubbing it into Lyla's cheek with her thumb. "You'll be all right?"

"I'm fine," Lyla said. "Don't worry about me."

Starting for the coat check, Lyla passed a table of barons with many gems studding their earlobes and noses. Their eyes flicked over her ragged curls and her windburned face. They scanned her baggy, worn coat sleeve where it fell over her wrist.

I'm not a slagging failure. I'm serving a tour. She wanted to say this. And if the tour didn't begin for real, and soon—if the evening of the shadow market didn't arrive quickly—she was going to start raving.

The other coat-check girl wasn't around: Sisley was probably sneaking drinks. Lyla quickly stepped into the closet and changed into the Beacon shirt that fit her best, its flared hems hiding her undershirt and a good bit of her trousers. She let her arms hang so the wide sleeves covered her wrists completely.

She stepped up to the polished granite counter. She looked out as usual, but instead of enjoying the music and the dancing, she just wished the night would hurry up and finish. The rectangular-faced chronometer had long, slender hands she could see from the coat check; they'd barely moved at all since she arrived. She had hours and hours.

Lyla breathed in the delicate breeze of briar rose scent that the owner's air perfumer blew across the room, and she tried not to look at the chronometer. Across the dance floor towered the music booth. The owner's spiral ampliphones lined the top of the booth, and they sent music thudding throughout the room. Inside the music booth, the music mixer stood over the table of thin panels. Lyla hadn't ever seen this mixer before. His shirt and trousers were all black, and he wore a thin cap pulled low on his forehead. Studying the discs he spun, instead of the dancers, he tapped a few switches so bright, they looked hot to the touch. A new song began—slower drums and horns, a deep voice singing in a patois.

Around the dance floor, servers carried their trays. The barkeep poured drinks, bathed in the glow of the large orb directly above him. The sheets of waterfall-like glass within the orb shone patterns on his skin—watery light and shadow. On the dance floor, couples in silky shirts drew together. Lyla longed to be among them in her own silk shirt, wrapped up with a tall student from the university, maybe one who looked a little like Pirate Jackman.

"I'm going to invite Marc over to have a drink with us." A slight baron with large beautiful eyes and several diamonds in one ear stood at Lyla's counter. Beside her stood a baron with hair that flopped over his forehead. His bent nose looked like it once had been broken. The woman faced Lyla, as though they'd been speaking together.

"Pardon, mistress?" Lyla asked.

The man said, "Tickets, for our coats. That's what you're here for, yes?"

"Yes, sir."

"It's a good night?" the woman asked her.

Surprised by the question, Lyla wasn't quite certain how to answer. "Yes, fine. Thank you."

The owner stalked over. "What's wrong?"

"Nothing, I was just speaking to your girl. No hello, Marc? No kiss?" asked the woman, laying a hand on the owner's arm.

The owner dropped his head and laughed. "I'm sorry, Clara." He kissed her twice on both cheeks, then also kissed the man.

The man spoke, saying things in a language Lyla couldn't understand. The owner answered, "Good," and started toward the bar.

The woman leaned a little nearer to Lyla. "The thing to remember with Marc is that his bark is worse than his bite."

"Clara." The man sounded disapproving, but the woman only smiled at him.

He drew off her wrap, then thrust it and his coat at Lyla. She took them, careful to keep her mark hidden.

The man began to follow the owner to the bar, but the woman said to Lyla, "Do you go to the secondary school?"

"Yes, mistress."

"Do you know Raven Slate?"

"Do you mean Teacher Slate?"

"*Oui,* who teaches in the Bright."

Lyla had never heard a grownup call the Advanced Studies room the Bright. "Yeah—yes, mistress."

"Could you please tell him hello from Mistress Regin?"

"All right."

"And good luck with your studies. Be a better student than I was." The woman laughed.

Lyla forced a smile. "I'm doing my best, mistress."

Mistress Regin left the counter as Lyla hung the coats on the long, half-full rack. They had an oddly smoky scent for barons' coats, like open wood fire. Glancing around to make sure nobody was looking her way, Lyla leaned close to smell the coats better. Instead of smoke, she smelled damp wool and cedar. Lyla pulled back and caught the smoke scent again. Beyond the counter, the air was slightly hazy.

"Fire!" a voice cried.

The music stopped abruptly; all the dancers stilled; at tables, barons rose. The owner stood beside his two baron friends. "But there's no alarm," someone said, as if fire gave off alarms rather than smoke.

"Out! Get out!" the owner yelled.

"Red Fist!" someone cried. "Slagging thieves!"

Everyone started to run at once. Lyla darted away from the coat-check counter. "Hope!" she yelled. She didn't see Hope anywhere.

Barons pulled out pistols. One pointed his in the direction of the servers, and then he aimed at the barkeep. A bang and the sounds of shattering glass halted Lyla. Yet the barkeep stood before whole glasses and bottles.

Uncertain of what had just happened, Lyla fled. She still couldn't see Hope, not at the bar, not among the barons streaming toward the dragon's mouth. The crowd of barons at the opening surged backwards. Peace officers pushed into the room. One officer began helping people step out through the dragon's mouth, saying, "Slow down. Stay calm." Several officers ran down the hallway toward the bathrooms, stun clubs in their hands. No Hope at the doorway; no Hope caught in the crowd.

Lyla remembered the back exit, through the kitchen, and she ran past the barons. She slammed through the kitchen door, haze clogging her throat. She coughed. The cook was scooping up copper pots and piling them in a box full of shining pots and pans. He was the only one standing amid the cluttered counters and stovetops. "Have you seen Hope?" Lyla asked, her eyes tearing.

"Haven't seen her," said the cook as he yanked open the knife cabinet. "Get going, Northstrom."

Lyla spun toward the door to the main part of the Beacon. "Don't be dim," the cook barked. "This door's your closest exit."

"But—" A siren began to wail.

"Out!" ordered the cook, dumping knives into the box. "She's not stupid enough to stay in there looking for you. She'll expect to find you outside."

Alarms suddenly started to scream. Lyla's ears rang as the cook pointed at the door and mouthed, *Slagging get out.*

Lyla fled through the back door, into the clear night air, her eyes streaming.

—CHAPTER NINE—

OUTSIDE the Beacon, the metal landing creaked under Lyla's boots. Night had turned the sky blue-black, but the escape lanterns someone had hung by the Beacon's door cast some light. Lyla clattered down the metal steps.

A couple of fire officers burst from the mouth of an alley and crossed toward her and the Beacon. Starting up the metal stairway, one demanded, "Anyone inside?"

"The cook," Lyla said, stopping. "Have you seen another girl who looks sort of like me? Taller, with less curls."

"No," said one as they passed her.

"She's a server, wearing a black velvet shirt."

Without answering, the officers reached the landing and disappeared through the kitchen's doorway. Above the roof hovered thick gray-black smoke. Hope couldn't be inside with that smoke. She had to be out front.

A siren and indistinct shouts blared from somewhere. Lyla rushed toward an alley. Before she reached the opening, she heard someone inside the alley say, "Quit!" She stopped.

On the alley wall before her, lantern light flickered over thick black letters painted on the brick: BURN THE BARONS. Beside it, Red Fist's tattoo, the fist dripping blood. Lyla reread the words—BURN THE BARONS. It reminded her of battle broadsheets in *Pirate Jackman*—BURN THE UNIVERSITIES. As if Red Fist weren't just angry guys thieving from barons, but were instead some kind of soldiers, like Gray Cloaks. She backed away from the words.

Then she halted. She was supposed to spy on Red Fist. And Red Fist was here. Finally, finally, her tour had actually begun.

An indistinct murmur drifted from the alley opening. Lyla crept forward.

Peering around the edge of the building's corner, she wasn't sure exactly what she was seeing. Light from the alley's opposite opening, from the street, shone into the narrow gap between the buildings. At the outer rim of this light crouched two guys in well-worn coats and trousers. A couple of girls climbed metal escape steps toward a top window or the building roof. The girl farthest up the steps looked like the Beacon's other coat-check girl, Sisley, who always wore her shirt and coat overshort, to expose a bare strip of back and belly. The crouching guy, in a long ragged coat, gestured to the bigger guy, and then he hoisted himself up the ladder. Lyla didn't see any weapons.

A siren screeched from the street, and snow-cruiser lights shone down the alley like glittering prism eyes. The bigger guy stood, and instead of climbing the metal steps with the rest, he began to run toward Lyla. An officer dashed into the alley, chasing him. Lyla scrambled away from the building's corner and heard a voice yell, "Halt!"

She ran.

Bolting down a different alley, she stumbled over chunks of ice. Ahead, a peace officer snow-cruiser blocked the exit to the street. The alley was dark and silent. There weren't any officers nearby, but there weren't any Red Fist to spy on, either. She gripped a metal escape step, and its cold stabbed through her hand.

"Hey. Hey," a hushed voice called, as if to her.

No one was ahead of her. Behind, back in the Beacon's alley, the guy who'd run toward her was kneeling with his forehead on the ground and his hands flat in front of him. A peace officer laughed as he pulled the guy's arms behind his back and locked metal bands around his wrists. "Yeah, I heard you. You got *nothing* to do with this. You just happened to be passing by."

"The roof," the hushed voice called. Lyla looked up and saw a dark shape leaning over the edge of the roof. "Lyla, it's Gill."

After a day of wanting to find him, here he was at a Red Fist attack—and she wished he wasn't. *You stupid slag.* "Gill?"

"I saw you both bolting. You and Hope. Hope's out front. I can get you to her from the roof."

"Oh. Sure," Lyla said, caught off-guard by his offer. "Thanks."

She began to climb the metal steps. Shouted commands to either side of her sounded close. "Sit." "To your left." "This way." She climbed faster.

Above, moonlight and the flash of orange alarm lights from

the street dimly illuminated the rooftop. Gill crouched near the roof's edge, a large bulky shadow. "Quick," he whispered down to her. "You want a hand?"

"I'm fine on my own," she told him. He shifted out of her way as she hauled herself over the roof's cold brick edge.

She crouched next to him, and her heart knocked against her breastbone just as it had when they were kids in the woods pretending to hide from Gray Cloaks. She tried to think of what to say.

A voice called from somewhere beyond Gill: "Leaper." In the dark sky, a roof-leaper glided in the direction of their roof. The bright orb on its nose swiveled, a huge, searching eye.

Gill reached for Lyla's arm. She drew back, and he held both gloved hands palms up, saying, "It's officers. We gotta get in a hole." He pointed to a square shadow. "Take that one."

She scrambled toward a small square storage box. She clambered into it, her boots slipping on the floor's grit. Webs caught in her hair. Gill crawled into other shadows and disappeared.

Her square hole didn't have quite enough air; she breathed shallowly. The roof-leaper's eye gleamed stark and white.

The stark light shone down the alley Lyla had just been in. It shone on the edge of the roof where she'd crouched with Gill. Its glare swept toward her too-small box.

Though she could barely breathe, she curled into a tighter ball. Like an angry kid. Like someone the officers would mark again and haul off to prison. That's who she had to convince Gill she was—she was hunted. She was trouble.

The leaper's eye soared above Lyla's hole. She heard the thud and the creaking roll of the leaper's wheels hitting a rooftop, maybe the next building over. The engine roared and its propellers whirred; the machine leapt on.

Lyla was lightheaded from lack of air. Her skin crawled as she thought of spiders scuttling off their webs into her curls, but she stayed crouched for a moment. The dim roof before her was still, as if deserted.

Then Gill's bulky form climbed out of a rectangular shadow. "Lyla?" he called in a hush.

Lyla pulled herself out of the box, and her chest suddenly released from her lungs' squeezing grip. She filled with cold air.

Ahead of her, a couple of shadowy figures climbed from behind stacked boxes. They were ragged and thin, squatties like the ones in front of Cheap Feet. In fact, she saw they were two of those same squatties: the girl with the dragging trousers and the thin guy who kept sniffling. They must have attacked the Beacon. Them and Gill.

Don't ask Gill why. Don't tell him he's a slagging idiot. Lyla couldn't look at him.

The squatties, half-bent, crept toward her, their footsteps silent.

"Keep low," Gill said to Lyla in a hush.

She dropped beside him, not too close, near a large metal bin. As the girl and the skinny guy knelt in front of them, the girl pointed to Lyla. "Scribbler." The girl seemed to be speaking to Gill. "What's your slagging problem?"

"No problem, Spinner. I know Lyla from way back. She was trapped in the alley. So I brought her up."

Spinner shook her head. "Good. Fine. Girl, he kept your skin clean," she sneered. "So now you can blow away."

"Actually—"

"'Actually.'" Spinner mocked her. "*Merde.* Don't tell me she's a Bright girl, Scribbler."

"I'm—" Lyla broke off as the skinny guy leaned his face too close to hers.

"Haven't I seen her somewhere before?" He wiped his nose on his sleeve. "Somewhere."

"She looks like a Hill girl," Spinner said. "Not a squattie."

"But she isn't a squealer," said Gill.

Look them all in the eye and agree. Lyla looked at the other two, not Gill. "I'm no squealer."

"Right. Sure. See—" The girl dropped lower suddenly; Gill and the skinny guy froze. "Did you hear that?"

Lyla listened hard for whatever the girl had heard. Lights from the street flashed. Sirens wailed, several sounding strangely far off. Lyla wished she could go over to the roof's edge and make sure Hope was all right. Instead, she peered around the metal box. "Nothing this way."

"Quit jiggling your leg against me," Spinner snapped at the guy.

"Shouldn't they be back already?" he asked.

"Shut your mouth," she said, with a glance at Lyla, who kept her face a blank, as if she weren't really listening. "You're a slag, Nose."

Gill laughed a little, softly. "Nose, man. You're gonna drive her crazed."

Then there was a scuffling sound nearby, and Lyla tensed. A bulky shadow launched around the metal box. As Lyla and Gill jumped up, the shadow landed on Nose, knocking him over. Spinner rose, and another shadow grabbed her from behind, hugging her. She kicked back, and it lifted her off her feet.

Lyla squinted. The shadows were the two other squatties guys. Before her, the whole pack.

The guy holding Spinner was the one with the slicked-back hair. He whirled Spinner around. "Zeb. You—" She squirmed, and he gave a soft cackle.

The other guy, stocky and broad, lay on top of Nose, who was face-down. Nose thrashed, and the guy pushed his face against the rooftop. "Eat it."

"What are you trying to do, Jit?" Gill asked. "Kill him?"

Jit laughed, and he ground Nose's face harder against wood and grit. "I said, eat it."

"Quit," Gill ordered.

"Jit, man." Zeb set Spinner down. "You're slagging crazy." He grabbed Jit's arm and yanked.

Jit half fell to the side, and Nose scrambled up. Cupping his hands over his nose, Nose leaned over, maybe dripping blood. "Slagging *merde*." His whispering voice was shaky. "Jit. You freaky slagging bastard. I think you broke my nose."

Jit shook off Zeb. "I didn't break nothing," he said in a loud whisper. "I'd have to hit you hard. Red Fist isn't never going to tattoo you unless you toughen up."

"I don't want them tattooing me," Nose protested. "Running free's better. Right, Scribbler?"

"Free's the best," said Gill.

"Free to get knocked around," mused Zeb.

"Yeah!" Jit cried. "Zeb's speaking it. If you don't got a tattoo, Red Fist can stomp you whenever they want. If you're Red Fist, *you* get to do all the stomping." He stomped his feet against the rooftop.

"Not what I meant," said Zeb.

"Quiet, Jit," said Spinner.

Jit grabbed her in a hug, his hands on her ass. "Hey, sweet."

"Quit." Spinner smacked his face.

Zeb yanked Jit by the collar of his coat, and growled, "Get off."

"All right, all right. I know she's your territory."

"I'm no one's territory." Spinner swung at Jit again, and he deflected her, laughing.

Lyla noticed Gill had shifted closer to her, putting himself between her and Jit. *This guy's your friend?*

Jit whirled toward Nose, who leaned away, but Jit still put an arm around him. "And you're my territory. You do what I tell you. 'Cause I can break your nose, and you can't break mine."

"Man, Jit." Gill shook his head. "What powder did you snort tonight? You should go run it off."

"Enough." Spinner gestured at Lyla. "Could we get rid of the Bright girl and finish here before we get grabbed by the blue-coats?"

Jit looked at Lyla as if noticing her for the first time. *"Merde."*

They all looked at her.

"I'm not a Bright girl," she said. "I got booted."

"My heart weeps," said Spinner.

Jit laughed, sounding like a coydog. Zeb hit his arm. "Shut up."

As Jit tried to stifle himself, Gill asked her, "You got booted? For what?"

"The night I saw you at the shadow market, I was caught."

"That's tough," Gill said.

"Not really." Lyla tried to sound as if she really meant this. "I wasn't any good at primary alchemyks anyway. I bet I forgot it all already."

"If you say so." Gill shrugged. "Probably for the best. Everyone's getting marks. You wouldn't want to be left out."

"Let's see it," said Zeb.

"Scuse?" Lyla said. "The mark?"

"Yeah, let's see it all." Jit thumped Nose on the back, and Nose grunted.

"If you don't stop being such a slag, Jit," Zeb said softly, "Scribbler and me'll push you off the edge of this building."

"You could try," said Jit.

"So, let's see that mark, Bright," Spinner taunted.

Lyla felt an almost overwhelming urge to hide her wrist behind her back. *No hesitating.*

She forced her arm to stretch out in front of her, underside up, and she tugged back her sleeves. A scrawny wrist, and there, in the light flashing up from the street, the blue line, like a strip of someone else's skin.

"A mark for the Hill girl," Nose taunted in singsong.

"One whole mark," said Jit. He thrust out his arm: five marks.

"If you're smart," said Spinner, "you do whatever you want and get none. Like Zeb."

Zeb raised his hand and bowed his head. Then he dropped it. "I guess we don't have to shove you over the edge to keep you from running to the bluecoats," said Zeb.

Lyla couldn't tell if he was japing or not. "Thanks."

"We've been here too long," said Spinner.

"You all go on," said Gill. "I'll send Lyla down and catch up."

Spinner and Zeb started walking off. "See you," Nose said to Gill, and he followed the other two.

Jit swerved over and snapped his teeth at Lyla. Gill shoved his shoulder.

"Your territory. Got it, got it." Jit swayed away.

As the pack drifted off, silent, Zeb stopped at a broken metal door and pulled a can out of his pocket. He used it to spray something on the door. Lyla couldn't see what he'd written.

Then he melted into the shadows with the rest, and Lyla felt she'd lost or missed something. They weren't going to beat the crap out of her, but they also didn't care if they ever saw her again. Not exactly a spying triumph.

"I'll get you to Hope," Gill murmured.

Lyla wondered what the squatties were doing here, exactly. That's what Riverton would want to know.

She slipped after Gill. At the broken metal door, she saw Zeb's message: END THE RULE OF BARONS.

All that told her was they wrote Red Fist messages. She jogged to Gill. "Jit doesn't seem like a great lookout."

Gill gave a soft laugh. "No. He's the one who leads the blue-coats on a long chase."

"While you set fire to the Beacon," she said lightly, as if this didn't trouble her at all. "Did you know I was in there? And Hope?"

"If I had, I would've warned you."

"Thanks." *Slag.*

Gill knelt near the edge of the building and sat back on his heels. "You like Marc Dulac?"

"No. But I'd rather not die just because I work for him."

"You weren't gonna die. Nobody was. It's mostly smoke." He nodded beyond the building's edge. "Look at that."

The town was like a *Pirate Jackman* picture of a Gray Cloak invasion. Downhill, near the river, one of the Lift's baubles hung motionless on its cable, stopped midtrip. Uphill, on the hillside's dark slope, the red-orange lights at the Project wavered. A black-ness—smoke—rose in a narrow stream. And across the ridge from the Project, at the university, another stream of smoke spiraled upward. Suddenly, it billowed, a dam cracking and releasing torrents.

Red Fist was breaking the entire town. It was breaking everything.

Lyla worked at finding her voice. "Why?"

"Red Fist wants the barons to see that they can't just do whatever they want anymore. They'll see Red Fist can really hit at them."

"I thought you weren't Red Fist."

"I'm not. They're slags. But barons are bigger slags. It's good to see some of their glitter burn, isn't it?"

She was breathing in too much smoke; her throat felt clogged. "I wouldn't mind living with glitter."

"Yeah. Imagine how much decent stuff from tonight will be at the next shadow market."

"This attack—it's big." Lyla hadn't gotten a chance to help stop it, to help Riverton impress his captain. "They . . . Were they planning it for ages?"

"Sort of. They been working on something bigger."

"Bigger than this?" She hadn't failed yet. "Like what?"

Gill shrugged, and she wanted to shake him. "Don't know. Red Fist has got this guy who plans the attacks here. He goes on and on about changing Hill's Ridge for good. Trying to take over stuff like the mines or the Project, and have inventors work for Red Fist. He talks big, you know? It should be a decent fight— Hill's Ridge Red Fist versus Hill's Ridge barons and bluecoats. Who you bet will win?"

Lyla looked out at the smoke rising across town. "If Red Fist wins, everything will be a mess."

"Yeah. But marks will be good. An honor." Gill laughed. Then he looked carefully down over the building's edge. "Hope's still here."

Lyla peered down the three stories to the street. The officers — or the bluecoats, as the squatties called them — and the barons looked like toy children. A haze of smoke blurred them, and the lights on top of the healers' and the bluecoats' rectangular trailers flashed across everything: bright, dark, bright, dark. Several people knelt on the ground. One was the guy Lyla had seen captured in the Beacon alley, the Red Fist. His wrists were still locked behind his back.

She didn't see her sister. "Where's Hope?" Lyla heard how high-pitched her voice sounded, and tried to lower it. "Gill, where do you see her?"

"It's all right. She's there." He pointed. "With the crowd across the street."

Then Lyla saw her, wearing only the Beacon's black velvet fitted shirt, no coat, a brown blanket half wrapped around her. She didn't look hurt. She paced, staring toward the smoking Beacon.

"She's worried. I've got to get to her," Lyla said, and tried to think how to arrange to see him again soon without sounding odd or suspicious.

"This way."

At the building's corner, they both crouched. Lyla could see that between this building and the Beacon lay an empty alley, which opened onto the street. "Look." Gill hung his arm down the side of the building and pointed out a series of crude metal steps that led from balcony to balcony.

"Getting down's easy," Gill told her. "I'll show you how to climb to the first one. You can take the rest of it on your own."

"Thanks, but I don't need help getting down the steps. I got up those others all right."

"Yeah." He cleared his throat. "Hey. Do you remember the name of that heron, in the stars?"

"Stars?" she asked. She thought perhaps she hadn't heard right.

"You know, little lights, in the sky?" He gestured upward.

"I know what stars are. You're the one who always knew the names, though." Lyla looked up at the smooth arch of blue-black, the many white glitters. The scattered stars seemed to have lost their pictures. They lay strewn as though kicked around, then abandoned. "It wasn't just Heron? Or Flying Heron, or something? I don't even see it."

"There." Gill pulled off one mitten. He pointed up and off to the right, so far away from the alarm lights and sirens. His finger moved as if sketching rather than finding shapes. Three beak points, the round of a neck, wings fanned wide.

He sketched again. "Bear." Two raised paws, a large head. "Otters." Pointed noses, long sleek bodies, tails streaming. Lyla leaned farther back. Wind brushed her face. The blue-black sky stretched to each side, behind, beyond her.

"We're so small." Gill's low-pitched voice said the exact words in her head.

His arm dropped. He looked down at her, his eyes shadow blue, like a piece of night sky.

"Gill—" What was she going to say?

At the same time, he said, "I—"

"Sorry," she fumbled. "You go ahead."

A siren shrieked, a long, piercing wail.

Gill shook his head, and she caught a glimpse of scarred skin at the corner of his mouth, whirled ridges and ruts. "It's nothing," he told her. "Say hey to Hope for me."

"All right," Lyla said slowly. She began to lower herself to the ladder.

Then she stopped. "Will you be at the next shadow market?"

He looked at her, eyebrows arching. "Me? Yeah." He pulled his cap a little lower. "Will you?"

"Yeah. I'll see you," she promised.

"See you." He smiled.

She smiled too, triumphant.

—CHAPTER TEN—

AHEAD on the street, a trailer's orange lights flashed. Sirens bleated, and bluecoats cluttered the sidewalk. Lyla crouched in the alley's shadows, as alone as Lady Captain in *Threatened Alchemyks,* and also *Dark Days, Lost II,* and *POW.* No one knew where Lyla was or what she'd done. No one knew she'd succeeded, a little. No one was allowed to know, except Riverton.

Hope was speaking to a bluecoat near the Beacon, a stocky man with spectacles and an arrogant face. Lyla wanted to run over, but then the bluecoat might start questioning her—where had she been, why had it taken her so long to get out of the Beacon, what had she been doing all this time?

She waited. Smoke filled her nose.

On the sidewalk, the owner and the cook dug through the box of pans and knives the cook must have saved. A couple of bluecoats hauled the Red Fist Lyla had seen earlier from his knees. They dragged him toward their trailer. His arms and legs hung heavy, dead weight. He started to chant, "Burn the barons! Burn the barons!"

If he thought others would start chanting too, he was wrong.

People just stared. He suddenly struggled, pulling both bluecoats off balance. One lost her hold on him, and he began to scramble away. The other still gripped his arm and stumbled behind him. Someone shouted, "Pistol! The Red Fist has a pistol!"

Everyone scattered. Hope ran behind a snow-cruiser. Lyla crouched lower. The bluecoat who'd let go of the Red Fist ran after him, pulling her stun club from her belt. She hit him, and must have jolted him at the same time. The Red Fist shuddered and fell forward, his hand releasing a metal tube. Somebody shrieked, but the cylinder simply hit the ground and rolled until the curb at the opposite side of the street stopped it. No fire, no shots.

The bluecoats held the Red Fist face-down. The one who'd hit him pulled a cloth bag from her belt, then slid it over his head. Both bluecoats yanked the Red Fist up and half walked, half dragged him.

The Red Fist shouted hoarsely through his hood, "Burn the barons!"

Lyla felt burned, her lungs seared.

Someone yelled, "Ignorant slag!"

"Arsonist!"

"Killer!"

As the bluecoats pulled the Red Fist up the steps of their trailer, a merchant started to bang against the side of the trailer with his hand. "Butch-er! Butch-er!"

The crowd of barons, university students, and merchants pushed nearer to the trailer: a gathering wave of red, blue, black, and orange. It poised at the bottom of the trailer's stairs.

"Butch-er! Butch-er! Butch-er!"

The merchant's chant drew Lyla up. As no one was looking her way, she left the alley. She started toward the poised crowd.

"Butch-er. Butch-er."

"Stop," ordered a voice. "We have to take him to tribunal."

A slight baron, the lovely baron who'd spoken to Lyla at the Beacon's coat check, broke from the crowd. The chanting merchant stopped.

Mistress Regin stepped in front of the merchant and began to speak, the wind blowing her sheer blouse so tightly against her, it was like a second, emerald skin. Yet she didn't appear to be cold at all; she even rolled up her sleeves, as though warmed by whatever she was saying. A guy held out a blanket to her, but she pushed it away. Her hands gestured, short sweeping cuts. The crowd pulled slightly back from the trailer and from her.

The stocky, arrogant bluecoat took the arm of the hooded Red Fist and said or did something to the Red Fist, who sagged to the steps; that Red Fist sure wasn't any danger now. The baron didn't notice. She went on speaking to the silent crowd.

Lyla walked closer, like any other straggler, straining to hear. She was almost knocked over by Hope, who grabbed her in a hug. "Where have you been? I looked all over!"

"I was looking for you!"

They hugged each other.

"I'm sorry." Hope smoothed Lyla's curls away from her face and tucked them behind her ear. I looked for you. But some university students at one of my tables convinced me you must have already left. They got me to dash out the front with them."

"I couldn't find you. I ended up in the kitchen. But you weren't there, either. The cook made me leave through the back."

"Have you been questioned yet?" Hope pointed toward the trailers. "Do you need to get in line?"

"Let's just go." Lyla started leading Hope away, toward the part of the sidewalk still hazy with smoke and shadows.

"But—"

"If they stop us," Lyla whispered, "I'll say you didn't know I was trying to leave without a questioning."

"Lyla, I can't—"

"Or say I made you go. That's the truth."

"Lyla—" Hope broke off as a bluecoat walked near them.

Once he passed, Lyla stopped Hope and whispered, "I don't want to talk to them. I'd rather not have to lie."

Lyla could tell from the worried look on Hope's beautiful face that she wanted to ask, "What would you have to lie about?"

Lyla wanted to tell her. It was so hard to keep secrets from Hope.

"Yeah. Probably best to keep quiet," said Hope finally. She took Lyla's hand, and together they slipped away from the screaming sirens.

———

Lyla opened her eyes. She was lying in the darkness, on hard wood floorboards, cold and bare. The dim ceiling hovered above her nose. She was shut in a wooden cell.

No air. She panted—useless breaths.

She battered her fists against the low ceiling. Her mark split open, and pain stabbed, wrist to elbow, elbow to shoulder. It sliced into her rib cage. She opened her mouth, a soundless gasp.

The ceiling dropped.

Lyla woke with a cry.

"You all right?" came Hope's voice from the other side of the room. Hope didn't sound like she'd been sleeping.

Lyla sat up. She tucked her marked wrist between her bent legs. "Yeah, I'm all right."

Hope's breaths were long and slow. As Lyla matched hers to Hope's, Hope asked, "You sure?"

"Yeah," assured Lyla.

She wasn't, though. After the attacks on the Beacon, and all the rest, the other night, the town councilor had issued a town-wide curfew. She and Hope had reached home, but then the school and everything else had been shut down, so that the blue-coats could scour the streets, alleys, and rooftops for Red Fist. The mines had stayed open, and all the diggers had to stay at the mines. A messenger had come to the farm to say Ma and Da were all right, and to take the message that Lyla and Hope were fine back to them. Ma and Da still weren't home, and the town was still under curfew. Lyla wasn't supposed to leave the house, but tomorrow was the day of the shadow market at the Spice Shack, where she had agreed to meet Gill.

Moonlight shone in around the sack curtains, and Lyla saw that Hope was sitting up with blankets wrapped around her. Se-crets usually lurched out of them when they were both awake in the middle of the night. Hope had told about the young piano teacher who'd worked at their school only a few months before leaving. He'd kissed Hope at the end of every piano lesson for weeks. And they'd *only* kissed, though he was almost twenty-five. Hope hadn't seemed able to explain why. "It was like playing music together. Not like a smash or wrapping up."

Lyla wanted to tell Hope about finding Gill, about everything. She buried her face in her pillow.

She fell in and out of sleep, off and on, and the next morning, a messenger came around to announce school was open. The curfew was lifted.

But town, as she and Hope passed through, was different. Bluecoats stood watch on every street corner, and roof-leapers crisscrossed overhead. At the newszine stands, headlines announced, "Red Fist Burns Project and University Guard Towers," "Red Fist Explodes Piece of Lift Tower," "Beacon and Several Baron Homes Scorched," "Prime Councilor Calls Town Councilor and Town Peace Officer to Capital—for Testimony on the Failure of Safety Laws."

Also, during the curfew, the bluecoats had hung new broadsheets. STAY VIGILANT. REPORT RED FIST. Some broadsheets were all white, with a single black eye. The narrowed eyes were somehow painted so they stared directly at Lyla, no matter what direction she moved. Beneath them: WE WILL FIND YOU. She wasn't the "you" they meant, but she couldn't help feeling she was.

School had changed too. Bluecoats stood at the entrance and checked through all the students' bags and coat pockets. A tall female bluecoat drew the Marked to the side, and she roughly patted down the girls while a male officer patted down the guys.

As Lyla leaned a little forward, against the school's brick wall, she spread her legs wide. The woman's hands began to search her body. Lyla didn't look at Hope or the others standing around. She also didn't look at the bluecoat, especially when the woman's hands slid up the insides of her thighs, where almost no one else had ever touched her. She forced herself not to squirm away. She thought only of Lady Captain, captured and searched, of Lady Captain's bored face. The officer's searching hands didn't matter.

Finally, the bluecoat stepped back and said, "You can go." Lyla kept her face blank and bored as she pushed away from the wall. A number of the school's ski racers—merchant kids—were watching her. Despite the frigid wind, they wore their sleeves turned up. One she didn't really know grinned at her and waved, showing off his bare, clean wrist.

Lovely. Is it worth the frostbite? She took Hope's arm and headed into the school.

All day, Lyla had to sit through classes and pretend to pay attention to lectures on Gray Cloak attacks and weather patterns, while all she could think about was Red Fist. What if Red Fist didn't hold its planned shadow market because there were so many bluecoats everywhere? What if, after Gill had left her, he'd been caught?

Finally, finally, the school day ended. In the school's chilly hallway, Hope said, "Oh, I forgot. You'll have to walk home alone today." Lyla almost said, *I'm not going home. I'm going to the shadow market.* Hope continued, "I have to stay after. The music director asked me to play piano for a show. It's an older show," she explained, speaking faster and higher than usual. "The tunes have this great rhythm. Syncopated. It hangs back, but moves. I can't explain it. And in one tune, the melody's sweet but sad at the same time. Anyway"—she stopped and folded her arms like a shut gate—"playing in the show could actually help me get a patron. Some barons like to see you do extras, not only study."

Lyla was tempted to pull Hope's arms apart and ask, "Why can't you just say you like playing piano? You love it, don't you?" But asking would upset Hope, and Lyla had upset Hope enough recently, so she said, "Sounds good. Meet you tonight, back at home."

Lyla left the school, bursting out the doors, running over the path through the pines into town. There had to be a shadow market today, and Gill had to be there. He had to.

She turned down Digger Street, heading toward the river. A couple of bluecoats were walking up the street in her direction. She tucked both her hands into her pockets, and then she realized this was probably what all Marked did when they saw bluecoats. Hiding her marks was like a bird's call or an animal's track; it told everyone watching what she was.

Before they could catch sight of her, she veered down a side street. She ran to the end of it, crossed some lane she didn't know the name of, and entered another, which she thought would take her to Skullcap Street. The lane was crooked, so dim and small that it was more of an alley. Lyla glanced behind her. No blue-coats.

Dusk was darkening the blue of the sky. She ran out to Skull-cap Street, and she passed a mine-stained digger, who stopped to cough and then spit in the gutter. She passed turret-shaped brick buildings with broadsheets: WE WILL FIND YOU. She reached dockside and the row of large square warehouses. A few blocks upriver, a Lift bauble lowered into its tower, which stood at the side of an ice-ship the size of a warehouse. The ship's lights shone like fire sparks. Music drifted from its high deck: old jive. Guards in black ringed the base of the ship, standing by parked black snow-cruisers. Lyla passed lit-up warehouses, and at the doors of each stood guards with rifles. Guards on roofs aimed their ri-fles in her direction. There seemed to be a lot more guards than there'd been before the Red Fist attacks. A lot more guards, a lot more bluecoats. Red Fist couldn't possibly hold a shadow market tonight.

Still, Lyla kept running forward. She reached the edge of town and the old abandoned warehouses. The padlocks on the doors made her laugh; the warehouse walls were so rickety, any-one could easily find a way to climb them. One was plastered with REVITALIZE! broadsheets. Another was covered by painted fists dripping painted blood. She was close now.

She rounded the curve, passing the town's last abandoned warehouse. It was quiet on this almost-empty edge of town.

Ahead stood a tall rectangular building with thin rectangular windows, old like the old warehouses, but brick and solid—the Spice Shack. And hidden inside, maybe, the shadow market.

A large guy stood on the curve up ahead. He spotted her and began loping over. Gill, Lyla realized. It was Gill.

He stopped in front of her. His eyes were storm-cloud gray, and he held his head a little tilted, so she couldn't see the ruined stretch of cheek and neck.

She said, "Here I am, as promised."

"Hey." He looked beyond her, up the street, down the street.

"Hard night?" she asked.

"Bluecoats are nervous." Gill grinned. "You slipped away from the Beacon all right?"

"Yeah. I climbed down and found Hope."

"No more marks?"

"Just the one."

"One's not so bad," he said. She wondered how many he had, but asking felt odd, like asking him about his underclothes. "I'm almost done with my shift," he said. "Then I'm going to meet up with Spinner and them."

"Can I come?"

"Sure—it'll be fun."

How could he actually think she'd find it fun? Did he remember anything about her?

"What's my favorite color?" she asked.

Gill arched one slender eyebrow. "Purple-blue. The color of those little flowers. What're they called?"

"Ne'er Forgets," Lyla answered. He was right. "My favorite *Pirate Jackman*?"

"Girl in the Tunnel."

"Yeah. Yours is *Grounded*."

"Used to be. Now that's my second favorite. *POW II*—it's the best."

"*POW II* is my second favorite. Definitely a close second."

"I almost said it was your favorite."

She laughed. "Did you?"

He seemed to spot something behind her. "All right. I'm done here. You ready for an adventure, Cap?"

"Sure, Jack." Her hand rose to her mouth. She'd forgotten—when they'd played Pirate Jackman as kids, that was what she always used to say.

"You certain?"

"Are you suggesting I might *not* like an adventure, Jack?"

He grinned. "My apologies."

"I'll consider forgiving you." Her heart was like a bird veering back and forth through her rib cage. "Where are we going?"

He leaned forward on his toes. "It's a surprise," he whispered. "This way, kid."

Lyla laughed as she began to run.

—CHAPTER ELEVEN—

AS Gill led Lyla up a narrow alley, Cornelia Millener passed by the alley mouth, walking in the direction of the Spice Shack. Lyla veered into the darkest side of the lane. "I know her."

"Oh, yeah? Why're you hiding?" Gill whispered, one side of his mouth quirked upward. "You scared to be seen with me, kid?"

As she said, "If Cornelia sees us, she'll ask what we're doing," something seemed to crack open inside her, a long-shut, forgotten doorway. Gill had asked her the exact same question once before. When they were eleven. After his family had fallen onto Digger Street. His clothes had gotten dirtier; he'd stopped bringing any midday food to school. He'd started to look like Digger Street kids, except worse because of the wasteland covering half his face and neck. Most of the girls kept away from him, and Lyla sometimes did too. One day, he'd jokingly asked, "You scared to be seen with me?" And she'd said, "I'm not scared. It's just my other friends don't talk to me much when I'm with you. You know, because of your face."

The words hadn't seemed mean to her at the time, but Gill

hadn't responded. After that, she now realized, he hadn't really spoken to her much. She'd rarely seen him at school.

He didn't seem to be thinking of these things now; he was simply sneaking down the alley. His shoulder was higher than the top of her head, and though the good half of his face was nearest her, even this more reassuring side was wind-roughened, his cheek a little sunken as though he never got quite enough to eat.

"Do you think I should be scared of you?" she whispered, only half joking.

"Maybe. I did get myself tattooed."

"Pardon?" she asked, startled.

He laughed. "On my arm. You wanna guess what it is?"

A red fist.

"Well? You want to know what it is, or not? Knowing might be dangerous. I might have to kill you after I show you."

Lyla smiled. "You go around killing people every time you pull up your sleeve?"

"I'll consider sparing you." Gill shoved his sleeve up to his elbow and held his forearm out, the left arm, not the one the bluecoats usually marked. The tattoo was hard to see in the dimness, but she could tell it wasn't a fist. At first she thought it was an elongated diamond, the narrow top and bottom angles pointed, the wider side ones rounded. Then she realized the diamond was made of two hats, their broad brims outward — the brims' edges forming the diamond's outer edges — and their crowns aligned to form the diamond's center. One was black, and one was brown. Pirate Jackman's hat, and Lady Captain's.

Lyla reached to trace the inked picture, but then, suddenly aware of his bare forearm, she dropped her hand. "I've never seen one like that."

"Yeah?" Gill sounded pleased. "I designed it."

"It's great." There was something better to say, but she couldn't think of it. "It's so great," she repeated. "Where's this adventure you promised?"

He looked away a moment, smiling slightly, like he used to when he thought up a new scheme. "I want to stop somewhere first."

"Where?"

"Somewhere." Obviously Gill still loved surprises. He started off. "Come on."

She flew after him, like she used to, unsure where they were going or what they'd find when they got there. As if he were leading her to a rock ledge to look over, or a tree to climb, or a waterfall to stand in, water slipping through her hair and down her shoulders.

Gill turned sharply into a lane between two leaning warehouses. One had the newer bluecoat broadsheet, the watching eye. WE WILL FIND YOU. Another said MARKS FOR YOUR PEACE OF MIND. Across "Marks" was painted "I'm a Slag."

Gill grinned over his shoulder at Lyla. Then he took a couple of long steps, pulled open a side door far shorter than he was, and bent low to get through. He disappeared.

"Gill," she whispered as loud as she could. He didn't answer.

She folded her arms to keep them from touching the walls, and she walked down the lane. She paused and listened. No sound at all.

Steeling herself, she stooped and went through the small doorway.

Before her, within tall charred walls that ended several stories up, lay a wide expanse of snow and trees. The warehouse roof was gone. Long trunks stretched toward the sky, crooked branches pointing to the winter-blanched sun.

"See?" Gill said. He put one hand on a smooth white trunk. "Underneath the snow's a lot of broken tile and concrete. The wood grew up through the cracks."

Slender trunks swayed slightly, and branches reached for the vast expanse of indigo. The tree nearest to Lyla had white bark, with strips that had pulled free and hung in ringlets. Their undersides were pale orange. She slid off a glove and ran her fingers along the ringlets' pale orange softness.

Wind rattled boughs and last summer's dried-out vines, which clung to the brick walls. The faded red bricks had cracked in places, but none had broken completely apart. Boards covered every single window. Outside, passersby would see an old shell of a warehouse but no trees, only four stories of solid walls.

Lyla rested against a trunk. Here, no one was peering at her.

Gill came over and actually sat in the snow, not far from her feet. He leaned back and stretched his legs out. He lowered his head onto one folded arm, his face to the sky.

There was a space beside him, on his good side: her space. When they were kids, she'd lain in it a million times, her shoulder near his shoulder, her head touching his head. That space was warm. She had room to lie down inside it, one foot tucked around the other. She always fit.

That space was too close to him now. That space didn't belong to her anymore.

Lyla draped her arm around the tree next to her and pressed the side of her face against its chill.

Gill let out a long exhale, a white smoky cloud. "This is the only place I don't feel watched."

"Yeah?"

He laughed. "I'm telling you, now that you're Marked, the bluecoats'll always be squinting at you. And Red Fist'll spy on you. Even if you're just working for yourself, taking on jobs and getting paid. Even if you're not trying to earn a tattoo. They'll spy on you to see if you're a good recruit. Or if you're stepping out of line. You'll have to get used to it. The spying."

She had the crazed urge to laugh.

"But here"—he swept his free arm through the air—"I can say anything. Do anything."

Lyla hugged the tree so tightly its bark dug into her cheek.

"No one will see," he said.

"Except me," she warned.

He laughed again. "Yeah, and you'll run right off to Red Fist. Report to them all about the way I lie in the snow."

"I'd never spy for Red Fist." *Or for peace officers,* she should say. "See—" She looked up toward the indigo sky and its white glitters. "I'm not even looking at you."

"Not looking at me is definitely easier than looking," he remarked.

"That's not what I meant."

"Really?" He sounded dubious.

I meant I'm not spying on you—the lie stuck in Lyla's throat. She stared at the sky.

"You aren't a liar, Cap." Gill's voice was japing, but it cut at her too. "That's why you're such a good friend."

The wind blew down inside her coat collar, an icy breath against her throat. She said, "It's a little cold."

"Yeah," he agreed.

He didn't say, "Sit over here. We might warm up." She didn't say it either.

———

Back out in the alley, the hidden wood didn't seem real. It was like the stories Lyla and Gill had made up when they were kids. Once upon a time, through a little doorway, there was another land. The land lay inside four tall walls, where a wood grew through the concrete. Inside that wood, wind whispered among the branches and vines. The sky above the branches was purple and black, and stars shone white. No one lived in that land and no one could travel through the door—only Gill and her.

The real world in the alley outside the wood had narrow eyes painted on walls. They watched Lyla and Gill pass. WE WILL FIND YOU.

Gill stopped in the shadow of the last building at the edge of town. Beyond lay the hillside, where a few scattered warehouses jutted up among the rocks. He scanned the almost-dark landscape. Lyla heard the whirring of roof-leaper propellers and pressed herself flat against the building. Gill crouched in the shadow of a trash barrel.

Lyla held her breath as the bright beam of light shone near them. It passed over the wall of the building across from her. It slid onto the rooftop.

A shout, and then, "Stop!" A bang echoed through the alleyways.

"What was that?" she murmured. What it sounded like was a pistol shot.

Gill was staring up at the rooftop. "Somebody shot something."

His face was more grave than she'd ever seen it before. The wood they'd just been in seemed days and miles away. Maybe she'd even imagined it.

"Let's get on. Carefully. As quiet as you can."

She nodded.

He backed away from the mouth of the alley and began to pull himself up a ladder that led toward the roof of the building. She climbed after him, trying to keep her boots from clanking against the metal rungs. He stopped short of the roof, and he did something to a tall six-paneled window. The window swung open like a door, and he hauled himself inside. Lyla scrambled after him, into the dark room.

"This way," he whispered. Lyla crept after him toward a faint thread of light coming from a doorway. Gill rose as he went through the doorway, and she stood too. Pulling off their gloves, they slipped into an interior room without windows. It was bare except for a table, where a candle sat flickering. Instead of Jit and the rest, two guys stood in front of them, big guys like the Red Fists who guarded the shadow market.

"Hey." Gill sounded fine, but he stuck his hands in his pockets, his shoulders hunching slightly. "We're meeting Jit and Zeb."

"Jit told us, Monster. We asked where you'd be, and he told us," said the one with a wide, flat face. He sounded angry. Lyla tried to catch Gill's eye, but he was staring steadily at the Red Fists.

"Shut the door," the taller one ordered Lyla. "Wait . . . we know you?"

"She's looking for work," Gill said. "I know her from way back, so I brought her along. She's not a recruit. She can leave if you want. She's got nothing to do with anything."

"You want to work for us?" the tall one asked her.

No flinching. "Yeah."

"Fine. Pay close attention," he said.

"She's not—" Gill broke off as the one with the wide, flat face pushed him. Gill stumbled into the wall. The Red Fist palmed the back of Gill's head and pressed the good side of his face into the boards.

"What're you doing?" the tall Red Fist asked Lyla.

She'd taken a step toward Gill. "I'm—"

"I told you, she's new," said Gill, not really looking at her.

The Red Fist said to her, "Get against the wall."

As she nodded, he shoved her shoulder. She stumbled, her forearms bumping the boards. The man began to run his hands over her body, searching for weapons.

No shaking.

She locked her knees to stop the shakes. She heard scuffling from the other direction, where Gill was. She tried to turn her head but the Red Fist gripped the back of her neck and pressed, pinning her to the wall.

A grunt, two thuds. She pushed back against the gripping hand. It shoved her against the wall again. She couldn't swallow.

"Quit squirming," the Red Fist said in her ear.

Another thud, like something hitting the ground. She forced words out. "You're choking me."

His gloved fingers dug into the back of her neck. They pinched like a mouth biting, teeth digging into her skin.

"Fine. Keep out of the way." He let her go so she could turn around. Gill was kneeling, forehead resting on the ground, arms wrapping around his belly, eyes squeezing shut.

The Red Fist standing over Gill said, "Get up, Monster."

Gill didn't move, so Lyla reached for his arm.

"I said, stay out of the way." The tall Red Fist shoved her.

As she hit the wall, she swallowed a yelp.

Gill pushed himself to his hands and knees. He rose slowly,

as if something inside his belly or chest was broken. The Red Fist with the wide face hit him in the lower back, and he half collapsed. Gill stayed on all fours like some scrawny school kid who knows that anything he does or says will only make the battering worse.

The tall Red Fist leaned over Gill. "That hurt?" He laughed. Then he said, "Monster, you deserve to lose your hands."

Lyla thought she hadn't heard right.

"Or maybe just your fingers? I can give them to your girl here in a box."

No. No, no.

"You know why, don't you?" the tall one asked, quietly. "You remember that sketch you sent around? Red Fists as swaggering bulls. Braggarts."

Gill didn't answer.

"You insulted brave men." The Red Fist sounded quietly, dangerously furious. "Men who're risking themselves to liberate ungrateful slags like you from barons."

"I didn't send that around," Gill said.

The Red Fist kicked him in the stomach, and Gill grunted, folding so his head rested on his knees.

"Yeah, I drew it," Gill said. "But I didn't send the sketch around."

"You think I'm stupid? You gave it to that kid who snorts too much powder, Monster. You knew he'd show it around."

"Nose is an idiot," muttered Gill.

The Red Fist leaned over Gill and grabbed Gill's left wrist.

"Open your hand," he ordered. Gill opened it, palm pressed to the floor, long fingers spread out. His fingers were stained black with what must be ink.

The Red Fist drew a knife from his belt, and he set the edge against the second knuckles of all four of Gill's fingers.

Everything seemed to stop: all sound, all breathing, Gill's heart—Lyla was sure Gill's heart must have stopped.

The Red Fist with the knife edge against Gill's fingers said, "Monster, you need these?"

"I can't work for you anymore if you cut off those fingers." Gill's voice was flat, frozen or dead.

"I asked if you need these," repeated the Red Fist.

"Yeah."

"You want to keep them?"

"Yeah."

"There are plenty of other kids who could work for us if I have to slice off your fingers." The knife bit slightly into Gill's skin, droplets of blood welling from the cut.

"I hear you," said Gill.

The Red Fist let go of Gill's wrist and patted his head. "Good, Monster." Both Red Fists laughed. "That's our good, good boy."

—CHAPTER TWELVE—

LYLA kept completely still while the Red Fists quietly left. Gill hugged himself, as if he hurt badly.

When their voices faded, Gill sat back on his heels, and Lyla murmured, "Slagging hell, Gill."

Gill slowly stood, moaning a little. She stepped toward him.

He took a step back, turning the bad side of his face away from her. "I'm fine."

She studied his long nose and hollow cheek. Then she whispered, "Those guys seem like they think they're soldiers or something."

"A bunch of the Red Fist guys think they get to do whatever they want, 'cause they're heroes for attacking barons."

"Who were they?"

"Knife." Gill's voice was soft. "And Pug."

"You don't know their real names?"

"What do you want their real names for? To report them to the bluecoats?" For a frozen moment, Lyla thought he suspected her, and then Gill laughed. He stopped short, hissing. "*Merde*. I think they broke one of my ribs."

She reached out to him. The brush of his coat sleeve made her hand pull back. Instead of taking his arm, she asked, "You all right? Should I do something?"

"There's nothing to do. Except keep from getting hit in the ribs again for a while."

"Better to get hit than to get your fingers cut off."

He gave an odd, gasping laugh. "You gotta stop. *Please.*"

"All right. All right," she said, though she hadn't actually meant to be funny. "Do you wish the bluecoats *would* catch them, though?" she whispered. "Lock them up forever?"

"Why?"

"To get back at them."

"I'll hit back at them." He sounded angry. "I'm not Red Fist's whipping dog."

"I wasn't saying you are."

He limped toward the doorway and peered through. "Where's Zeb and them?"

"That's not what I meant," she insisted.

"I heard you," he said without looking at her.

"Sure. Listen, Jack—" She heard a slight thud from the other room.

"There," whispered Gill. Then, "Hey," as he drew back from the doorway and leaned against the wall.

Nose, his nose swollen and one eye bruised, came through the doorway, Zeb and Spinner following. Jit came after, capering on his hands and feet like a kid doing the bear walk for some game.

He stopped near Gill, then crouched, saying, "You look like crap, Scribbler."

"Did you take a hit tonight?" asked Zeb.

"Yeah," Gill said, and he shot a glare at Jit, who didn't seem to notice.

Zeb, scowling, shook his head. Lyla couldn't tell whether he was unhappy with Gill or the Red Fists.

"Jit, they knew I was meeting you," said Gill. "They talked to you. You could've warned me."

"Don't come wailing to me. You're the one who was stupid enough to give that sketch to Nose."

"Nose—" Gill said, and then stopped, staring at Nose's bruised face. Then he started again, his voice less angry. "You all right, man?"

"Yeah, yeah."

Jit suddenly caught sight of Lyla, and he grinned. On all fours again, he began to creep toward her. She stood her ground.

"Scribbler," Zeb said, smoothing his slicked-back hair. "You need a little something to take the edge off?"

"Zeb, man, yeah, I do. If you got something, I'll forever worship the dirt your boots touch." Gill leaned his head back against the wall.

Lyla watched Zeb hand Gill a tin. Gill took a couple of pills out of it and swallowed them. The night was going from bad to worse.

Jit crouched in front of her, his grin reminding her of a dog's. "Hey, Bright. What're you doing here?"

"I came with Scribbler."

"You lost?" Spinner's voice climbed high, sickly sweet and breathy. "You need help?"

"No. Scribbler promised an adventure."

Nose laughed. "An adventure. Working for Red Fist's always an adventure," he said, wiping his nose on his sleeve. "Plus, they're the only ones that can pay us a wad of points. Which I sure need."

Zeb frowned. "You're out again? Already?"

Nose shifted from one foot to the other.

"What did you blow them all on?" Zeb demanded. "You better not be snorting powder again. That crap'll kill you. The pills were supposed to help you stop."

"I didn't blow them on nothing." Nose shifted faster. "Trousers. I got some trousers. In the market. A couple pairs." He plucked at the ones he was wearing. "Not these."

"Who slagging cares what he spent 'em on?" Jit said, and sat back on his haunches.

"Just forget it for now, Zeb." Spinner studied Lyla, her eyes heavy-lidded like a cat's, watching without seeming to watch.

Yeah, I see you.

"For now," Zeb said. "Sure." He crossed his arms and leaned against the wall, next to Gill.

"I still have points," said Spinner. "So does Zeb. I bet Scribbler does too." Gill nodded. "We don't have to go scavenging tonight. I got some great discs from the trash outside of the Beacon. Only a little warped. Nothing that really shouts out against barons. But city beats, horns—great. We could head to my room and I'll spin them. We could dance." She gave Zeb a little smile, and he gave her a little smile back. Spinner said to Lyla, "There's not a lot of space in my room. If you don't like city beats"—her tone saying, *If you don't like city beats, you're an idiot*—"you might just want to head home."

It had never occurred to Lyla that squatties might sit around cranking a spinner and listening to music. Which was stupid—why else would the girl be called Spinner? "I like city beats. I heard them at the Beacon." She rattled off the names of some troupes she liked. "I like to dance."

"Those are decent troupes." Spinner still studied her with those watchful cat eyes, but Gill wore this smile as if Lyla had said the exact right thing.

Jit crept closer to Lyla. "Spinner, whatever music Bright likes, she still could be a squealer."

"She's no squealer," said Gill.

Lyla looked only at Jit, with his big ugly grin. "You really think I'm a squealer?"

Jit rose directly in front of her. His pupils were huge; he was definitely flying on something. "Bluecoats've been knocking Marked around. Beating on them till they promise to squeal." The beatings had to be a Red Fist lie; Lyla hadn't heard about any. "We should see if they been thumping you. I'll check you over." He leered at her chest.

Spinner said to Jit, "We'd have to check for bruises. That's all. *Not* check what size she is."

"Bigger than apples," crowed Nose.

"Shut up, Nose," said Gill.

"But smaller than melons," Nose went on.

Lyla resisted the urge to cross her arms over her chest; if they knew they were bothering her, they'd never stop.

"What are those fruits called?" Nose persisted. "From the southlands?"

Gill pushed himself off the wall. His face grim, he took a step toward Nose. "I said, shut up."

Nose skittered back.

"Nose," Jit said, laughing. "Looking at sketches in the nasties don't make you any kind of judge. You need a guy who knows what he's doing."

"Jit." Gill said it like a threat.

"You're a pig, Jit," said Spinner. "You and Nose both are. Neither of you is going to look her over."

Jit shoved Spinner. Zeb's fist shot out, hitting Jit in the gut. Jit grunted and doubled over, as Zeb said quietly, "I told you to slagging quit pushing Spinner around."

Gill walked over to Nose, and Nose held both his hands up. "I was just japing, man." He said in Lyla's direction, "Sorry."

She shrugged.

Gill murmured to Lyla, "We should'a just stayed in the wood."

She smiled.

Spinner looked from her to Gill, eyes cat-sly again. "You planning on bringing her to everything, Scribbler?

"She needs work."

"I can look out for bluecoats," Lyla said. "Or whatever you need."

"I don't know, man, about bringing along Bright," Zeb said to Gill. "We do good as we are."

"Yeah," Gill agreed. "She's quick, though. And she's smart."

"We're all quick." Jit clapped his hands. "We're all smart."

Zeb and Spinner shared a look. Spinner said, "Sometimes we could use someone small and fast. And she doesn't seem Marked, so people won't suspect her right off."

"I'm vouching for her," said Gill.

"You don't have to," Lyla insisted. "Look, you want me to prove myself, I will. Ask me anything."

"Bright," Jit said suddenly. "You were in the Bright."

"Yeah."

"You know where it is. In the school."

"Yeah," she said again.

He grinned at her, a feral dog smile. "We've never scavenged there before. I bet it's got some stuff Red Fist'll pay for. You can show us where it is. Where the best stuff to take is."

Lyla started to nod, to keep her head from shaking no.

Spinner said, "That's a decent idea. We could lay some paint on the walls while we're there."

Zeb added, "Speak a little truth."

Whatever that meant. "Burn the Barons"? "Sure," said Lyla. "Sure. Though Teacher and the rest at the school, they're not barons."

Jit grinned wider. "You don't want to steal from them, Bright."

"I'm just saying if you're trying to hit at barons, Teacher isn't one."

"You like Teacher," Nose chanted like a kid in the schoolyard.

"No," she said. Beside her, Gill cocked his head, looking her over. Mistrusting her? Or silently telling her to toughen up.

"You liked licking that Bright teacher's boots," Spinner mocked. "And you really thought that if you kept his boots clean enough, he'd find you a baron—so then you could lick that baron's boots too."

You'd rather lick Red Fist's boots?

Jit stepped close. He was staring at Lyla's temple, rather than her eyes. His breath was terrible, as if food or a tooth was rotting in his mouth. "You don't want to steal from some bootlicking teacher?"

Lyla kept her own stare steady. "All I was saying was he isn't a baron. But, yeah, he's got all kinds of inventioneering stuff. If you're looking to scavenge, it's a great place to go."

Jit smiled and shook his head. "The Bright," he called. "We're going to take apart the Bright." He raised his arms. "Rip it to shreds."

Lyla kept a smile plastered on her face. "Great."

—CHAPTER THIRTEEN—

AT the edge of the pines, the pack of squatties stopped. Ahead lay the snowy slope, blue-white in the darkness and moonlight, and at the slope's peak stood the low, rectangular school. Spinner glanced at Lyla, that watching-cat look. Lyla simply met her gaze; you had to earn a cat's respect, not beg for it.

Zeb stopped here and there to spray paint on walls: THE MINES = SLAVERY and QUIT DIGGING — START SINGING, whatever that was supposed to mean. Lyla was just following the pack; she wasn't part of it.

Beside Lyla, Gill tapped his gloved fingers against his knees. Jit and Nose shifted their feet and jostled each other.

"Is there a guard, Bright?" Zeb murmured.

"I bet there is," whispered Gill. Since taking the pills, he talked so quickly. "Is there?" he asked her.

"A bluecoat?" asked Spinner.

The pack's faces, splotchy in the moonlight, stared at her.

"We were searched by bluecoats when we got here the other morning," she told Spinner. "So, maybe."

Spinner nodded. "Where would a bluecoat stand guard?"

"They were at the entrance. At the doors."

"A guard wouldn't stand there all night." Spinner's cat stare asked, *So? Where?*

"On the roof?" Lyla suggested.

Spinner shrugged. "Maybe."

There must be something more clever to say.

"I'll find him," said Jit.

"Oh, no," Zeb told Jit. "I'll find him and lead him off. You stay."

Jit muttered something Lyla couldn't hear, something guttural and ugly, while Zeb bolted off, up the slope. Zeb bent, kind of skulking, though he was in plain sight. Lyla was reminded of birds that pretended they were hurt, to get you to walk away from their nests. A form, a bluecoat, leaped from the tree that stood by the school. He yelled and began to chase Zeb. They ran over part of the field, strangely silent, as if neither had a voice. Zeb led the bluecoat into the pines, a distance away. Lyla rose.

"Wait," whispered Gill and Spinner.

From the trees, not far from where Zeb disappeared, a small column of flames shot upward.

"What was that?" Lyla asked.

"Something borrowed." Gill laughed, and so did Jit and Nose. "A fire-shooter. Guess we're not giving it back."

Another flash shot upward.

"All right," said Spinner.

The pack leaped forward, and Lyla scrambled after them. *Catch up.*

Jit passed Spinner and led them to the school's side entrance. The double doors were locked together, a chain wound around their handles.

"Pick it, Spinner," chanted Nose. "Pick the lock."

Gill stopped beside Lyla, swaying a little on his feet. She glanced at him but couldn't tell if he still felt pain or didn't feel anything. *"Merde,"* he said, staring off toward the pines. "Green flames."

Either she'd missed a flash or Gill was starting to see things because of the pills. And also not see things, like Jit sidling up to her so close, she could smell his rotten breath. "What'll we find in the Bright, Bright? Decent scavenge?"

"Yeah." *The orb.* What would happen to Teacher Slate if they stole the orb? "I could go in and bring stuff out on my own. Or me and Scribbler can."

"She wants to get you alone, Scribbler," said Jit. "You're into ugly, Bright?"

"Shut up." The words were out of Lyla's mouth before she could stop them.

"Hey—Bright's got a little spark."

Nose laughed.

"She just doesn't want to listen to your yapping all night," said Gill, without looking away from the trees.

Jit whined like a dog. "You wound me, man."

"Don't we need lookouts?" Lyla asked. "Out here, in case the bluecoat comes back?"

"Doors are open," said Spinner. She unwound the chain. "I

want to lay a little paint out here. You can lay some inside, Scribbler? I'll be lookout."

Before Lyla could suggest Jit be the lookout instead, Jit and Nose tromped into the school. Gill drifted behind them. All Lyla could do was follow.

As she passed Spinner, Spinner gave her a small, brief smile.

Lyla matched Spinner's smile — small, brief, not too eager.

They stepped into the darkness. Jit lit a match, and then a lantern so small, he must've been carrying it in his pocket. "All right, Bright," he said. "What good are you?"

"This way." She started fast down the cold hall. Maybe she could get enough ahead to hide the orb before they saw it.

"Still stinks the same in here," said Gill as Jit grabbed the top edge of an AIM HIGH — BECOME AN INVENTOR broadsheet and yanked, ripping it into ragged strips.

"Scribbler, you came here a long time," said Nose.

"Until the winter I was a tenth year."

"Tenth year!" Nose exclaimed as Jit shredded the next broadsheet. "I dropped out of eighth. I kinda miss running races on the field," Nose admitted. "I won a bunch."

"Yeah?" said Gill. "I didn't know that."

"Why'd you stay so long?"

"My ma's idea. Not mine."

"Awww. Your ma," mocked Jit.

Gill veered in front of Lyla, and without saying a word, he slammed Jit against the wall, pinning him easily, both wrists in one hand. Gill's other hand pressed Jit so his chest was flat against the wall. "What are you slagging doing, Monster?" Jit demanded.

Gill pressed one knee against the back of one of Jit's knees, pushing it against the wall, and Jit's face spasmed.

"I was just kidding around." Jit's voice was actually pleading, the best sound Lyla had heard all night; it made Nose grin. "I didn't mean anything."

Gill studied Jit's face from the side. Gill's knee shifted, digging into the back of Jit's knee.

"Ah!" called Jit. "Slag it. I didn't mean anything." He grimaced, eyes squinting. "Don't break it."

Lyla stifled a laugh; he must not know Gill very well if he really thought Gill would break his knee.

Gill smiled. He drew back his leg, and Jit sagged a bit. Then Gill swung his knee sharply into the back of Jit's, striking it; it hit the wall. Jit shrieked.

Lyla stared, disbelieving.

"Nice," said Nose.

Gill let Jit go, and he crumpled to the floor. Hissing, Jit clutched his knee and rocked.

"What if you broke it?" Lyla asked.

"It isn't broken," Gill said, though he didn't sound as if he cared one way or the other. "Get up, Jit. Let's go." He nudged Jit with his toe.

"It *is* broken, you slagging monster."

"If it is, that's your own fault. Quit beating on everybody. You've been such an ass lately."

Gill and Nose began to walk off, leaving Jit alone in the dark. Lyla trailed behind, keeping her distance.

Gill slowed and swayed toward her. "We going the right way?"

"No." She stopped and glanced back, into the dark where Jit moaned. Then she glanced ahead, beyond the light from the lantern Nose held. The hallway looked as strange as a street she'd never been down before. *Pull yourself together.*

They were in the hall leading from the side door, so they had to turn ahead. "Yeah, this is the way."

She took the lead, walking fast. She didn't want Gill too close to her.

From behind came the sound of limping footsteps, and then shredding paper. She turned and walked backwards. Jit was leaving a torn broadsheet. He gimped to the next, and he raked the paper.

Lyla turned and sped up, feeling chased, though she was leading the pack. The door to the Bright was locked. She had to stop and wait while Gill and Jit smashed it down. Gill grunted as they broke through, finally seeming to feel some kind of pain. He stumbled a little, but then he caught his balance.

Nose shoved past. "Bright got us to the Bright."

Lyla stepped through the doorway and then stopped. The guys were silent—Gill swaying a little and studying the room, Jit glaring at Gill, Nose drifting toward the stove. The Bright was cleaner than she remembered. The floor was so smooth. The windows were whole, their glazed panes reflecting the lantern's flickering candlelight. Beyond the wood stove's grill lay glowing embers; the air was still a bit warm, though the school day had ended hours ago.

Not a single one of the pack seemed to notice the orb above Teacher's desk. Its dimness and its rectangular paper shade hid it, so it looked only like an overlarge rectangular lantern. But it wasn't. It was the best thing in the room to steal. It was the thing that would make the pack praise her.

"There's nothing decent here." Jit limped forward and slammed a desk with his fists, toppling it.

"What do you mean?" Nose skittered to the side, keeping well away from Jit. "It's something. Some-thing."

Jit sneered. "We been in abandoned warehouses with better scavenge."

"You just never been to school," said Nose. "There aren't rooms like this for anybody regular. If there were, maybe I would've kept studying the crap they teach."

"Aren't we wasting time?" Gill was still swaying a little on his feet. "We're wasting time. And I want to leave a few words on the walls. Words to the wise."

"Your girl should'a told us the Bright wasn't nowhere good. We got better places to go." Jit hurled a chair at the desks, and they crashed, toppling over.

Gill shook his head. He asked Lyla, "Where's the best scavenge?"

Look up.

"There's the cabinets along the walls," she said. "And the

shelves. All those have metal and tools. Also there's a locked one near the closet. I don't know what's in it. Or in the closet. I don't know what's in there."

"You don't know much." Jit limped to her and Gill. "You don't know anything."

"She hasn't been a thief since the cradle," remarked Gill.

Jit spat on the floor, near Gill's boots.

"If you want to spit at me, why don't you go ahead?" Gill pointed to his own face. "Right here, man. I dare you."

Jit pointed to his own face. "I dare you," he mocked.

"Teacher's got leaflets in his desk," Lyla said quickly. "Alchem-yks sheets, I think. He locks the desk."

"You know where the key is?" demanded Jit.

"No."

"I can break into it, simple," said Gill.

Jit limped to Teacher Slate's desk. He yanked on one of the desk drawers, which stayed shut. He pounded on the desktop with the flats of his hands. "This is gonna be a crap haul!"

"We haven't even looked yet." Gill gestured at the cabinets, and Nose took a bounding step toward them.

"No," ordered Jit, and Nose froze. "This is a slagging waste of clicks. Let's bolt."

"There's scavenge to collect, you stupid slag," said Gill.

"There's nothing good here." Jit grinned, teeth bared. "*Your* Bright, she's led us bad. *Your* Bright, she don't know nothing."

"You've got piss for brains," said Gill.

Jit started toward him.

"You both are slagging idiots," Lyla said, trying to distract them from another fight.

Jit whirled toward her.

"You can't even see what's right in front of your nose," she said.

Jit stopped. All three guys stared at her.

She looked at them, only them, not up at the orb. "What's inside the shade? Above Teacher's desk."

Jit and Gill looked up, staring as if they didn't know what they were seeing.

"What?" Nose asked, shuffling over. "What is it?"

Gill started to grin.

Nose reached him and peered up. "No way."

Jit smiled so widely, Lyla could see a couple of his rotten teeth. "Bright, I was kind of wrong."

She held her ground as he came closer to her with his foul breath. "You're not totally useless," he said, slapping her on the shoulder.

"Thanks." She smiled. "That's such a sweet compliment."

Jit laughed. Then he launched himself toward Teacher's desk, jumping on top of it. He reached over his head for the orb's shade and tore the paper. The orb hung above: the smooth oval of glass and the colored moths with outstretched wings, ready to fly off.

But there was no way to escape.

Threatened Alchemyks, episode 5

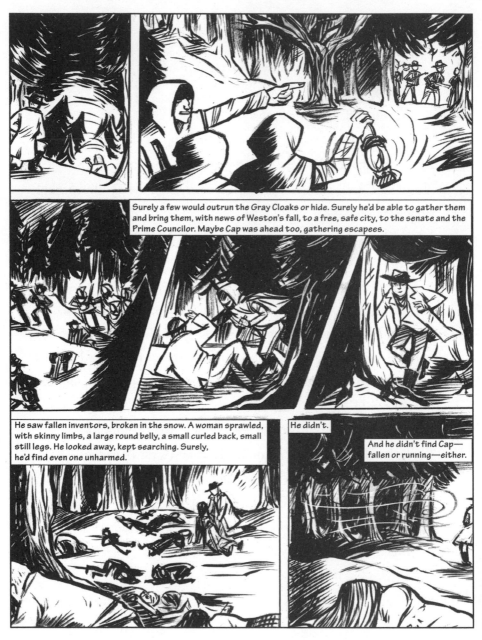

Surely a few would outrun the Gray Cloaks or hide. Surely he'd be able to gather them and bring them, with news of Weston's fall, to a free, safe city, to the senate and the Prime Councilor. Maybe Cap was ahead too, gathering escapees.

He saw fallen inventors, broken in the snow. A woman sprawled, with skinny limbs, a large round belly, a small curled back, small still legs. He looked away, kept searching. Surely, he'd find even one unharmed.

He didn't.

And he didn't find Cap—fallen or running—either.

—CHAPTER FOURTEEN—

IN school the next day, Lyla sat in dull classes as dull teachers droned on. She didn't listen. Instead, she daydreamed about Pirate Jackman's search for Lady Captain—and she also kept seeing the night before, in the Bright.

Lantern light had flickered. Jit and Nose had hurled chairs and stomped on graphites. Gill, using a spray bottle from inside his coat pocket, painted on the walls: WAKE UP! BREAK THE BOOTLICKING SYSTEM! Her own gloved hands collected bits of metal, coils of wire, and leaflets covered with primary alchemyks symbols. She touched the sleek glass of the orb carefully, carefully, though its Protean was fixed, solid, safe. She couldn't help thinking that the orb's sliver of Protean, somewhere within it, was enough to explode her and all of them. Teacher Slate had told her once that the casing around the Protean sliver would break only if it grew too hot, as hot as the hottest heart of a fire of burning chemyks, or too cold, as cold as a midwinter nighttime blizzard. Still, holding the orb felt risky.

She cradled the glass. When the others weren't looking, she

caressed it with her cheek. Cool and silky smooth. She unbuttoned her coat, held the orb against her belly, and rebuttoned the coat over it as best she could, to carry it easily.

Outside the school, in the cold, they met Spinner at the school's door. Painted there: DON'T WASTE YOUR LIFE IN THIS PRISON. Spinner asked, "How's the haul?"

Nose jumped up and down, the metal in all his pockets clanking. "I got alchemyks sheets in my trousers."

"We should get on before someone sees us," Gill said softly. He slouched, as if the pain from his beating was breaking through the pill-numbness.

"Bright surprised us." Jit swooped down and kissed Lyla's orb-belly.

Lyla unbuttoned her coat a little, and Spinner leaned over to look. *"Merde,"* Spinner whispered. "Bright, next time you come out to play, the drinks are on me."

The pack surrounded Lyla on all sides, hiding her from any passersby. They hid her at their center through the pines, through the alleyways, and up to a maze of rooftops. All the way to a warehouse, where they set their scavenge in a closet, for Red Fist to collect.

She had taken the orb. She was quick. She was bold. She was a thief.

And in all the school hallways today, everybody whispered about her without knowing she, right beside them, was the one they were whispering over. *Red Fist? Squatties? They broke down the Bright door. They thieved everything good in there. They thieved an orb. Did you know there'd been an orb in there? Me neither.*

Hope usually took the same hallways Lyla did so they could say hey between classes, but Lyla didn't see Hope, not even once, not even a glimpse. Lyla had kept everything she'd done secret, just like Riverton wanted. What could she have said, anyhow? Especially because Hope had already been upset; they'd received a message from the owner saying he wasn't going to reopen the Beacon. So neither of them had a job, but they needed credit points to help with the farm debts. And now that Hope had seen the broken-apart Bright, Hope was avoiding Lyla, suspecting her. Whenever Lyla thought on this, she felt ill. Triumphant and sly, but ill.

The day moved so slowly, as if clicks had somehow slowed for good. Lyla just wanted to reach the last chime, when she would finally meet Hope at the doors. Even if they fought, that was better than not seeing Hope at all. Plus, on the way to school, Lyla had spotted Riverton's initials in the old tree at the edge of town: the signal to meet. She wanted to get on to the meeting. But the clicks kept crawling.

And then, as Lyla was dragging from one endless class to another, bluecoats burst into the school. They swept through the hallway with rifles swinging back and forth, like hounds hunting prey. Their faces were grim. One stopped right in front of Lyla, and she started: Junot Riverton.

"Hi," sprang out of her mouth.

He shook his head once, *no*, as she remembered too late that she wasn't supposed to know him.

"Get on, Marked." He jabbed at her with his rifle, hitting her rib.

She winced and stepped back.

His mouth opened, softening, and he looked as if he was about to say, "I'm sorry." Then his mouth closed. "I said get on."

Lyla turned and walked, refusing to rub her aching rib. Riverton followed her down the hall with the rifle pointed at her back.

He gathered other Marked in the hallways and in classrooms. Then he herded them all to the eating hall, where a bluecoat checked names off a list he held. There, in black letters, "Lyla Northstrom," with all the rest. *Lyla Northstrom — Marked.*

A stocky bluecoat with an arrogant face and spectacles walked over. "I don't know why we even bother to send them to school."

Riverton and another bluecoat gave the one with spectacles brief respectful bows. "Captain." Riverton's voice was awestruck.

"Bag the guilty ones," the captain ordered, gesturing to a table with a pile of cloth bags, the kind that bluecoats put on the heads of Red Fists. Lyla's rib cage narrowed around her lungs. "Then give them to me."

"Yes, sir."

Riverton shoved the Digger Street kid beside Lyla toward the center of the candlelit room, where bluecoats surrounded a cluster of Marked. Lyla went before Riverton could shove her, finding a place with the others. One guy near her smelled sour, like the way Da smelled when he was sweating from fever. Lyla shifted a little, but she couldn't get the stink out of her nose. She also couldn't stop staring at the rifles.

The captain stood in the corner, his eyes hidden by his spectacles, which reflected the candlelight's flickering glare. Riverton kept taking Marked to the side for questioning. "You," he said to the guy beside Lyla, and then, "You," to the guy on the other side. "You," and then, "You," and then, "You." But not her. He didn't even look at her. The Marked stood before him, and he asked questions Lyla couldn't hear. One eighth year tried to bolt, and swiftly, gracefully, Riverton grabbed the kid's arm, knocked him to his knees, and forced his forehead to the floor. Another bluecoat locked the kid's wrists in metal bands and drew a bag over his head, the cloth sagging sideways.

The bluecoat yanked the kid up and then led him to the captain. "Sit," ordered the captain, and as the kid lowered himself, the captain grabbed a handful of the kid's cloth bag. He jerked the kid back, and when the kid yelped, the captain said, "Against the wall, mine rat." The kid scuttled to the wall.

"You," Lyla heard, and she tore her stare from the captain and the cowering kid. Riverton was finally looking at her. "Well?"

She walked over to where he stood, a bit away from the rest of the bluecoats, and from the captain, whose glinting spectacles turned in her direction. Still, she expected Riverton to mention her tour somehow. Instead he began firing questions at her, barely giving her enough time to answer. He asked who she was, where she lived, how she'd gotten herself marked the first time.

She paused, surprised. "You caught me at the shadow market, sir."

He narrowed his eyes, as if trying to remember. Then he shrugged.

Not even some small hint that the tour existed.

"Where were you last night?" he asked, and she told him she'd been at home. He said, "With anyone?"

"My sister."

"Your sister's here?"

"No. Well, yes. She's at the school, but she isn't Marked. She's in Advanced Studies."

"Who's your sister?"

His graphite was poised, ready to write the name, as though he didn't already know it. The captain was watching, listening for her answer. "Hope Northstrom," Lyla said very quietly.

Riverton wrote down *Hope Northstrom*. "If you're lying, you'll get in less trouble by confessing now," he warned.

His face was so smooth, so blank.

"I was home last night, sir," she repeated.

He put something down next to Hope's name. "We'll speak with her." He said it like a threat. Then he held up his papers, and the captain started over. "Get out of here."

"But Hope didn't do anything wrong. Not at all."

"I said, get out of here, Northstrom. That'll help your sister most."

All Lyla could do was leave, sidestepping out of the captain's way like any other Marked. She had to warn Hope that the captain might question her about last night. Or Riverton. And that Riverton would pretend, so completely, that the tour didn't exist. But he was only pretending it didn't exist. He knew it existed. He knew.

The last chime of the day rang. Lyla waited at the school's front doors for Hope as everybody jostled past. Cornelia Millener walked by, her eyes puffy; she'd been crying. She was probably coming from the Bright. Dane shoved through a group of seventh years and hit the doors so hard, they flew open in front of him. They banged somebody outside, who yelled, "What the slag are you doing?"

No Hope. The ski racers clattered by in their blue snow trousers, jackets, and hats. They wore their right sleeves rolled up a little to show their clean wrists. Lyla looked away. A couple of teachers came toward the door, leaving for the day. If she kept standing here, she'd probably see Teacher Slate.

Lyla pushed off the wall, toward the exit. Then she stopped. She had to warn Hope about the questioning.

She started down a hallway, unsure where she was going. She took the turn toward the performance hall, though Hope hadn't said earlier that she had a rehearsal. Hope sometimes snuck into the hall when she was upset.

Lyla opened the performance hall doors a crack and heard the rise and fall of quick scales. She hesitated. Then she slipped into the darkness.

Ahead, beyond the rows and rows of seats, on the wide empty stage, stood the scuffed piano, a lantern resting on top of it. Hope sat on the piano's old bench, and her hands flew up and down the keys. She was playing scales so fast, they sounded like running and running until you could barely breathe, but still running because you had to get away.

Hope stopped abruptly, letting her hands drop to her lap. She was silent, but her shoulders heaved as if she couldn't get enough air.

Lyla wrapped her arms around herself. *I'm sorry about the Bright.*

Slowly Hope's breathing steadied. She kept staring down at her hands in her lap.

I'm sorry.

Hope straightened. She shut the curved top over the piano keys, grabbed the lantern's handle, and started up the aisle between the rows of seats, staring down at her own boots. She reached Lyla and stopped dead, looking up at her, lantern half raised, eyes wide and mouth a little open.

I'm sorry.

No sound came out. None.

Hope blinked, her mouth closing. The shadows were somehow darker around her eyes, or maybe it was her skin that was shadowy, as if it were worn out or bruised. "You know about the Bright."

Lyla nodded.

"You know it's terrible." Hope's tone was accusing. "It's a ruin."

Lyla cleared her throat. "It can be picked up, right? A lot's just a stupid mess."

"No," Hope argued. "Not all of it. Teacher Slate's desk— He yanked out all the drawers, they were so smashed, and he threw them into the corner of the room. Really hurled them. It was awful."

"But the rest of the desk is all right?"

"What use is it without the drawers?" Hope's voice climbed high. "Of course the orb's gone. Of course. But why wreck so much? Why ruin everything?"

Lyla shook her head. Not everything. She had made sure Jit didn't ruin everything.

"Teacher Slate paid for lots of supplies in the Bright, or he convinced barons to." Hope kept on and on. "Most of what's wrecked won't get replaced. Who would want to donate now? Everything might get stolen again."

"They might still donate. It wasn't his fault."

"That won't matter," Hope declared. "You know it won't."

"It should matter—blaming him is wrong."

"You know people will anyway." Hope thrust the lantern closer to Lyla's face; Lyla tried to blink away the light's glare. "Unless the officers find out about the thieves."

"Find out about the thieves," Lyla repeated faintly.

"You talked to the officers, didn't you?" The light shook. "Earlier?"

"Junot Riverton brought me to the eating hall to be questioned. Yeah, I talked to him."

Hope held the lantern so close to Lyla's face its glare stung. *Well?*

"Would you put the light down? It's hurting my eyes."

"Sorry," said Hope, though she didn't sound like she meant it. She let the light sink a tiny bit.

"There wasn't much I could tell him."

Hope's mouth opened a little, soundless.

"There were a lot of people in the eating hall," Lyla said, but Hope only gave a "So?" shrug. "They brought in every one of the Marked. It was crowded. And there were lots of bluecoats—officers—all around." Also that scrawny eighth-year kid with his head bagged, who had to scuttle to the wall. "A captain was bagging some kids."

"So?"

"Everyone could hear everything I said."

"The officers don't know who did it?" whispered Hope. "They aren't even out looking for the orb?"

"Well, they probably are out looking."

"But they don't know where to look."

"They might. I don't know. How am I supposed to know?"

"It's *gone*."

Lyla struggled to keep her voice soft. "I'm doing what I'm supposed to do."

Hope shook her head.

"I am."

"We should get on," Hope said flatly.

"Fine." Lyla started fast for the door so she didn't have to walk with Hope or say another word to her.

But at the door, she heard voices and stopped. Coming through the wood, the words were unclear. She and Hope waited as the voices drifted away.

"Wait," whispered Lyla. "Did Riverton question you yet?"

"Of course he hasn't questioned me. Why would he question me?"

"It's not so ludicrous. Unmarked sometimes break laws too."

"I haven't. Lyla, why does he want to question me?"

"Maybe because you're suspicious." Lyla flared at Hope, but then her anger snuffed out. "Actually—it's not so big a thing. I told Riverton I was home last night with you."

Hope didn't move. "You what?"

"Hope, it's *Riverton*."

"Why did you say that to him?"

"I already told you. The eating hall was crowded." Lyla dropped her voice lower. "I'm meeting him later. That's when I'll explain."

"What if he doesn't question me? What if someone else does?" Hope whispered angrily. "Do you expect me to lie?"

"It'll be him."

"You don't know that for sure."

"It will be. He has to know it's gotta be. He's not stupid."

"This isn't right. None of this is right." Hope pushed past her, yanking open the door. The sudden light blinded Lyla.

Hope stepped out and slammed the door shut, leaving Lyla alone in the dark.

—CHAPTER FIFTEEN—

LYLA tried not to think of Hope as she climbed the Hill path on her way to meet Riverton. She didn't see Hope ahead of her. After Hope left the performance hall, she must have dashed quickly, or taken a different route, or hidden herself away somewhere.

If you don't want to see me, fine. I don't really want to see you, either.

Project Road lay ahead and to the left. Lyla stepped to the side, almost into the ditch, then stopped. Through the trees, she could glimpse the tops of the Project's towers and its fence; also, strung across the end of Project Road, the edges of the flapping banners: THE TOWN COUNCILOR'S PROJECT: PROTEAN POWER FOR EVERY HOME. YOU'RE INVITED—4TH MONTH 4—THE PROJECT UNVEILED!

Lyla stayed at the edge of the road for a moment, scanning the path and trees. She seemed to be alone. *Quick and careful.*

She leapt over the snow-filled ditch and reached a cluster of pines with boughs so thick, the ground beneath them was almost bare. Like Lady Captain, she jumped from pine to pine, landing in a crouch. She stopped a moment to listen, and heard nothing.

Then, a roaring sound made her drop to her knees. Back on the Hill path, a machine growl—rounded metal and glass, peace-officer blue, hurtled up the hillside. A patrol.

She waited until she couldn't hear the roaring anymore, and then longer. Nothing around her moved.

She rose and slipped to the edge of the small clearing. She could make out the cellar hole where they were meeting, a large concrete square. The snow inside was untouched, as smooth as milk in the bottom of a mug. The cellar's far end actually had a roof: a section of the floor from the house that had once stood on top of the hole. She considered quietly calling Riverton's name.

But to her right side, through the trees, stood the Project fence and its towers. The top windows of the towers gleamed with red-orange light. Shadowy forms—guards or inventors—moved across the light, unhurried. She crouched more deeply within the pine branches. She couldn't let anybody inside the Project catch sight of her.

The light between the towers, above the building, was odd. The dusk seemed to flicker, bright and then dim and then bright. As if the air, or maybe the sky, was shaking.

What's going on in there?

That wasn't her concern right now.

She crept to the covered edge of the cellar hole. At one of its corners, there were steep steps, brushed clean. She hesitated and listened; wind murmured in the pines. No footsteps, none that she could hear. She climbed down the stairs, slowly, silently.

She reached the bottom, a stone slab that lay before a wooden door. She listened again: still nothing but wind. She eased the door open.

A couple of candles lit the dirt and stone cellar, and across from her, at the opposite wall, crouched a man, who began to rise. Instead of peace-officer blue, he wore trousers and a coat, dusty gray and faded. She stepped back.

"You made it." He sounded relieved. As he walked forward, she saw his face: Riverton. He smiled, then said again, "You made it." His pace quickened. "You came."

"Didn't you leave your signal, sir? Your initials?"

"Yeah. But you could've changed your mind." He stopped so close to her, she could see his eyes were mismatched—one dark brown, one brown-green—like the eyes of two different people. "Hey— I . . . Earlier, at the school," he said. "I didn't mean to hit you with the rifle. You're all right?"

The rib ached. "Yes. Fine."

His mismatched eyes studied her. "You're a better liar than I thought. When I questioned you, you sounded like any other Marked."

"I thought . . . You said you didn't want anyone to learn about the tour."

"I don't. They can't."

"So. I mean, I have to be a good liar."

"You do," Riverton admitted. But he kept looking at her, looking, looking.

What? she wanted to ask. *What do you see?*

"I found the squatties, sir," Lyla said. "Waterhouse took me to them. We were the ones in the Advanced Studies room."

"I thought so. That's great." He reached for her arm, and she flinched. "Are you all right? Did they hurt you?"

"No. I mean, yes. I'm all right," she said. He took her elbow as if she were a little kid, rather than someone just a few years younger than he was, and he pulled her over to the crate with the candle. "Really. Nothing's wrong with me. I'm fine."

He squinted at her in the candlelight. Then he nodded slightly. "All right. The attacks the other night on the Beacon and the Lift—"

"They weren't the big attacks. Red Fist has a bigger scheme."

"Yeah. There are a lot of whispers going around about a Project attack. Maybe Red Fist here is planning with Red Fist in the capital to attack a bunch of places at the same time. But we've only heard rumors." Riverton spoke fast. "Did Waterhouse talk about that?"

"Gill—Waterhouse—did say that this one Red Fist who leads attacks goes on and on about trying to take over. Like, take over the mines and the Project. So inventors will have to work for Red Fist. They'll be, I guess, like barons. He talks big. But he basically just knocks people around."

"Oh, yeah." Riverton slumped a little. "They're always

sounding off like that. My captain's already heard a lot of Red Fist bragging from squatties he's questioned. None of it useful."

"The captain from the school? The one bagging kids?"

"Yeah, that's Captain Dyre. He's tough to impress, Northstrom. Believe me," Riverton said with awe. "He takes no mouthing off, no excuses. If you earn his respect, you know you deserve it. He's so great. The best."

Maybe they somehow weren't talking about the same captain?

"Waterhouse didn't tell you anything else?" Riverton asked urgently. "About . . . anything important?"

Lyla tried to remember exactly what Gill had said, every single thing. "He didn't say more stuff about the attacks, sir. Jit, this other squattie, he did say how great it was to be a Red Fist, so you could stomp on everyone." There had to be something else, something important.

"Who were they, the squatties? Were they Red Fist?"

"No, but Waterhouse and I met some Red Fists. Before the squatties."

"Really?" Riverton straightened.

Lyla let the silence hover, and he waited for her. This moment, when she knew something and he didn't, made her pulse tap faster. If she asked him for something extra—a bit of food, a better hat or coat—in exchange for telling, would he get it for her?

Don't mess around. Not if you want your mark scraped.

She told him that she met Gill at the shadow market and that they went to the abandoned warehouse. She didn't say a word about the hidden wood, but she told him all she could remember about the Red Fists who'd attacked Gill, all she could about their voices, their sizes, the insults and threats, the knife cutting into Gill's hand, poised to slice off all his fingers.

She told him how the squatties came next. She mostly described Jit. The way he capered around and shoved Nose for no good reason. "He's the worst."

"'The worst'? What are the others?" Riverton asked slowly. "Sweet?"

"No. But he's really the scariest. Nose, too," Lyla added. "Except he's a . . . He's one of those following guys. He tries to get the strongest guy in the room to like him."

"And the rest?"

"Zeb's quieter. He's more careful than Jit." She paused. She wasn't going to say that Zeb obviously liked Spinner or that Spinner spun music discs. "Spinner kind of bosses them all. Jit's a pig to her, but she hits back at him; I mean, with the things she says. Gi— Waterhouse, he's big enough to keep Jit from messing too much with him. Waterhouse schemes with Spinner and Zeb. Those three are more—well, Jit was the one wrecking things in the Bright. But not Spinner and Zeb and Waterhouse. Spinner and Waterhouse painted on the walls. You saw the school door."

"They're angry."

"Yeah," Lyla said slowly. "They want to speak out—"

"They're liars. They're thieves," Riverton went on. "Jit and Nose are the thugs."

"Yeah," she said. "Though what Gill and Spinner wrote weren't really lies. I guess."

Riverton studied her again. His eyes went a little back and forth like he was reading a zine. "You guess?"

"Jit is definitely a thug."

"And the others?"

"They just don't scare me," she said. "They mostly want to tell everyone what's unfair. That's all I meant." Riverton was frowning. Lyla said quickly, "Also, they're thieves. Spinner, Zeb, and Waterhouse." She was a thief. "And me."

His fingers on her elbow gripped her a little more tightly. "Did they give you some kind of trial? You passed it? You're in with them?"

"Because I helped steal the orb. Yeah. They seemed— I think I'll be able to run with them."

Finally, he smiled. "That's great, Northstrom. Really great."

"Thanks."

He let go of her. He took a deep breath in, and then he let it out slowly. "I think this is going to work."

"Yes. It is."

Riverton actually grinned at her, and Lyla grinned back. *This is going to work.*

He bounced a little, slightly bending and straightening his knees. "So then you took the orb to one of the places Red Fist hides in?"

"No. We brought it back to an abandoned warehouse. I can show you which one. We left it so Red Fists can come and pick it up."

His grin faded. "They didn't take you to one of the Red Fist hideaways?"

"I'm not sure they go to those places. Red Fist hires them, but they aren't tattooed. They aren't really Red Fist. Spinner, Zeb, and Waterhouse don't seem to like Red Fist very much."

Riverton paced away from her and then paced back. "You'll have to find a way to get to the hideaways."

"You want to know where they are?"

"We know where most are. At least somewhat. After we raid one, they make new ones. No, here's the thing: Squatties we catch on the street talk about rumors, but they don't really know the plans for Red Fist's big attack. So I bet only a few Red Fists in Hill's Ridge are planning. They won't plan in public. We have to be where we can hear what they're saying."

Riverton reached for Lyla's arm again, her marked arm. She slid it a little behind her thigh, but he grabbed it like it belonged to him. It did belong to him, until she finished her tour. "All right, Northstrom. Listen. If Waterhouse can't get you closer to Red Fist soon, you have to start running around with someone who can. Maybe that other guy, Jit?"

No way.

"Jit sounds ready to get himself tattooed. He'll lead you into the hideaways, I bet. You'll learn a lot more there than on the street. Jit could be better for you to run around with."

Lyla couldn't even imagine what she'd have to do to run around with Jit.

"I'll get myself closer. I'll sort it."

Riverton's one brown eye and one brown-green eye stared at her.

"I will."

"If you can find out more of Red Fist's big scheme, that'd be a real triumph. Especially if you find out about a series of attacks across Highland. My captain, all the captains, could really target Red Fist across the whole land—really hit them hard."

"Okay." *But not by running around with Jit.*

Riverton said, "If we're able to stop the big attack—Captain Dyre, he'll be impressed. Truly, truly impressed. And I'll be able to scrape you clean. I might even be able to scrape you early. You wouldn't have to serve the full year."

"Really?"

He dropped his eyes, and for a long moment. "I mean—" He met her stare again. "I'd have to arrange that. But I would."

"You don't know if you really can."

"If you find a way to keep the Project or the university, somewhere important, safe, I will," he vowed—steady and certain. "You'll get clean early. Unmarked."

Unmarked and free. "Deal."

—CHAPTER SIXTEEN—

LYLA stood on the bottom step to her house, in the dark. Yellow candlelight shone from the small windows. Someone was in the kitchen. Hope.

Lyla took in a deep, cold breath. Around her, the frigid air was vast and silent, as if she were the only person on the Hill, the only person in all of Hill's Ridge, in all of Highland.

She climbed the steps. Inside, she was surprised to see Da, only Da. He stood by the window, at the sink basin, and he was smoking his pipe, though Ma didn't let him smoke in the house. "Little Girl," he said without trying to hide the pipe. The window near him was a bit open, and he exhaled a slow stream of smoke out the gap. His eyes were puffy; he was either very tired or he'd just woken. "We have to keep quiet. Your ma is sleeping."

"Where's Hope?"

"In your room, I think." He put the stem of the pipe in his mouth and he stared at the window as if searching for something important, although all Lyla could see in the glass, all he must be able to see, was his own not-so-clear reflection.

Something was wrong. "Da, have there been cutbacks at the mines?"

"Not that I've heard." He turned to her and frowned. "Have you heard of any?"

"No. But you're smoking in the house."

"Oh. Yeah." He rubbed at his tired eyes with one hand. "Little Girl—The soothers they're giving out at the mines still aren't working good for Ma and some others. The overseer dismissed her, for now. Said she should stay in bed a few days. She doesn't have the Cough, though," he added quickly. "None of them do. It's a breathing problem. They can't quite get enough air. The overseer's ordered another kind of soother for them, but it isn't here yet."

"Did the overseer say to see a healer? Have the others gone to healers?"

Da exhaled smoke, forgetting to blow it out the window, so it drifted around his face. "I talked to a digger who had. It didn't really help. And it cost an arm and a leg."

If Ma was in bed for more than a day or two, they wouldn't have enough for all of this month's debts. Especially because the Beacon was closed, because she wasn't bringing home credit points and neither was Hope. "Hope and I—we can try to find more work."

Da tapped the bowl of his pipe against the sink basin. "I might take a position with the northernmost mines for the rest of the winter. They always need diggers, and I'd earn enough to cover all our debt payments."

The northernmost mines. Where diggers worked long hours, and slept at the mines in shelves built into the rock. You awoke in the dark, you worked endless hours in the dark, you went to sleep in the dark. "Da, really, Hope and I can find something."

"To be honest, Little Girl, you can't cover what we need. Especially as you have your tour to serve."

She wanted to slice the skin off her wrist and begin fresh.

"Little Girl, it's all right. Don't look so sad."

"Da, you'll hate the northernmost mines."

"Come here." As she walked over, Da smiled a little. "You think your old man is too broken down to dig in those mines?"

"No. Of course not."

"You think I'm just about ready for a wheeled chair and gruel for dinner?"

Lyla rolled her eyes. "Da. No."

"A cane—Were you planning on getting me a cane for my birthday?"

"Da."

Da put his hand on the top of her head, kind of cupping it like he used to when she was small. She let him shake her head slightly from side to side. "It'll be all right, Little Girl. We'll make it through."

We will. We have to. She nodded, his hand still on her head. "I should talk to Hope."

"Let her be, Little Girl," he warned. "She's upset with you." His eyebrows raised, a question.

"Da— I—"

There wasn't anything she could tell him.

He dropped his hand. Then he took a deep drag on his pipe. "You got homework?" he asked.

She said, "Yeah," just like usual, and he said, "Get on, then," just like usual. He didn't look at her or ask about her day. He didn't ask why she was so late. There was nothing for either of them to say.

———

Lyla and Hope walked down the Hill path in silence. Sometime late last night, Lyla had quit trying to talk to Hope. Now she thought of Gill's map, which she'd found in the message rock early this morning. She'd hidden it in the Aerie, in her stack of old *Pirate Jackman*s. As kids, she and Gill had left each other messages in a rock by the stream, but until the other night, when Gill suggested that they use the rock again, she had forgotten about it and all their little notes: "Meet me in the tree"; "Gathering berries for dinner"; "Captured!" The map he'd left her said that he could meet at dusk this evening. Dusk was such a long while away.

"Have you gone to see Teacher Slate?" Hope asked suddenly.

Lyla's step faltered. "Pardon?"

"Did you go see him yesterday?"

Lyla shook her head. *No way.* Hope was looking straight at the Hill path, rather than at her, so she added, "No."

Hope made this sound in the back of her throat, a *hunh* of disgust.

"Why should I talk to him?" Lyla demanded.

"You could say you're sorry."

GILL'S MAP

"For what? What do you think I should be sorry for?"

Hope crossed her arms and started walking faster. Then, abruptly, Hope stopped. She pointed.

Ahead lay Project Road. All its banners were gone, except for one, which was large, bright-white, and new: 4TH MONTH 4. The date of the Project's unveiling.

Next to Project Road stood a new shed: a wooden shelter, narrow and tall, with a window facing the Hill path. One side was open to the wind, and a young guy stepped out, holding a rifle. He wore a black cap and coat, the kind worn by private guards. He studied the sisters, shifting back and forth from one foot to the other.

"This is all new," Hope said. "When did they put it up?"

Lyla shrugged. Beyond the shelter, the Project stood just as silent and full of secrets as always—fence and guards; the tall gabled towers at each of the buildings' corners, with triangular windows that shimmered red-yellow.

"Hey," called the guard. He aimed in their direction. "Come here."

"Yes, sir," said Hope.

There was a thudding sound behind them. They turned and found another guard, standing in the path, with another rifle. Above him, a wooden platform rested on high tree limbs. Several trees back, a third guard crouched on another platform in the treetops, watching them, just as he must have watched them and listened to them when they'd passed beneath him. Hope's hand grasped Lyla's, and Lyla silently went over everything she and Hope had just said—nothing, really, about the tour.

The guard behind them on the path gestured toward the shelter with his rifle. "Get on." Walking toward the shelter, Lyla tried to keep her face smooth.

Rooks above the guard who stood on the tree platform bickered and squawked. The guard raised his rifle and aimed. There was a loud crack and the rooks shrieked as one fell. Hope jerked Lyla away from the headless bird lying in the snow.

"Oh, yeah," said the guard who'd shot the rifle. "That's one rook won't swoop at me no longer."

"It's dead?" asked the guard following the girls.

"Shot the head off."

"You gonna put it in the pot?" asked the guard by the shelter.

The other two burst into laughter. "'The pot'? You're guarding the Project, man. You'll have plenty. You don't need to eat rook."

"Girlies," called the guard behind Hope and Lyla. "You like fresh meat?"

"Yeah," called the one in the trees. "You want to eat my bird?"

The rest guffawed, one calling, "My bird!"

Another gunshot echoed, and the girls both flinched. A second rook fell. Two black headless birds lay in the snow, wings and feet splayed, necks spilling blood.

Lyla and Hope reached the guard by the shelter. He tapped his foot unsteadily. "Wrists."

Again. Lyla began to hold out her arm. Hope said softly, "Yes, sir, though we're not going to the Project."

The guard thrust the rifle forward, and they stepped back, away from it, but the guard following stopped them. "Hey there. Not that way."

The guard in front of them said, "You refusing to show your wrists?"

"No, sir."

Lyla tugged up her sleeves just as Hope tugged up hers. Hope's slender wrist was clean. Lyla stared down at her own, which had gone numb in the cold: one blue mark.

The guard spat on the ground not far from Lyla's feet. He said in Hope's direction, "You can go."

"I have to wait for her," Hope said faintly.

"I'll watch the path," the guard behind them said to the guard in front of them. "You pin her to the wall." He pointed his rifle at Lyla and grinned.

Hilarious.

The guard in front of them looked at Hope and gave a little exhale, a laugh or a wordless answer.

Lyla didn't want that guy getting too close to her sister. She whispered to Hope, "They said you can go."

"No, I'll stay with you."

"It's all right," Lyla said. "I can find you a little later."

Hope shook her head, her hand clasping Lyla's tightly.

"Get on," the guard ordered, and they followed him. He

stopped at the shelter. "In." His twitchy eyes looked Hope up and down.

Hope walked straight in as if she didn't notice. Lyla walked in too, making sure she stepped between the guard and Hope. The shed was cold and, with the three of them standing in it, crowded. No tables or chairs, just three walls of bare wood, except for one stretch of wall to the side of the window, where a line of pages hung, most with spectographs of people who lived on the Hill. At the top of each page, in capital letters, "OFFICIAL RECORD"; and in the top right corner, blue prison-bar marks. Every page had a different number of marks, usually one or two. Some had as many as four.

"Name?" asked the guard.

"Northstrom, Lyla."

He found one of the pages on the wall, her official record, with its one blue mark. Lyla stared at her own name: "LYLA NORTHSTROM." Maybe Riverton himself had given out her name and mark number to the guards. She suddenly wondered how many people in Hill's Ridge knew she was actually serving a tour. If anything happened to Riverton—if he were hurt or went away or started up some new scheme and forgot about her—who would know that she wasn't just running around with squatties and Red Fist? That she was actually working to get herself clean? Riverton had said he'd gotten approval from his captain for her tour. So maybe Captain Dyre? That was all?

The guard looked at Hope again. Lyla shifted so she blocked

his view. He reached outside the shed and leaned his rifle against the outer wall. "Stand there," he said to Lyla, pointing to the back wall of the shed. Then he said to Hope, "Let go of her hand."

The sisters hesitated, and then let go. Lyla backed all the way to the wall. *Don't touch my sister, creeper.*

The guard leaned toward a dim corner, where there was a crate that she hadn't noticed before, and picked up a machine the size of a loaf of bread, made of paper-thin metal. It had a long nose, and at the end, a round lens of glass or polished translucent stone. Needle-slender lights gleamed along its top edge. It was a spectograph machine, the kind inventors made for barons. He said to her, "Face forward. Look directly at me."

Then he held the machine up to his face, the nose and lens pointed at her. He pressed a button. Nothing happened. She expected him to say it hadn't worked right, but he didn't say anything. He only placed the machine on the crate.

"Raise your arms. Spread your legs."

Lyla hesitated. She'd never been searched by a guy; only by women.

Hope looked out one of the doorways, as if she expected some woman guard to appear and perform the search.

"I said—" the guard began again, with a slight waver, as though he was nervous or scared.

What else could she do? Lyla extended her arms and spread her legs. The guard stood directly in front of her, almost entirely blocking her view of Hope. He was at least a head and shoulders taller than Lyla, and wider. As he began to pat at her arms, she stared above his shoulder, at the opposite wall and the "official records." She was getting so used to these searches that she could easily half disappear inside herself. She felt his hands on her, but faintly, as if through a thick blanket. Her—the real her—was sunk deep inside.

You're the slowest yet, creeper. Would you get on with it?

His hands wandered from her ribs to her breasts, and she startled. He cupped her breasts, and then he squeezed.

His face was blank—he wasn't staring or leering. He didn't smile. His hands slid back to her torso.

Beyond him, Hope's expression was still watchful, but not outraged. He was mostly blocking Hope's view, but still, wouldn't Hope have seen something if there was anything to see? Maybe he didn't realize what he'd done? Or maybe Lyla was somehow mistaken?

The guard's hands slid down to her legs. Lyla tried to disappear inside herself again, but she felt the press of his fingers. He pinched her inner thighs. Then one of his hands brushed the crotch of her trousers.

Lyla stepped back. "That's not part of your slagging job, creeper."

The guard's mouth dropped open. Hope stared at her with wide eyes.

"Lyla—" Hope whispered, her voice high-pitched.

"What's your slagging problem?" His voice was high too. He looked at the floor, not at Lyla.

"You're groping me." Saying it out loud felt good; it felt slagging great. "Is that the only way you get to touch girls?"

"Lyla!" Hope stepped around the guard and tried to grab Lyla's arm.

Lyla shook Hope off.

I'm a thief. I'm trouble. So Lyla said right in the guard's twitchy face, "You gotta force yourself on girls. They won't come near you otherwise."

"Marked trash." He shoved her against the wall. The back of her head struck the wood, a starburst of yellow light and pain.

Hope called out.

The yellow light faded, and Hope wasn't anywhere in the shelter. Lyla started to dash for the door, but the guard grabbed her hair, yanking it so pinpricks of pain jabbed into her scalp. She scratched at his hand.

He pushed her into the wall again, and he leaned into her, a heavy weight crushing her to nothing.

"Quit." All the air disappeared.

She kicked and kicked. He yelled in pain and sagged, his grip loosening.

She slipped to the side, out from under the heavy weight, and she gulped in a deep breath.

But then he slammed into her. She kicked out again and shouted, "Quit! No!"

Men's jumbled voices; and then Hope's voice, nearby: "He's hurt her. He's hurt her."

Hands from behind Lyla grabbed her arms and pulled her back, as the guard from the trees yanked that guy—*him*—away from her. He grimaced, teeth bared.

One of the other guards shouted at her, "Quit!"

The hands pulled her backwards, out into the snow. Hope stood there. She stared beyond Lyla, at whoever was tugging her sister away from the shelter, and then said, "Where are you taking her, sir?"

Lyla began to turn, but a bag came down over her head: darkness, the smell of apples, her own hot breath. No air. She was a fish, mouth open, chest heaving.

—CHAPTER SEVENTEEN—

A HAND gripping Lyla's arm dragged her—scrambling, stumbling up steps—into an echoing room. The hands shoved her down onto a hard seat, and then yanked the bag away. A dark chill. She coughed and swallowed, deep sobbing breaths.

"*Merde*. Easy," said a guy's voice. "Try to breathe slower."

In, slow but shaky. Out, slow but shaky. Lyla gripped her own knees. They were knobby and solid. "I'm all right."

"Stupid," he said about her, or maybe about that guard.

"Is my—" Before she could finish asking for Hope, Lyla heard his footsteps. The door swung open, and light stabbed in. She saw the back of him—tall, wearing black. He slammed the door shut behind him: darkness. Her chest felt too tight.

In, slow but shaky. Out, slow but shaky.

———

The bench was metal, and the walls, and the floors. She was sitting in a small metal box. A bluecoat trailer? The Project fence's guard tower? They hadn't walked that far with the bag over her head.

No heat. The metal under her backside was icy; cold seeped through her trousers and coat. She stood and began to walk. Five steps forward, turn, five steps back. Ten lengths, then twenty. Her fingertips were numb, and she had to pee. She had yelled at a Project guard, scratched and pushed him. He deserved it. He deserved it.

―――

The tall guy came back, and, towering over her, he tied a blindfold tightly over her eyes. "Don't tell anybody I took off the bag but didn't put the blindfold right on. You live around here, don't you? I'll make you hurt if you get me booted from this post," he threatened.

"I hear you, sir."

"Sit," he ordered, so she sat on the metal bench.

The door clicked, and then came the clomping of a few sets of footsteps. "Cold in here," said a voice that sounded a little familiar. Maybe Riverton?

Lyla held on to her knees, solid bone.

A woman started questioning her, and Lyla could tell by the questions that the guard had said she had attacked him. She had shoved him for no reason, and hit him.

"I didn't hit him, miss," Lyla said calmly, steadily.

"So nothing happened? He made this whole thing up? He and your sister, who came running out of the shelter shouting for help?"

"No, something happened, but I didn't hit him, miss."

"What did you do?"

If Hope had already said it all, lying wasn't going to get her out of this. "I shouted at him, miss. I called him a creeper."

There was a little sound—a snort.

"Why did you call him that?"

Lyla suddenly wondered how many other guards were in the room.

"Well?" the woman demanded.

Come on, Bright. "He groped me."

"He groped you?" the woman asked, disbelieving. "Where?"

Lyla's face felt hot. Were the guards standing around her mostly guys? Was one of the guys actually Riverton? *Who cares, Bright? Convince her.* She told the woman exactly what happened.

After she finished, there was a long silence.

"Your sister didn't see any of this."

"He stood between her and me, miss," said Lyla. "He's a lot bigger—" A waver. Lyla cleared her throat. "She couldn't see around him."

"He scared you." The woman sounded amused, and somebody gave a muffled laugh. "He was just playing around."

"Your boys sound distracted," said an arrogant voice.

"They do their jobs fine," the woman countered.

"It's understandable," the arrogant voice said, "that your boys want to play around with a mine rat. But who knows what crawlers she's picked up from other mine rats?" *Slag off.* "Your boys'll be better off if they keep themselves clean."

Lyla gripped the edge of the bench hard.

"And *your* boys all keep themselves clean, Captain Dyre?" demanded the woman.

"I choose my boys for their discipline," the arrogant voice—Captain Dyre's—told her. "Riverton, he wouldn't ever play with a rat, no matter how high she lifted her tail at him. He wouldn't risk his mission for a rut that's over in five clicks."

"No, sir," pledged Riverton.

"Captain Dyre the Pure," the woman said dismissively. "So, what will you do with this mine rat? She fought with my boy. You saw the scratches on his arm."

"I'll take care of the girl, sir," said Riverton.

"I asked, what'll you do?"

"Riverton said he'll take care of it," said Captain Dyre. "Is your commander here? In the tower?"

A complete and total hush; not one whisper. The woman said, "Yes." She sounded angry. "He is."

"I need to speak with him about your boy's conduct. You'll join me," ordered Captain Dyre.

Quick footsteps headed for the door, several pairs. The door creaked, the footsteps thudded, and the door banged so hard that the bench underneath Lyla shook.

She tried to lift her eyelids against the tight blindfold: only a crack. Yellowish light, the metal floor, Riverton's boots. With her fingertips, she pushed a little at the cloth, trying to shift it, to see Riverton—did he really think she had been "lifting her tail" at those guards like his hero Captain Dyre thought?—but the blindfold wouldn't budge.

"You all right?" Riverton's voice was quiet, nearby, as if he didn't want anyone to overhear them.

"Yes," Lyla said in the same hush. "Fine. I wasn't playing around with those guards."

"I know you're not mine trash."

"Captain Dyre thinks I am."

Riverton hesitated. "Captain Dyre's seen a lot of kids mess up. Thieve, lie, cheat. You just got to prove you're better than them."

"And he knows that guard's a pig," Riverton whispered. "I can't believe you shoved him—" His whisper changed, some way. "Just like some angry squattie kid." He sounded odd, kind of praising but also kind of wary.

"I didn't plan it, sir," Lyla assured him. "When he . . . I was so mad."

"You acted from your gut," Riverton said, a little accusingly.

In my gut, I'm a squattie?

"Which is good," he assured her, or maybe himself. "Red Fist is always looking to recruit angry kids. What you did was good."

"Yeah, sir."

"We should finish up, Northstrom. I'll send a recommendation for expulsion to the school—"

"Wait—"

"*Shhh*. You don't want to be expelled?" Now he sounded more sure of her. "I know it'll be tough, Northstrom. But it's that or I haul you in for a few nights. Which would lose you time on the streets. And you'd end up expelled anyway."

"But after I'm clean—"

"Our agreement stands."

"Expelled," she murmured. "I can't tell my family why."

Riverton was quiet a moment. "Once the tour is over, you can tell them. They'll be proud of you." His hand grabbed her wrist; she jerked back and the hand tightened. "Northstrom," he said, exasperated, "I need to mark you."

"I can't see."

His grip loosened. "I didn't mean to surprise you. I can't take that blindfold off. In case one of them walks in."

"A second mark." Her hand was clenched; she eased it open.

Metal clanked. He took her wrist more firmly, turning it underside up. As he pushed back her sleeves, her bare skin immediately chilled.

Cold metal pressed against her wrist. Needles stabbed, so sharp.

The stab ended. The cold metal drew away, leaving a rhythmic pulsing ache.

Marked twice. Expelled. Bright wouldn't care in the least.

———

From memory, Lyla followed the map Gill had made her through alleyways, as quiet as smoke, so no one would see her. She'd had enough bluecoats for one day. Especially Captain Dyre.

Riverton had spoken to Hope before entering the trailer, and had sent her off to school. After Lyla got her mark from him, she had left a note at the house for Hope that said she'd be back late tonight. Without thinking, she then had started on the route toward school, but stopped, suddenly remembering she didn't have to go. There was no point in going. For now, she was done.

No job, no school. She knew she should feel bad. Instead, she felt as if school had been a wool coat—long, soaking wet, heavy. Without it, she was so light, her feet barely grazed the ground. All afternoon, she had drifted from alleyway to alleyway, careful not to snag the attention of any bluecoat. She skimmed the surface of the packed dirt and ice. Nowhere to go; nothing to do.

At dusk, she turned down the final alley where Gill's map led her. Ahead stood the little door to the hidden wood. From the walls, the narrowed eyes on broadsheets watched her pass. WE WILL FIND YOU.

Not tonight.

She slipped inside the wood, clicking the door shut behind her. That guard from this morning and Dyre and the rest were far away. They couldn't find her here.

She'd forgotten how big the wood was, bigger than her house. Dusk had turned the snow bluish. The trees were dark figures, reaching for one another like dancers reaching for partners as music began to whirl. Above, no roof-leapers. The sky was darkening from blue to purple, and the night's first two stars shone.

Gill hadn't arrived yet. Lyla raised her arms, stretching the tense ache out of her shoulders and spine, and her sleeves dropped a little. One clean wrist; one wrist with two blue marks. If she'd never gotten herself marked, she'd never have known this wood existed.

"Hey."

She startled, dropping her arms. Gill's voice had come from ahead of her, not behind at the door. He was crouching high up in a tree, his back against the trunk. Lyla stuck her hands into her pockets, her marks reburied in a couple of layers of wool. "You've been here this whole time?"

"I didn't notice you'd come in. I was kinda drowsing," he admitted.

"Eagerly anticipating my arrival, apparently."

"I was. But I also didn't sleep so good last night." He lowered himself until he hung from a tree limb, his long body swinging. Then he dropped to the ground with a grunt, and he hugged his ribs.

"It still hurts?" Lyla asked. "Or did you get hit again?"

"Still hurts from the other night. I'm fine."

As Gill walked over, he didn't seem to be flying on pills. He stopped right before her, slightly turned, as usual, so she could only glimpse the scars at the corner of his mouth. He looked sleepy, his eyelids heavy. A feeling opened inside her chest, like wings unfurling; something would happen tonight, an adventure.

"So, Jack, what's our mission?"

He leaned down toward her. His eyes had dark streaks, radiating from the pupil through the pale gray iris. "I got a little scheme some guards won't like. Wouldn't you like to know what it is?"

"Yeah, I would."

"This is gonna be fun. I get to torment you."

"Ha," she said. "Come on, Jack."

"You wouldn't want me to ruin the surprise by telling you before you saw on your own."

"I'd forgive you, Jack."

"But I could never forgive myself," he said, teasing her.

He lay down on the ground. Stretching out his legs, he crossed his ankles and folded one arm under his head, a pillow. "The others'll be ready to meet us a little later."

"Where are they?"

He shrugged, smiling a little, and then he pointed up at a cluster of faint small stars. "Those're called Snowdrops," he said. His hand lowered to the two stars shining just above the wall. "The Pearls."

Lyla stared up at the two identical stars. The Pearls glittered.

"More'll be out soon," said Gill. He dropped his arm so it rested on his belly.

There was her space beside him again, the space where she used to fit. She lowered herself into it, but she didn't lie down; she sat cross-legged, careful not to touch him. He smiled at her, a small, sweet smile. Strangely, wings inside her chest opened wide, though she and he were still only waiting for tonight's adventure to begin.

Lyla looked up at the branches and the sky beyond: indigo was turning black. Gill pointed again. "Coyote," he said softly. "Fleeing Geese."

A tail, four legs, pricked ears, and a snout. Three small heads, three long necks, three triangles of wings, soaring away from Coyote.

"Why do the stars all have serious names?" Such a silly thing to ask, but she couldn't seem to stop herself. "Whoever named them wasn't very funny."

Gill gave a laugh. "What would you name them?"

"I don't know. Pebble Eyes?"

"'Pebble Eyes'?" He guffawed. "That's not funny. It's just terrible."

"All right," she said, laughing. "So you come up with something better."

"That won't be hard." Wincing, he sat up. "Baby Teeth."

"'Baby Teeth'? Are you kidding?" Lyla started to laugh so hard, she had trouble speaking. "That's no better than Pebble Eyes. It's not funny at all."

"You're laughing. You just don't want to admit I'm funnier than you are."

"I'd admit it, if you actually were."

"I'm very funny," he insisted. He reached for her kneecap and squeezed it.

"Gill!" she cried, scrambling back. "That tickles."

He scooted forward, one outstretched gloved hand grazing her calf. She leapt up with a little shriek.

"Shhhh," he warned, still laughing.

Stifling giggles, she tried to run, but he caught her hand. He stood and pulled her closer, tickling her side.

"Gill!" she cried again.

He whispered, "Sorry. Shhh, shhh."

Their laughter quieted. He was still holding on to her, his fingers clasping hers. Moonlight shone on his slightly peaked eyebrows and long nose. Shadows hid his scars.

Lyla stood still. Within her rib cage, the wings swept wide.

Gill leaned close.

I'm a spy. She jerked back.

He dropped her hand, and he looked down and away so his scarred side was hidden.

"Gill, sorry, it's—"

"I was looming"—he joked, but he hunched his shoulders a little—"which I've heard is slagging terrifying."

"You weren't—"

"We should get on."

"No." *No?* "Yeah, I mean. Yeah. We gotta go."

—CHAPTER EIGHTEEN—

GILL led Lyla through a tangle of passageways, crouching when several bluecoats walked close, pressing up against a wall when a roof-leaper and its searching eye soared overhead. Lyla couldn't take her eyes off his upturned collar and the bottom edge of his cap: a scrap of skin and stubbly hair, bared to the cold.

Quit staring at him. You're lonely. That's all. Don't slag things up because you're lonely.

She couldn't say, "Gill, it's not your face." There was no good way to say this. Because then he would ask, "Yeah? What is it?"

They reached a tall, narrow building with windows boarded over. Across one of its brick walls: WE WILL FIND YOU. Gill climbed down a couple of steps to a set of bulkhead doors, which seemed chained shut. He knelt and, after picking the lock, began to unwind the chain from the handles.

"Jack," Lyla whispered, without looking at him, "who are we about to meet?"

"You'll see."

"I don't have to worry about you getting your hand cut off here, do I?"

"I don't think so."

"Wait. How did they re-chain the door once they were inside?"

"There's a second way in." He tapped softly on the metal door, a complicated pattern. From the other side, more clicks and clinks: another lock and chain.

Lyla started to reach for one of the bulkhead's handles; Gill's hand was there, reaching too, almost underneath hers. She pulled away. "Oh. Sorry."

"That's all right. I got it." He sounded odd, awkward.

Gill, it's not your face.

He eased the bulkhead doors up. Below, shadows and a form that was backing off the steps. Beyond the form, deeper in the cellar, light wavered and danced, a yellow-orange warmth.

Lyla climbed down the stairs and stopped. The shadowy figure ahead of her was Zeb. "You weren't who I thought," he said. "Hey, Bright."

"Hey," she said. Beyond him stretched a large cellar room lit up by candles. Spinner sat on the floor; next to her crouched a woman wearing a long coat and baggy trousers. Spinner and the woman were studying pieces of metal and scraps of paper scattered around them.

"Hey, Preacher," Gill called, not seeming at all troubled by the sight of the woman. Without looking up, she raised one hand and gave a wave.

Lyla noticed a couch, a couple of crates, a chair, and a huge spool tipped onto its side like a table. Against the cellar wall stood cement-block-and-board shelves, which were filled by neat stacks of some kind of thin square board. Nearby sat a bunch of rectangular metal machines with hand cranks and bell-shaped horn mouths. Beyond those spinners—that's what they had to be—a pallet lay on the floor, covered by a worn blanket. This must be Spinner's squat.

All around, painted words shouted from the walls: MARK ME—'CAUSE I'LL NEVER LICK YOUR BOOTS; RAGE; HAVOC; WILD THING. Lyla knew Rage was a Red Fist music troupe that played secret shows in secret places.

Lyla started toward Spinner. Spinner moved the metal fragments on the floor together and apart, as if they were pieces of a puzzle. The woman studied a slender metal tube.

Lyla stared at the tube. It was the length of a pistol, but it didn't seem to have a trigger. Not yet, anyway.

Behind her, Gill said, "So where are Jit and Nose? I thought we were going running."

"They haven't showed yet," said Zeb.

"Man," said Gill, sounding irritated. "I got something I want to put up."

The woman rotated the tube. Lyla shifted a little so neither end of it pointed at her. What if the squatties asked her to help build some weapon and use it?

Gill said, "I'm not waiting around all night while Jit kisses Red Fist's ass."

The woman said, "I sure don't want you kissing my ass."

"Preacher," Gill said with a smile, "if *you* ask me to go running, I'll go running."

Zeb asked, "Are the workshops short on anything?"

"We always need scavenge," said the woman, squinting at a paper and turning the tube back over.

Don't point that thing at me.

"Knife gives you the scavenge we get, right?" Gill asked. "He's not keeping it?"

The woman laughed, but she sounded more bitter than amused. "He gives it over. What else would he do with it?"

"Use it to beat someone," said Gill.

Again, the bitter laugh. They seemed to be making fun of Knife and the other Red Fists. Lyla tried to hide her surprise.

The woman looked up at Lyla. "You aren't aiming to become a soldier, are you?"

Lyla expected Spinner to say something sharp about her, but Spinner just kept working on the puzzle. Lyla answered, "A soldier? Like Knife and them?"

Gill was shaking his head. "No way."

"Bright's a friend of Scribbler's," said Zeb.

"Good," said the woman. "That's good." At the base of her throat was a tattoo of a red fist. "They'll all tell you how great and heroic it is to knock people around. Don't you listen to their crap."

"Yeah," Lyla said slowly. "I'm not planning on it."

"They've gone around the bend," said the woman, sounding more like Teacher Slate or Riverton than a Red Fist. "The Red Fist 'soldiers.' At least in Hill's Ridge, they have."

"You should take over," remarked Zeb. "You all in the work-shops."

"Gen'ral'd have them fight us. They'd all be happy to do what he told 'em," said the woman. "And we aren't fighters."

So you just let them do whatever terrible things they want?

The woman set down the tube and stood. "I'm sorry, Spinner. I don't know what a lot of this is. I don't think I can help you."

Spinner didn't look up from her puzzle. "Yeah. I just thought I'd ask."

"Stop by the workshop soon. And stay away from the soldiers."

"My sisters gotta eat," said Zeb.

The woman nodded, and then shook her head. "Yeah. Well. Stay safe."

She walked off into the shadows, toward the stairs and the door through which Gill and Lyla had entered.

Lyla glanced at Gill. "That's Preacher," he explained. "She stays in the Red Fist workshops most of the time. A lot of people in the workshops—they don't like Knife and them much. She's pretty genius. She's figured out a ton about Protean. She's always trying to get her hands on some that's unharnessed, so she can try to harness it."

Suppressing a shiver, Lyla managed to joke: "And she's telling *us* to stay safe?"

Gill smiled. "I know."

"Too true," said Zeb.

"Enough!" Spinner shoved all the metal away from her.

She pushed the papers so they slid across the floor. "You know what's the worst? There's probably books in that slagging university library that tell how to build music recorders and ampliphones and magniphones. But I gotta figure it all out on my own."

Lyla looked at the tube on the floor, the one that she'd thought was part of a pistol. "Magniphones?"

"Things that make your voice louder when you sing into them." Spinner stood. "The Project is such crap. If it actually works, we'll have power but no good machines to use with it."

"You'll build some," said Zeb.

"I guess." Spinner headed toward the old couch, which was lower on one side than the other. She smiled at Zeb, and he smiled too, before looking down at his boots. "Yeah. All right," she said. "I will."

Spinner reached down to a crate, pulled a large brown bottle out of it, and popped the bottle's lid. Taking a long drink, she knelt on the couch.

"I got something I want to hang tonight," said Gill. "Let's go running. Just us four."

"Sure. After we finish this." Spinner held up the bottle, then held it out to Lyla. "I heard the Coats hit the school."

Lyla took the bottle but didn't drink. "Yeah. A questioning."

"They think it was you?"

"I said I was home with my sister," Lyla said as Zeb climbed over the back of the couch and sat beside Spinner.

"Your sister'll lie for you?" asked Spinner. "My brothers wouldn't."

Gill lowered himself into the rickety chair and stretched his legs out in front of him. "Hope won't want to lie."

"No," said Lyla. "She's mad at me."

"Sisters." Zeb shook his head.

"Zeb's got five older sisters," said Gill. "That's why he's so quiet. They do all the talking."

"And fighting. And crying. And whispering," said Zeb. "Best to just sit back."

Gill held his hand out to Lyla. She started to pass him the bottle.

"You didn't drink." Spinner sounded a bit accusing.

Lyla held on to the bottle, and Gill laughed. "You don't have to," he told her.

"Though Brewer's stuff is decent," said Zeb.

"I don't think that's what Scribbler means. He means she doesn't have to share spit with me," Spinner said, her voice sharp.

Zeb shook his head, smiling a little, as Gill said, "Spinner, that's not it."

"She doesn't have to touch my dirty glass with her lips?"

Lyla raised the bottle, and as she took a long gulp, Gill said, "Wait." A billion tiny bubbles exploded in her throat and surged up her nose. She sneezed as someone grabbed the bottle from her. She sneezed again, three more times, her nose and throat burning.

Eyes watering, she finally straightened. Gill and Zeb snorted a little as they tried not to laugh.

Spinner was grinning. She stood and walked close to Lyla. "Bright, you should've said it's your first time." Spinner linked arms with her and brought her over to the couch, squeezing close to Zeb to give Lyla room to sit on the other side. One arm still linked with Lyla's, Spinner elbowed Zeb with the other. "Quit laughing."

"I am." His voice wavered.

"You had a first time too."

"I didn't almost fall over sneezing."

Gill laughed.

"No, but there were things you had to learn how to do"— Spinner pointed as she teased—"your first time."

Zeb shook his head and didn't meet Spinner's eye, but he smiled a little. "All right. Yeah, yeah. I hear you."

Lyla looked down in embarrassment as Gill said, "More than I needed to know about the two of you."

Spinner said, "You don't want to find out what he had to learn?"

"That's all right. That's fine. I'm sure it was . . ." Gill stood abruptly. Even in the candlelight, it was clear he was blushing. He crossed to a candle that had gone out. "Where's the matches?"

Spinner laughed. "The matchbox is on the spool. Right next to you."

"Oh. Yeah." Gill took out a match and struck it against the side of the box. A flame illuminated his hands, his long fingers splotched with ink stains. Lyla watched as one of Gill's hands deftly shielded the match while the other steadily held the flame to the candle. Its teardrop of fire flared.

Spinner leaned close to Lyla, maybe to say something, but Zeb said first, "Spin us a disk." He ran his hand down Spinner's thigh. "Let's dance."

"Sure. Give me a hit first." Spinner reached, and Zeb handed her the bottle.

"We oughta go running," Gill insisted as Spinner sipped.

A scraping, metal-wrenching sound came from way off in the shadows. It sounded like someone shoving open a door. "Jit's decided to honor us with his presence," Gill said.

"I was hoping for a night off from his crap," said Spinner. "Is he ever going to be fun again?"

Gill said, "Not if he actually gets himself tattooed."

"He wants us all licking his boots." Zeb grimaced.

"I'm not licking his anything," said Spinner, and the rest of them laughed. "Here, Bright." She handed the bottle to Lyla. "Sip it slow this time."

Lyla raised the bottle, letting some of the bubbles into her mouth. They swirled over her tongue and down her throat. Her limbs felt oddly loose.

As she handed the bottle to Zeb, Jit and Nose sauntered into the candlelight. "I got orders," Jit announced.

"Orders?" Gill scoffed. "You looking to turn us into your soldiers?"

"I don't care what you turn into, Scribbler." Jit stared at Lyla and Spinner. Spinner stared blandly back, though she held on to Lyla's arm sort of tight. "You two keeping each other warm? I been out in the cold. You could warm me up."

"Where'd you get that coat?" Spinner asked.

Jit grinned, teeth bared. "You like it?"

It was thick brown wool, long, with a wide collar. It flared out at the bottom like merchants' coats did. "Where'd you get it?" Gill echoed Spinner.

"It's sharp, isn't it?"

Nose hopped from one foot to the other. "Gen'ral gave it to him. Red Fist has got others like it."

"What'd Gen'ral give it to you for?" Gill asked, sounding like he already suspected the answer.

"Red Fist was happy about that orb," said Nose, as he hopped quicker. "They'll earn a lot for it. Maybe from the baron who owned it in the first place. The lady who lent it to that Bright teacher." He laughed, a kind of choking sound. "She'll pay to get it back."

Zeb was shaking his head.

Gill said, "They know the rest of us were there, in the Bright." He spoke each word quietly and distinctly. "So—why'd you get the coat? Did you say you led us there or something?"

"I'm the one that remembered Bright could show us what was good in the school." Jit held his arms out wide. "That's leading."

"Are you japing?"

"What do you care what I tell Red Fist, Scribbler?" Jit

stepped directly in front of Gill. "You don't want to earn a tattoo."

"You're a lying slag," Gill said mildly, standing. "That's all."

"Is Red Fist still paying all of us our cut once they sell the orb?" Zeb asked as if Gill and Jit weren't standing there arguing.

"Yeah, yeah. Your sisters need some points. We all know what a good baby brother you are," Jit taunted. "Of course you'll get your pay. Gen'ral knows you all helped. Especially Bright." Jit leered at Lyla.

Gill shoved Jit's shoulder.

Before Jit could shove back, Lyla said, "Scribbler, if I want him knocked around, I'll knock him around myself."

They all stared at her, and Nose stopped bouncing. Lyla started to laugh. Zeb held a fist out to her. She bumped it with her own.

"Bright's the one who should be wearing the coat," said Spinner. "She's the one who got us that orb."

"Bright don't want to get herself tattooed," said Jit, though he didn't sound certain. "Do you?"

No. "I guess I just wonder . . . It would be an adventure," she said to Gill, "to see one of the Red Fist hideaways."

"Especially the workshops," he said to her. "Those are an adventure."

"They're pretty wild," Spinner agreed.

"I don't know if you're ready," Jit said. "Red Fist won't invite in some Hill girl who messed up once and got herself a mark."

"Two," Lyla said, correcting him. "I got another after I shouted at a guard. And fought with him. Fought him off."

"You what?" Gill asked. "What did he do to you?"

"He was supposed to be searching me. This Project guard." The next words got stuck in her throat. She looked down and shrugged. "He was a pig."

She held up her wrist, pulling back her sleeves: two blue marks.

Gill had an odd, startled look on his face.

She said quickly, "I wasn't doing anything. I was just standing there. I didn't want him near me."

"So you hit him?" Jit asked, grinning.

"No. I asked him if groping girls was the only way he got to touch one. That's when he shoved me."

Gill's mouth fell open, and then he began to laugh. They all laughed: Zeb, silently; Jit with a coydog yip; Nose made that choking sound. Spinner kissed Lyla on the cheek and then handed over the bottle. "You look so sweet, Bright. So dreamy. But you're sly."

Lyla tipped the glass up, and the tiny bubbles seared down her throat. The bubbles were warmth; they were light.

"Wait. Why were you searched by some Project guard?" Jit asked.

"She's a Hill girl," Spinner said with a condescending catlike purr. "Which means she lives on the Hill. Which means she lives near the Project."

"That's great." Jit grinned wide. "You're slagging perfect for our mission."

—CHAPTER NINETEEN—

ON the Hill, on a winding narrow path that Lyla hadn't known existed, Jit ordered them to be quiet. Shielding the tiny lantern he held, he said, "Get down."

Lyla and the rest dropped. She put her mouth against her knee to muffle her breathing, the air streaming in cold, streaming out warm and damp. All through her, she felt searing bubbles sparkle.

She listened. Tree branches clacked, and there was a snapping sound: wood or ice cracking. Otherwise—nothing.

"So?" Spinner whispered.

"'So?'" Jit mocked; he refused to tell them where exactly they were going and what exactly the Red Fist soldiers wanted them to do. Lyla had stopped asking him. He seemed to want them to beg, and she sure wasn't going to.

"Slagging fantastic we got you, a Hill girl. You see anything that isn't usual up here, you tell me," Jit said to Lyla for the hundredth time.

"Yeah, I already said I would."

"I gotta get to the Hill path, before we reach the Project's guard shacks," whispered Gill. "Out of sight."

"No, you don't," whispered Jit.

"Yeah. I do. I got something to take care of."

"No," whispered Nose.

Gill rose and began to walk.

"Scribbler," Jit called in a hush.

Gill veered onto a path of meandering animal tracks.

"That way. Yeah. Good." Jit popped up and capered in front of Gill. Nose half jogged, trailing them. Then Jit started to run, and they all had to run too, to stay with the lantern light.

"Jit's slagging loving this," whispered Spinner. "And so is Nose."

"Let's follow Gill if he goes up to the Hill path," whispered Lyla. "Jit will have to follow us. He needs us, I bet. I bet he can't do anything for Knife and them tonight without us. Otherwise, why would he have brought us along?"

"Nice," murmured Zeb. "Nice."

Through the treetops, a ways ahead, the lights from the Project towers glimmered. Crowds of dark trees on both sides of the path rustled. Ahead of Lyla, in the snow, lay two headless rooks with splayed wings. No, no, this wasn't where they'd fallen. Not rooks, but splotches of night.

Jit stopped, raising an arm as if this were some command for the rest of them to obey.

Gill swiped the lantern from Jit's hand.

"Hey," Jit said, too loud.

"Shhh." Gill held the lantern high, out of Jit's reach.

"What're you doing, Scribbler? You'll get us hauled in," Jit said in a hush.

"Not if you're quiet. Or just stay here. I'll only be a moment," Gill whispered, walking backwards. He tucked the lantern into his coat, so it cast light only around his feet.

Jit stood still, with Nose hovering beside him. Lyla walked past Jit, after Gill, and the slight crunch of Spinner's and Zeb's footsteps followed her. Then she heard louder crunching. Nose jogged up to Zeb, leaving Jit alone on the path.

As Lyla crept to the bank that Gill was scrambling up, Nose, behind her, whispered, "I need —" He sniffed twice.

"No," whispered Zeb.

"Come on. I'm climbing out of my skull."

"I told you I don't carry that anymore."

"The pills, then. My head's gonna crack open."

"Those are supposed to help you quit the powder. You can't take both. You'll slag yourself up."

"I won't. I won't. I just slipped. I'm quitting."

"Sure."

"I am."

Reaching the edge of the bank, the edge of the Hill path, Lyla said over her shoulder, "Quiet."

Nose shifted back and forth. "You see guards?"

"Not yet. We're still not near enough," she said. "But sound carries."

Gill took papers out of his coat. "You want to hang these?" he whispered, handing a couple pages to each of them, along with a couple of push nails.

Lyla took a page and looked at it. Gill had titled it "Guard Duty at the Project." And the picture was so great. Gill had drawn the guards as dogs. One gripped another's neck and pushed its head to the ground; a couple sniffed butts; the largest half-sat and licked between its own back legs.

"You're the best, Jack," Lyla said close to his ear, with its perfect arches and whirls. She pulled his cap down over it, to keep it from getting too cold.

"What are you doing?" he whispered.

Lyla leapt forward with a quiet laugh. "Let's hang these all across the path."

Gill put out the lantern. Lyla scanned the treetops for guards, but saw no one. Gill's sketches fluttered in her hands, and she stuck the sharp points through them, pinning their fluttering edges to thick tree bark. The thin gray-white paper gleamed in the light of the moon.

She and the rest drew back to the bank. They skittered down it, clutching one another's arms and hushing one another.

Nose bounded ahead as Lyla slipped, pulling Spinner down into the snow. They landed in a tangle, stifling giggles. Nose came back. "Jit didn't wait for us."

A real laugh burst out of Lyla. She cupped her hands over her mouth.

Zeb crouched, shaking with silent laughter, and Spinner hid her face against Zeb's shoulder.

GUARD DUTY AT THE PROJECT

"He could've gotten hauled off," Lyla whispered. A giggle hiccuped out of her mouth.

"We would've heard." Gill raised his voice above a whisper. "He's probably watching us. He wants to see us miss him."

"Too true," said Zeb. "But keep your voice down, man."

"Maybe he went off to the Project on his own," suggested Spinner. "You know what? I've never spied on the Project." Leaning against Zeb, she pushed herself up. "Let's go and spy around."

"No, Gen'ral wants—" Nose broke off.

"What does Gen'ral want?" asked Gill. "What are our 'orders'?"

"Shouldn't we try to find Jit?" Nose asked, tapping his hands fast against his coat.

"He's the one who left us," said Spinner.

"He'll be mad at us," Nose whispered, scanning the trees.

"So what?" Gill said.

"Let's just go, let's just go." Spinner started to walk backwards up the animal path. "Let's find Bright an adventure."

"I mean, if we don't do it right, Gen'ral will be mad," said Nose.

The rest all stopped abruptly, even Spinner, so Lyla stopped, too.

Gill whispered at Nose, "What did Jit promise Gen'ral for tonight?"

Instead of answering, Nose looked out into the trees. "He's gotta show up."

"Are we supposed to be somewhere at a certain time?" Spinner demanded. "This is a kind of mission?"

"It's a trial. Why would Gen'ral—Wait." Gill ran his hand over his face. "Is Jit trying to earn his tattoo tonight?"

"Slagging tell us, Nose," whispered Zeb.

"All right. Yeah," Nose said fast. "Yeah."

"I'm not getting the crap beat out of me because Jit's decided to play some game. And I'm not Jit's errand boy," whispered Gill. "He wants to earn his tattoo, he can do it himself."

"He's already slagging told Gen'ral we'll do it, Scribbler," whispered Zeb. "Whatever it is. So we have to."

"I'd rather take the beating."

"They won't go easy on you because of your rib."

"What if they hurt your hands?" Lyla asked Gill, remembering that knife across his fingers, pressing until the skin split.

Nose was rocking back and forth. "Let's just give Jit a click."

A huge shadow-shape plummeted from the treetops and thudded beside Nose, then tackled him. It was Jit.

Gill and Zeb grabbed at Jit's coat and hauled him off. He threw himself backwards, so all three sprawled in the snow.

Lyla stepped toward them. "You all right?"

Jit scrambled up. "Let's get on."

Gill grabbed for Jit. "Wait."

Jit pulled away and headed off.

Gill hit the snow with his fist.

Lyla asked, "What's he doing?"

"We don't have a choice," Spinner whispered. "Let's go."

"Come on," Gill whispered, following the rest of the pack. Lyla trailed after.

They began to run. The path was tough to see, splotched with shards of moonlight and shadow. Lyla flew over the splotchy snow. She stumbled, caught her balance, hurtled forward.

The Project lights shone through the treetops. A guard's voice called out, "Did you see that?"

They stopped, frozen.

Be a tree, a sapling swaying in the wind.

"Blue, yeah," called another voice. "I think I'm done betting on cards. You always win."

The pack crept forward. Jit led them past the guard shelter and through the woods that stood parallel to the side of the Project. He swerved wide here and there, to avoid passing beneath the tree stands where the guards perched. Other shadows flickered among the trees, but Jit didn't seem troubled. Maybe there were other squatties or Red Fist soldiers helping with this mission? That was likely, but Jit hadn't said anything about them. Lyla couldn't stop looking over at the Project fence and, rising behind it, the Project's sloped roof and the corner towers. Puffs of air rose above the fence, like white breath in the cold.

Jit led them almost all the way past, and then farther into the woods.

"Where are we going?" Lyla whispered to Gill.

He shrugged. All around the Project fence stood guards with rifles.

Two bluecoats strode toward one of the guards—the stocky one leading, the tall, upright one trailing. Lyla recognized Officer Riverton and Captain Dyre.

Jit, what the slag are we about to do?

Jit veered down a little slope and jumped into a pit. As Lyla and the rest followed, crouching on the snowy ground, she saw they were actually in a kind of earthen room, an old root cellar, maybe, with crumbling walls. It smelled like onions.

Jit stood at one wall, staring over the edge at the fence.

"This is it, this is it," whispered Nose, swaying back and forth. "Time to knock at some Coats."

"Shut up," Jit whispered.

"Where's Gen'ral?" whispered Gill. "He isn't coming? Don't tell me this was all some big lie." Gill started to stand.

"Get down," Nose told him.

"If you slagged this up because you had to mess around on the Hill path"—Jit spat at Gill—"I'll have the brothers gut you."

"Since when do you call Red Fist 'brothers'?" asked Gill.

"Like they're going to do what you tell them," whispered Spinner, with a quiet laugh.

Jit whirled and feinted a punch at Spinner. He sneered. "Think what you want."

"If Gen'ral isn't here—" Gill broke off as Jit pointed.

"He's out there. If you all don't shut it, we're going to miss the signal."

Lyla peered over the wall, though she didn't have any idea what Gen'ral looked like. Moonlight, snow, forest, the guards, and the Project fence. Riverton and Captain Dyre. "What are we supposed to do?"

Jit sniffed. "You'll see."

Gill leaned close to Lyla, his breath warming her ear. "If anything gets messed up, bolt for the message rock."

"Yeah. You too."

Jit turned toward Gill. "Scribbler, you got paper?"

"What do you mean?"

"You brought paper, right? That's what I mean. You always bring paper."

"What are you talking about?"

"What do you think?" Jit snarled. "You're supposed to sketch the guards, where they stand. Like a map. And what they do when they see us. Their plan—no, Gen'ral's got another word for it. Their *tactics*."

"*Merde*, Jit. Are you kidding?"

"This is what we came here for?" demanded Spinner. "To watch Scribbler sketch?"

"Gen'ral's gotta see what they do when we attack," said Jit. "For a plan he's got. But mostly our mission is *them*." He pointed at Riverton and Captain Dyre.

"'Them'?" murmured Lyla. "What do you mean?"

"'What do you mean?'" Jit mocked. "Little Bird told Gen'ral that Dyre has been here all day. We're supposed to lead him off into the woods. And that other bluecoat with him. His lap dog."

"If Red Fist gets them . . ." Nose was bouncing, a big grin

on his face. "That'll be a big triumph for Gen'ral. Divide and conquer."

"What do we do with them after we grab them?" Lyla asked.

"Don't mess things up, Bright," Jit growled. "Don't try to get all the glory. We have to lead them into the woods. That's our orders. Then a pack of brothers will grab them."

"This mission is trash," said Zeb. "We're not speaking out against barons. We're not scavenging anything for the workshops."

"We said we wouldn't take these snatch jobs," whispered Gill. "I don't want that kind of blood on my hands. Even if it is only bluecoat blood. Officer Riverton's blood."

"You know him?" Lyla asked, surprised.

"He's a slag."

"He's caught Scribbler twice," explained Spinner. "Riverton likes marking Scribbler."

"Riverton the Righteous," Gill said dismissively.

Lyla managed a nod. "But will Red Fist kill him and Dyre?"

"And miss a chance to get some gold?" said Spinner. "Oh, no. They'll take them off somewhere. They'll get information out of them and beat them raw. Then they'll ransom them."

"You're sure?"

"Town Councilor pays through the nose to get his bluecoats back," whispered Zeb. "Even if they can't walk anymore. Or one eye is wrecked."

"It happens all the time, Bright," Spinner told her. "Bluecoats keep it mostly secret. They don't want people hearing that Red Fist pounded any of them almost to death."

Lyla stared at Riverton, who stood by Dyre and a guard. He hadn't given her a plan for this situation. Nothing.

"You know I hate snatch jobs," Gill said to Jit.

"Quit being yellow," scoffed Jit.

"Scribbler," said Nose, plucking at his coat, "Jit already told Gen'ral we would. Red Fist is here. The soldiers are waiting. Probably watching us right now. Knife or someone."

"You aren't gonna get your credit points for the orb if you don't do this," said Jit. "'Cause Gen'ral will be pissed."

Gill, Spinner, and Zeb glared at Jit. Gill said, "Slagging bastard."

Nose was still bouncing, and Jit was grinning at them. "How frightened are you, Scribbler? You wet your trousers yet?"

"So what's your big plan, Jit?" whispered Spinner. "Where are we leading these bluecoats? How far into the woods? And where do we meet after?"

"Not Scribbler," said Jit. "He's gotta sketch the Project and what the bluecoats do when they see us — their plans, their tactics. Just lead the bluecoats off into the woods. After you're done, Gen'ral will be at the mineshaft up the Hill. Go there." Jit leaned close to Lyla, his breath reeking. "But don't lead anyone to the mine, the hideaway. You don't want Gen'ral pissed at you."

"I'm not an imbecile," Lyla whispered.

"'Imbecile.'" Jit laughed. "You still talk like you're in the Bright, Bright."

"It'll only work if we scatter," whispered Spinner. "Otherwise, it'll seem suspicious. But we can't seem like we're playing around. Or they'll just stop chasing."

"We run in together," Zeb said softly. "Except Scribbler. He stays out of sight. We sneak together like we got something to hit them with. When they see us, we scatter."

"I don't know where the mineshaft is," said Lyla.

"What do you mean you don't know?" Jit demanded. "You're from up here. That's why I brought you. So I wouldn't have to hold your hand."

"I don't know where every single thing is," Lyla said.

"The mineshaft is beyond the Glenwood place," Gill said to her. "You know the slope above the farmhouse? On that ridge."

"Sure." *Lead Riverton and Dyre into the trap, but warn them without getting seen by Red Fist, then go to the mineshaft and impress Gen'ral.* Lyla laughed. "Easy."

"We're getting paid for this?" demanded Spinner. "Even if it's your trial for your tattoo?"

"Of course. Yeah, we're getting paid," Jit sneered. "If you don't mess up."

"And you'll vouch for Bright? When we see Gen'ral," Spinner insisted. "So she'll be okay in the minshaft? She can come with us to the hideaway. Maybe even the workshops."

"Sure. Wait. That's it," whispered Jit. "That's it." He started to scramble over the edge of the root cellar's wall.

"Don't," whispered Spinner as Nose scrambled after Jit. "We got to creep together."

Jit and Nose both began to dash forward. *"Merde,"* whispered Zeb. "Quick."

Spinner and Zeb began to climb. Lyla glanced at Gill, who raised one hand, palm and fingers open as if they were pressed against a window. She raised her own hand—wasn't there something more she should say or do?—then she scrabbled up over the edge.

—CHAPTER TWENTY—

AHEAD, through the trees, Nose ran fast, a sleek, streaking animal. Jit lumbered behind. Outside the forest, at the Project fence, Riverton leaned toward a guard and pointed to where Nose and Jit ran.

Lyla stilled; Spinner and Zeb stopped. "If Jit slags this up," Spinner breathed, "and then blames us, I'll kill him."

"You won't have to," whispered Zeb. "Gen'ral will."

The guard started forward, raising his rifle. Abruptly, Jit and Nose halted.

Zeb murmured, "We gotta flush that captain."

"But that captain'll send Riverton, right?" Lyla knew this is what Dyre would do. "He'll be the one who'll come after us."

"If we get close to Dyre, he'll follow, too, I bet," whispered Spinner. "He won't just stand there."

"Two of us could lead the guards off," whispered Zeb. "Only one has to get close to the bluecoats."

I do.

The guard halted almost directly in front of Jit and Nose. He peered through the trees.

Lyla and all of them were statues, granite and marble. Cold, smooth rock.

Then Jit thrust his head forward and howled. The guard startled, half stumbling.

Jit bolted in one direction, and Nose streaked away in the other.

The guard shouted, "There!" He pointed toward Nose, and another guard ran from the fence. The first guard chased Jit, rifle raised.

Two out of the way. Three left, plus Riverton and Dyre.

"We have to get closer," whispered Lyla.

The other two nodded. Spinner started to creep forward, Lyla and Zeb close behind. A fox-like scream echoed through the darkness.

The crack of a shot. Lyla and the others froze.

"Did they hit Jit?" Lyla whispered. "Or Nose?"

"No. No, I don't know," Spinner whispered.

Lyla looked at Spinner, at Zeb. "If one of them's hurt," Zeb whispered, "the guards won't leave him bleeding in the snow. And if they have him, we can't help him."

A clanging sound—an alarm?—then the crack of another shot, and a long, taunting howl.

Don't look back. Lyla bent low, following Spinner and Zeb around trunks until they crouched across from the end of the fence. Lyla whispered, "I'll try to get to Dyre and his lap dog."

Spinner smiled. "That's our Bright."

"We'll draw the others off," whispered Zeb.

"Don't let that Dyre catch you, Bright," warned Spinner. "I've heard about him. He has a mean streak."

Lyla nodded. Something thudded inside her, a drumbeat she'd heard once at the Beacon.

Zeb cupped Spinner's face with both hands and kissed her, leaning forward as if he might fall through the surface of her. Lyla turned away, the drumbeat so loud, her ears rang.

Spinner whispered, "Come on." She grasped Lyla's hand, squeezed it, and let go.

They all bent again, and Lyla slipped around trees, watching Dyre, watching Riverton. Each held a pistol. She saw shadows flicker in the woods—other squatties? Red Fist soldiers? Dyre pointed to the opposite side of the Project, and one of the guards started for it, rounding the fence's corner. Only two guards left.

Riverton paced to the fence's corner, nearest the trees. Closer to the woods, easier to reach.

Walk out to the trees, Riverton. Near enough so I can warn you.

He didn't. She, Spinner, and Zeb wove past trunks, around knots of brambles, toward the guards and Dyre and Riverton. The two guards kept their rifles half-raised as they scanned the woods.

Shouts—angry, garbled—off in the woods. A loud yipping.

"Don't listen," whispered Spinner.

Lyla nodded. They crept up the little slope to the edge of the tree line. Ahead lay a wide expanse of snow, no decent cover.

"I'll go around this side," whispered Zeb. "Once they see me and chase, you two head out. Spinner, maybe a bit off that way. Toward that guard, so he'll come after you."

"Yeah," said Spinner, as Zeb dropped to his belly. He dragged himself forward, using the rise of the land to stay hidden.

The drumbeat pounded hard against Lyla's ribs.

Zeb got far, almost to the side of the building, before he was spotted.

"Stop!"

He leapt up and began to bolt.

"Take him down," ordered Dyre. "His leg."

A *pop*.

"That's a shot," Spinner whispered faintly.

"He's fine," whispered Lyla.

Zeb was dashing toward the woods, in the opposite direction from where Nose and Jit ran, with a guard following.

Only one guard left at the fence. One, and Captain Dyre and Junot Riverton.

"Let's go," Lyla and Spinner both said at once.

Lyla dropped, pulling herself along through the snow like Zeb had. Bits of ice flew up into her face, her mouth, her eyelashes. She blinked away the sting.

Spinner crept toward the guard, as Lyla slithered toward Riverton and Dyre. Riverton took a step forward, but he seemed to willfully fail to see her; he looked off into the trees. In the moonlight, his face below his blue cap had an odd blue-white sheen. "Come on, Riverton," Lyla murmured. "Look at me."

The last guard, so baby-faced, didn't seem to see Spinner, either. And then he started and stared. "Hey!" he called.

Spinner jumped to her feet and started to run. Riverton looked Spinner's way and took a step.

Lyla leapt up. He swung around, pistol aimed at her knee.

"Don't," she cried, and he looked at her face, his eyes wide like someone surprised, like someone seeing something he didn't understand.

She glanced in the direction of Spinner—running, running down the slope, but maybe still close enough to hear if Lyla warned Riverton.

"The girl's leg," called Dyre. Riverton stood between Dyre and Lyla, blocking Dyre's aim. Dyre hadn't recognized her. "If you can't grab her," Dyre shouted, "bring her down!"

Riverton stood motionless, eyes wide, as if he was waiting for her to give him some signal. But she couldn't. She knew Red Fist—Gen'ral—prowled somewhere near, watching.

Dyre shouted, "Riverton, what's slagging wrong with you? Grab her before she gets her wits back."

Riverton blinked. "Got her." He finally started forward.

Spinner was near the tree line. Out of earshot.

Lyla called in a hush, "You and Dyre have to come after me. But it's a trap."

Walking steadily toward her, Riverton whispered, "What kind of trap? Where?"

"Red Fist. In the woods. They'll try to snatch you. But you gotta chase me."

Riverton didn't nod, just kept walking, his pistol still aimed at her knee.

She turned and ran, plunging through snow.

Get away. Swerve. Don't look back.

Voices called out behind her; shouts, but no gunshot. She glanced over her shoulder. Riverton was chasing, and behind him, Dyre.

She grinned, running, swerving, scrambling down the slope to the tree line. She leapt over a snow-covered log and dashed into the trees. Ahead and off to the side a guard chased Spinner. Spinner wove through the trees like a deer bounding away, flickering among brambles and saplings.

A *pop-pop*. Spinner stumbled to her knees.

Lyla faltered.

Spinner staggered up.

Lyla glanced behind her: Riverton was closing in. She didn't see Dyre. Riverton's face was a set, intent mask. Like he was coming after her for real.

She looked to Spinner, but Spinner had somehow disappeared. Gone. Hidden in brambles, or down a bank. The guard was also gone.

Riverton, behind Lyla, was gaining ground. *Remember,* she urged him silently, *it's a trap.* Her elbow clipped a tree; pain flared up to her shoulder, down to her fingertips.

Riverton floundered; he was heavier, and bigger.

Head for deeper snow. Smaller spaces.

She dashed toward trees with larger gaps between them,

where the snow lay deep. She pushed through the snow as fast as she could, thighs burning, and then launched herself into a stand of dense trees. She slid through narrow spaces, tripping, scrambling up.

Pop-pop.

"Merde," said a guard, running up to Riverton. "The light's slagging bad."

"Hold your fire," said Riverton. "We want to question her."

"I've got orders to shoot."

"I order you to hold fire," said Riverton.

"You aren't my commander."

Riverton can't protect you from bullets.

She was prey. No, she was the trickster, a bird with a broken wing, leading hunters from the nest. That guard was the dupe. He was the fool.

As long as she didn't get shot. Her breath burst out of her mouth in ragged puffs of white. Her knees ached from hitting the ground when she fell and then rose and then fell again.

The guard ran to the side, trying to get in front of her. Ahead, there seemed to be no trees. The ground was oddly dark.

She ran to the edge of the gleaming snow, and she slid to a stop. A ledge, a long, steep drop. A ravine filled with shadows.

"Hands up. On your knees," shouted the guard, his voice breathless.

Riverton stopped next to him and held up both hands, as if Lyla were some wild creature he was trying to soothe. "That jump could kill you," he warned.

"On your knees!" shouted the guard. "On your knees!"

The Gen'ral could be nearby, judging her.

"It'll be easier if you surrender, and we take you," said Riverton.

"No. It won't," she told him.

She leapt over the edge, into the dark.

———

The fall didn't kill her. She plunged into darkness and then skidded down the side of the ravine, hitting the ice at the bottom. She crept through dimness, scraped and bruised, feeling her way along the icy bank as voices far above argued.

By the time she climbed the bank, Riverton and the guard were gone. Taken by Red Fist, or escaped?

She'd find out soon enough. She had slipped away through the trees, and she had almost reached the ledge, the meeting place; it was just up the slope.

She stopped at a tree and looked behind her. Clenching her teeth to keep them from chattering, she listened.

Wind rattled branches and caught up snow, whirling crystals into her face. Far off, a hound barked—maybe at the Project. Sound traveled so strangely on the Hill.

Lyla listened for footsteps following, the crack or slap of a branch. A shadow flickered behind her.

It was a long, lanky shadow. Bending low, it darted from one tree to another and disappeared inside drooping boughs. She counted for a long while, but the shadow didn't come back out.

Then it crept from the boughs and slipped up the hillside to the next tree. It disappeared.

It wasn't following her.

Lyla looked back down the slope and the shadow emerged. It clambered onto the ledge, then disappeared into the mineshaft, that Red Fist den. Gill, maybe?

She scanned the hillside, but didn't see other flickers of shadows, didn't hear other footsteps. The barking was still a long way off.

She scrambled forward, up the slope, over the ledge's jutting lip. In the rocky hillside yawned a hole framed by old timbers. It was small, a rectangular mouth just big enough to crawl into. *If Jack can fit, you can.*

Lyla crawled after him into the narrow tunnel. The rounded walls squeezed close. They shut inward, collapsing. She fought to take shallow breaths.

The tunnel went on and on. Then there was a dim pool of light ahead, a rounded opening. She reached the edge of a short drop, a kind of step. She scrambled into the light and stood.

"You hurt?" Gill's voice, oddly flat.

"No. I'm fine." She tried not to gasp. "Fine."

Riverton wasn't there, or Dyre. She and Gill stood before the tall Red Fist from the other night, Knife, who had threatened to cut off Gill's fingers. Monster, he'd called Gill, but *he* was the monster. He held his pistol like the gun was some other tool, a hammer he could raise easily. A ways deeper in the mine, a few Red Fist soldiers leaned against a wall. They talked quietly together, as though scheming. The mine was a dimly lit dirt room with wooden supports against the walls and ceiling. In front of her, Knife was looking at a scrap of paper held by another man, the tallest man ever, who had to stoop so he wouldn't smash his head. The tall man wore a wide-brimmed hat pulled low, so his forehead and eyes were hidden in shadows. He studied the page as if she and Gill weren't standing there.

She glanced at Gill, and he shook his head once. *Careful.*

The tall man turned the page over, frowning. "This is all you got?"

"They brought out dogs," said Gill.

"You're afraid of dogs?" Knife taunted.

"Jit asked for more," said the tall man.

Gill gave one abrupt nod.

Knife laughed. "What're you going to do, Monster, when you gotta take all your orders from Jit?"

"He'll have to follow," the tall man said in Gill's direction. "Not everyone has the nerve to lead."

Not everyone has the brains to lead. "Where is Jit?" Lyla asked. "And Spinner and them all?"

"Jit hasn't made it back yet." Gill's voice was still flat.

"It could be his first and last mission to command," remarked the tall man, untroubled, and Knife laughed.

"I saw Spinner get . . ." Lyla wasn't sure Spinner had actually been shot. "She looked hurt."

"She got grazed, but she's all right," Gill said, as though he didn't care one way or the other. He was blank, hiding away what he really felt.

"We sent them on," said the tall man.

Lyla wasn't sure what this meant. "To a healer?"

"Something like that."

"Zeb took her to get looked over," said Gill.

"What about Nose?"

"No, he got grabbed quick," Gill explained. "He had bad luck. He ran straight into the pack of hounds and bluecoats coming up the hill."

"He's in a cell by now," said Knife. "Unless he's squealed."

"Nose isn't dumb enough to squeal," said Gill.

"He don't always think," said Knife. "He's not some kind of smart-ass, like you."

"He's not an idiot," Gill said.

"Maybe. He's gotta know we'll hurt him worse than any bluecoat would." Knife grinned at Lyla. "We don't give squealers second chances."

"She's no squealer." Gill smiled. "She's like Spinner. Tough."

Don't. Just don't. Lyla looked away from Gill, at the tall man. "I can vouch for myself."

The tall man's thin lips pulled wide and thinner, like lines drawn on a face. "You're ready to prove yourself, girl?"

Which meant she hadn't already. Which meant the Red Fists must not have Dyre or Riverton. So they were safe. She'd kept them safe. "Yeah."

"We saw you—"

A clattering sound startled Lyla. The soldiers deeper in the mine fell silent. Knife raised his pistol.

The tall man said languidly, "Knife, there wasn't any alarm from the watch."

Jit tumbled into the mine. At the sight of Gill and Lyla, he smiled his wild grin. "I knew the two of you would make it," he said, and the soldiers went back to their scheming.

The tall man said to Jit, "The sketches aren't much. And you lost one of your boys."

"He'll keep his mouth shut. What about Dyre?" Jit asked quickly.

"No. The girl led him away from the Project, but he stopped following her too soon," said Gen'ral—the tall man, Lyla had figured out. "Dyre knows your face. If you had planned for him to follow *you*, instead of the girl, he would have gone a lot farther. We would've been able to grab him."

"That *was* the plan," Jit lied, staring accusingly at Lyla and Gill, as if they'd messed up. "Scribbler and them didn't follow it."

Gill shook his head. "Not true. Plus I didn't even know I was supposed to sketch before we got near the Project."

"You knew. I told you."

Gill glanced at Gen'ral and Knife. Knife was smiling wide, as if enjoying the argument. Gen'ral stood silent, watching and, Lyla thought, judging. "No," Gill said, deciding, it seemed, to continue arguing. "I didn't know. When you gave your orders, we were already in the woods."

"Scribbler said in the woods that you should've told him sooner," Lyla stated, matching Gill's even tone. "And you just ran out toward the Project. There wasn't any plan."

"Enough," Gen'ral commanded, his tone cold.

Jit nodded but said to Gen'ral and Knife, "They're lying."

Knife grinned wider. "Yeah?" he asked, not like he believed Jit, more like the fight entertained him. "Both of them?"

"Maybe that's what Scribbler told Bright, so she thinks it's true."

"Jit—" Lyla broke off as Gill shot her a look: *Don't.*

"Jit commanded the mission," said Gen'ral. "That makes Scribbler the liar. And the failure."

Knife slammed Gill across the face with the pistol, and Gill staggered. As Lyla took a step toward Gill, he bent, hands on his knees.

"I'm good," he stated without looking at her. But the others were looking, watching her. Gen'ral smiled slightly; the soldiers farther in the cave smiled; Jit and Knife grinned, while Knife twitched the pistol back and forth, as if eager to lash out again.

Bright, you are not shaky, you are not frightened. Lyla nodded. "Good."

Knife whirled and slammed Jit, who fell to one knee and then immediately forced himself up. Gen'ral said, "We didn't snag Dyre. You got a few sketches, not much. You lost a boy. One of your girls was grazed. You have to learn to keep your people in line. Too many failures like these could lose us this war."

Knife swung again, striking Jit's face. A couple of the soldiers laughed. Jit coughed, and spat a glob onto the dirt: blood, along with something hard and white—a tooth.

You are not frightened, you are not shaky, Bright.

"I hear you, sir," said Jit, glaring at Gill.

"Bright," said Gen'ral. Knife stepped toward her. She held her ground, and Gen'ral shook his head, his face still hidden in shadows. Knife stopped. "You could show these boys here how to obey orders."

"Sure," she said. Jit's glare swung to her.

"Dyre's started overseeing the guards. He'll change things at the Project. We gotta snatch him. Come to our refuge with Jit and the rest of your pack in two nights. You can replace Nose on the next mission to snatch Dyre."

She'd done it. *I'm in. I'm slagging in.*

"Sure."

Gen'ral added, "Maybe you should lead the pack that night."

"Me?"

Gill stared at the ground, breathing slowly as if he hurt badly. Jit, though bent and grimacing from pain, clenched his fists, like he had to force himself not to take a swing at Lyla.

Knife asked, "You looking to earn yourself a red fist?"

It couldn't be smart to say no. "I didn't think I ever could."

Knife laughed. "Jit, you might have to take your orders from her. You could be her lap dog."

Jit bared his teeth. "We'll see."

"That night," Gen'ral said mildly, "I'll decide who leads the mission."

Jit's teeth stayed bared, and Gill glanced at Lyla, his face a blank. She was suddenly flushed. She was dizzy, as if walking a narrow ledge with empty space below. *One foot in front of the other, Bright. And don't look down.*

Threatened Alchemyks, episode 6

—CHAPTER TWENTY-ONE—

LYLA waited in the cellar for Riverton, studying the zine strips, ripped from their newszines. She just wanted to find out what happened next. She had to know. A rattle startled her. Across the cellar hole, the door rattled as if some furious hand were trying to shake it apart. But the door didn't open. It was the wind's hand, not Riverton's.

She carefully folded the *Pirate Jackman*s that she'd found in the message rock this morning. Gill had left a note—"The hidden wood, dusk, tomorrow, before the hideaway"—and zine strips ripped from zines; he apparently had remembered that she had said she didn't have credit points right now to buy them.

Which confused her, because of what had happened last night after they left Gen'ral. She kept seeing what happened over and over in flashes she couldn't stop.

———

As Gill scrambles out of the mine, he is quick, as eager as she is, Lyla suspects, to get away from Gen'ral and the rest. They don't realize Knife has followed them until they are outside on the ledge. They stop, and Knife stops. Lyla stands still, her feet stuck to the ground. She doesn't want to go before Knife leaves. She doesn't want him following her to her house, to Ma and Da, to Hope.

Gill stands still too, studying the hillside. His head is tilted, so maybe he is listening for bluecoats. His good cheek and the edge of his top lip are swollen and reddish-purple where Knife hit him. Knife watches Gill, grinning.

"Monster," Knife says, "sounds like Bright's gonna join up with us brothers. If you join up too, maybe she'll give you a pity ride once in a while."

Lyla doesn't look at Gill. Knife laughs and laughs.

——

Finally, Knife has gone. Lyla and Gill make their way through the trees, heading in the direction of her farm. Gill's breathing sounds a little wrong to her, a bit shallow. "Jack, you all right?"

"Fine," he says curtly. Then he asks, "Do you want to get tattooed?"

"Me? Are you kidding?" Maybe Riverton wants her to. "Not at all. That thing never comes off."

"I hear you. Good. That's good." He pauses. "The soldiers're getting worse and worse. It used to be easier to avoid work like snatches. Dyre and Righteous Riverton are slags, but I don't want to help grab them."

"I don't want to snatch them either."

A smile flickers and fades. "'Cept now we're signed on to."

"If Gen'ral tries to fight some kind of crazed war against

barons, do you think other people in Red Fist, in the workshops, will try to get rid of him?"

"You heard Preacher. All the good fighters in Red Fist like Gen'ral. They all stand with him." Gill shakes his head.

He shakes his head again. "We'd be free if we didn't need food. Though if we lived on air, I s'pose Gen'ral and the barons'd both find a way to force us to pay for it." He gives a sharp laugh. "Once Gen'ral hands over our credit points for grabbing the orb, what'll you tell your ma and da about where the points come from?"

"Don't know. I'll make something up."

Gill is quiet, and then: "They'll guess soon."

"Sometimes I've bought things at the shadow market and just slipped them on the shelves."

"They'll still notice."

"I doubt they'll say anything. Ma's been sick, and Da's thinking of going up to the northernmost mines for the rest of the winter."

"That's tough." Gill exhales, long and slow. "Even if they don't say anything, they might . . . They'll cut at you, sort of. Say things that slice."

He is talking about himself, his step-da, Stan, who always used to cut at him for everything. Not Ria, who couldn't cut at someone even if she tried. Ria usually got sad, without ever saying why. She stared out the windows; she cried when she thought Gill couldn't hear.

"It was better for you to move out," Lyla says, realizing.

"I give Ma points and stuff when she visits. Right before she leaves. She gets upset." His voice has gone flat. "But she uses the points. So."

Lyla starts to reach for his hand, as if they are still ten, but she remembers in time they aren't and she is using him and he will find out someday. She can't touch him.

———

Lyla stands with Gill by the large tree in the moonlight. Her farmhouse is dark except for a flickering light in the Aerie window. Hope.

Gill turns his face so the bruised, swollen side is to her, the scarred side is away. He has a moonlit sheen.

"I'll see you," she says.

"Yeah," he says.

She doesn't walk off. Her Lady Captain voice says faintly: *You have to leave.*

Gill shudders. "Cold."

"Are you going to Spinner's? Maybe she and Zeb can look your face over?"

"No one should have to." He half smiles, half winces. "It doesn't even have a good side right now."

"Jack—"

"See, you're not gonna say I'm wrong, 'cause you know I'm right. I don't think I'll land at Spinner's. Jit might show up there, and I don't want to listen to his crap tonight."

"Could you go to your ma's?"

"No way. It's just bruises, kid."

"I could get you something from the house for the trip down the Hill. If you're cold, do you want a blanket to wear?" Though Lyla doesn't think she has an extra. "Or I could walk a little ways with you."

"That's sweet." He smiles, and then he reaches for her hand. She flinches back.

Dropping his hand, he looks down. He gives one bitter laugh. "I'm good on my own."

He walks off.

———

The cellar door rattled, and Lyla started. She was standing in the cellar hole, in the candlelight, waiting for Riverton. The wind was shaking the door. Still no Riverton.

Gill thought she wouldn't touch him because of his scars. *It isn't you. It's*—What? What could she say besides the truth?

And why did he leave her the note and the *Pirate Jackman*s? Wasn't he mad at her?

The cellar door swung open. Riverton, snowflake-covered, stepped in and shut the door silently behind him. He shook himself, snowflakes flying. His worn-thin pants were way too baggy, the way the guys at school wore them. It was strange to think that just a few years ago, Riverton had been at the school, going to classes and wearing those pants. The bluecoat uniform he usually wore made him look older than he was.

His mismatched eyes fixed on her. "You made it."

"Yes. I've been here a while."

"I wasn't sure you'd . . . you'd be able to come, since Dyre and me escaped last night. Did they punish you for losing us?"

"Not me. I wasn't leading the mission."

"'The mission.'" Riverton walked forward, staring at her as though he feared she'd disappear if he looked away. "Who was leading 'the mission'? Waterhouse?"

"No," Lyla said, too loud and quick. Riverton blinked, and she said more softly, "No, he didn't even want to be there." She explained how Jit had snared them all into doing it, to try to earn his tattoo. "Zeb, Spinner, and Waterhouse said they wouldn't. But Jit had already agreed. Gen'ral was already waiting."

"'Gen'ral'?"

"He talks like Red Fist is fighting a war against bluecoats. He wore his hat pulled low, so I couldn't see his face, but he's so tall. Taller than anybody else I've ever seen."

"Gen'ral. He used to be Captain. He must've given himself a promotion," Riverton said, with a laugh. "Waterhouse tried to snatch Dyre to save his own skin."

"Not Waterhouse; he didn't help. He had to sketch the Project. Or, no, he sketched the guards' 'tactics' when we showed up."

"Oh, yeah? Why?" Riverton asked. "Why was he making sketches of the guards' tactics at the Project? Are they going to attack the Project for sure? A coordinated attack, at the same time that other packs in other towns attack?"

She didn't want to admit she didn't know yet. "Last night you grabbed a squattie, didn't you? A thin kid. He sniffles a lot. What did he tell you already?"

"The powder-sniffer, right? He's got the shakes and the sweats. Does he actually know anything? He's barely said a word, and I been starting to think he's some kind of idiot."

Actually, he must not be an idiot, if he's gotten you to quit questioning him. "He was there. But, yeah, he isn't . . . Red Fist won't ever put a tattoo on him. I guess they probably won't ever tell him anything important."

"About what, Northstrom? They won't ever tell him anything important about what?"

Riverton leaned forward, waiting for her, and she paused; she wished she knew the answers. "I don't know what it is yet. But I will. Gen'ral invited me into a Red Fist refuge. And I'm going on the next mission. He still wants to snag Captain Dyre," she warned. "Because Dyre's been at the Project, bossing the guards, changing things. We discussed all of this at the mineshaft after the mission. There were a bunch of Red Fists there, probably planning." Lyla drew a quick map of the mineshaft for Riverton. He took it and smiled.

"So, they're going to hit the Project soon," he said triumphantly. "And you're all caught up in their plans." Riverton bounced a little. "This is great, Northstrom." He held out his hands, almost like he was going to hug her or something, but as she stepped back, he only stuck his hands in his pockets and bounced again. "You've done great."

"Thanks. What about Captain Dyre—"

"Oh, don't worry, he won't let this frighten him away; he'll still be at the Project. He's staying there. We both are. We can't let those guards the inventors hired mess up. Whatever Red Fist's scheme for the Project is, we'll be ready to hit them so hard, they'll break to pieces."

"And I—"

"Yeah, you'll be there to help us." He grinned.

Her, and Gill, and Spinner, and Zeb. How could she keep it from becoming a terrible mess?

"Oh, hey. I forgot." Riverton reached into an inner pocket, then extended his hand. On his open palm sat a red-orange oval.

"What is that? Is it a fruit?"

"A peach-cherry. From the southlands." He smiled, little-boyish. "You've never had any?"

"No." Lyla gripped one hand with the other so she wouldn't swipe it from him and stuff it in her mouth. "No, never."

"Go on. I brought it for you. When we grab thieved goods like this, stuff that'll just go bad, we get to divvy it up." He held it closer to her. "It's good, I promise. Sweet."

She forced herself to reach slowly. Its skin was so tender, she had to cradle it gently to keep from bruising it. She cupped the oval.

"Go on," he said. "You'll like it, I bet."

She bit into the soft, sweet flesh.

Riverton watched her eat. "Careful." He smiled. "There's a stone in the center. You don't want to break a tooth."

Lyla nibbled flesh away from the round brown stone until it was clean. She licked the juice from her fingertips and palms, and then licked a rivulet dripping down her wrist. Oddly, her marks didn't taste fake, like ink. They tasted exactly like the rest of her skin.

"See?" he asked, grinning. "I knew you'd like it."

"Thanks." She tucked the stone into her pocket, to put with her *Pirate Jackman*s in the Aerie.

"I'll try to bring another next time. Or something else. A couple weeks ago, I got to have a huge melon. It took me and my da four days to eat it all. We were almost tired of it."

"Thanks," she repeated. "I mean, but you don't have to."

"I know that. Sometimes, though, there's a lot, and other guys have wives. Babies. I just have my da. So, it's not a big deal for me to share a bit. You're—" He flapped his hands. Lyla nodded, though she didn't really grasp what he was trying to tell her. "You're my . . . responsibility." He shook his head as if the word didn't sound right to him.

"I'm your Marked."

"Yeah. I mean—No, not mine. You're not a hound or something. You've done a lot, really quick, all on your own."

"Thanks. You're decent, Riverton."

He smiled. "You know, I was a little troubled," he confessed, "about you and Waterhouse."

Lyla stared at him. "Oh, yeah?"

"There's his face, and he's working hard for Red Fist." Riverton grimaced. "But you were friends when you were kids. Sometimes . . ." He trailed off. Then he laughed. "I'm sorry I thought you'd roll like that in the muck."

Nod. Just nod.

Riverton stopped laughing. "Hey. Really. I'm sorry."

"It's all right. I know I'm not rolling in the muck."

"Once we shut him up in his cell, you won't even have to see him again. Not ever."

"*His* cell?"

"Since the day he was born, he's been doing all he can to get himself hauled into it, right?" Riverton gave her his eager little-boy smile. "You'll help shut him in for always—him and all the rest."

"Gen'ral and Knife."

"Definitely them, too."

No. Just them.

—CHAPTER TWENTY-TWO—

AFTER leaving Riverton and climbing the Hill, Lyla stood outside her home's door, in the cold, in the dark, looking through the window. Something in the kitchen was different, but she couldn't see what. The table was the same and the candle sitting on it, wavering and flickering, and the sink basin and the cookstove, the coats hanging on hooks near the door, the crooked rows of boots.

Something was different, though, so different, as if the house wasn't really hers, as if she should knock.

Instead, she eased the door open and stepped in, carefully, so no one would hear and so she could get to the Aerie without anybody seeing. She had done enough pretending and lying today already.

Voices toward the back of the house murmured. One voice went on and on, and then the other went on and on: probably Ma and Hope.

Lyla slowly, soundlessly peeled off her hat and gloves. She stepped out of her boots. The kitchen still looked different, but the pantry was the same, and the floorboards with the gaps between them where dropped grains of rice got stuck. The entire room looked familiar and unfamiliar, both at once.

Her hand, in her coat pocket, closed around the stone of the fruit she had eaten, Riverton's gift. She gripped it hard, so it dug into her palm, and then she put it in the pocket of her trousers. As she took off her coat, the *Pirate Jackman*s that Gill had given her made a crinkling, crackling noise.

The voices stopped, and Lyla went completely still.

"Lyla?" called Ma.

She winced. "Yeah, Ma. It's me."

There was a pause, as if what she'd said or the way she'd said it sounded odd. "We're back here. In my bedroom."

"All right." Lyla's voice *did* sound odd, even to herself, brash like Bright talking to Spinner and the rest. She cleared her throat. "In a click," she said, more softly.

Leaving the *Pirate Jackman*s in her coat, she walked down the hallway to Ma's door. "Lyla?" Ma called again.

"Yeah, I'm here, I said."

As Lyla went in, Ma asked, "Are you feeling ill? You sound like you're losing your voice."

"No, I'm not."

Ma was in bed but sitting up, pillows behind her back and head, her hair a tangle of trailing vines. Hope sat on the edge of the bed, near Ma's hip. They both stared at Lyla without saying anything, like they didn't recognize her, like *she* was the thing in the house that was different.

Then Ma held out a hand. Lyla took it and kissed Ma's forehead, which wasn't too hot or too cold. Ma smelled like the lavender they dried in the summers and sewed into the pillows. Lyla asked, "Are you feeling all right?"

Ma laid a hand on her own chest. "I can breathe."

"Da says you should stay home longer," Hope said to Ma. "You need to get all the way better."

"If I go back to work now, he won't need to head north," said Ma.

"But you could get sick right off again," said Hope. "I'm talking to the baron tomorrow, so I might start bringing home points soon." Hope told Lyla, "Teacher Slate has an old friend from the university who's a baron, Mistress Regin. She needs somebody to help in her atelier, to tidy and organize, so he arranged for me to meet her."

Mistress Regin—the woman at the Beacon who had asked after Teacher Slate. "That's great. Really, really great."

"Yeah." Hope smiled.

"Sit," said Ma to Lyla, patting the bed.

Hope shifted to make room, and Lyla reluctantly perched on the bed's edge. Ma took Lyla's hand and ran a thumb back and forth over her knuckles. The cracks in Ma's skin rasped against Lyla's skin. She tried to draw her hand away, but Ma held on. "Ma, I'm kind of tired."

"You've been out a lot."

Lyla shrugged.

Ma squeezed her hand and kept looking at her as if Lyla was supposed to say something else. "Sorry I haven't been home much," she finally said.

Ma nodded but didn't let go, and Hope said, "You should come with me to see Mistress Regin. Teacher Slate says she hires a lot of Marked."

"That won't work right now."

"It could. Teacher Slate says she likes to give Marked second chances."

"If she hires you, maybe I can meet her later."

Ma said, "She has positions now."

"A position, for Hope."

"You don't want to meet her?" asked Hope.

"This doesn't make any sense. She has a position for you, not me. And I can't right now."

"Why?"

"Hope, *I can't.*"

"You should check with Riverton. Maybe you can."

"It doesn't matter what he says. I know I can't."

"How can what he says not matter?" Hope demanded. "Isn't he . . . He's like a boss."

Lyla stood, but Ma clasped Lyla's fingers with both hands, holding her there. "Lyla, I didn't want you to get that mark." *Mark,* instead of *marks;* nobody had told Ma yet about the second. "But now that you have it, you don't have to . . . Maybe if this woman can help you, you could quit your tour. I think you should tell me what Officer Riverton is making you do."

Lyla pulled her hand away. "I'm doing what I'm supposed to do."

Ma pushed herself up, so she sat straighter against the pillows. "I never liked his plan to keep everything secret from us. That isn't right. All the lying."

"It isn't lying. It's just not telling."

"That's the same," Hope said, exasperated.

"No, it isn't. You don't always tell everybody everything."

Hope opened her mouth like she was going to speak, but then she closed it.

"And," Lyla went on, "Ma doesn't tell us everything."

"Lyla," Ma said, "now you're just being absurd."

"Why? We're not little kids anymore."

"All right," Hope said in her trying-to-fix-whatever's-messed-up tone. "We hear you. You've made your point."

"No, no," Ma snapped. Her breathing was suddenly wheezy, as if she'd been climbing the steepest part of the Hill path. "There are some things I don't talk about, because not everything has to do with you."

"Not everything has to do with you, either."

"Lyla," Hope said directly at her. "Would you stop being so awful?"

"All I'm saying is, I'm working to get myself clean." Lyla didn't understand why she had to explain this. And she badly wished she could also say that she was working to make the town safer. "I'll get clean, and I won't end up stuck down the hole."

"And stuck on our farm," Ma said bitterly. "Your family's farm."

"Ma, you always wanted me to get good scores. To leave the farm and go to the university."

"But this isn't getting good scores at school. It's nothing like that. I don't even know where you are most of the time," Ma said. "On the streets? Doing what?"

"You don't trust me."

Ma stared at her, shaking slightly, hair shifting against the pillows like rustling leaves. "Why is that, do you think? You knew I wanted you to stay away from shadow markets, and you went anyway. You got yourself a mark.

"But truly," continued Ma. "It's Riverton I don't trust. I really don't. He'd just send you off to do anything with anyone."

"You think I wouldn't be tough enough to say no? If I thought I should."

Ma slapped the bed with both hands. "How could I even tell? You don't talk about any of it. Not even to Hope."

Lyla shot Hope a glare. *You've been squealing what I do and don't do to Ma?* Hope looked down at her knees.

"There are worse things than being Marked," warned Ma.

"Yeah, I know that," Lyla informed Ma, and started for the door.

"Lyla—"

She left the bedroom, accidentally bumping her hip against the doorframe and not caring that it hurt, a sharp throbbing ache.

Walking fast, she headed straight into her room and to the Aerie's ladder. As she climbed, Hope came in. "Lyla."

Lyla paused on the rungs. "I just want to be on my own."

"You can't fight with her like that. She doesn't feel well."

"She seems pretty well to me."

"You couldn't hear her wheezing? She can't go back to the mines right now."

Lyla examined her own thumbs, curled around the top rung. "Hope, I truly can't go meet Mistress Regin with you."

A very long silence.

"Fine," Hope said, though she didn't sound fine at all.

Lyla heard footsteps coming toward her. As Hope stopped next to the ladder, she whispered in an angry hush, "You should know Ma was searching through your things."

It took Lyla a moment to make sense of the words. "Searching through my things? *My* things?"

"I told her you're not selling powders, or anything like that. But she's frantic. And you avoid her."

"So if I live here, she can just go through any of *my* things, any time she wants?"

"*If* you live here? Are you planning on moving out?"

"No. But did she go through my drawers? My undertrousers? Like I'm five or something?"

"She was in the Aerie. She had the *Pirate Jackman*s all spread out. And a map of the town? I think that's what it was." Hope's voice dropped lower, still angry. "The lines—they looked a lot like the way Gillis used to draw. When we were kids. Those little notes you used to give each other, when you were always doing all kinds of crazed things that could've got you drowned or broken into a million pieces."

"Is that what you told Ma?"

"No, I didn't. But she's guessed you're running around with Gillis, and she's been asking me to ask people what they've heard about him. To find out what kind of trouble he's in. If you want to keep your whole life secret," Hope whispered furiously, "you better start hiding things in better places than the Aerie."

Hope thrust a small, folded piece of paper toward her. "Also, there's this. From Teacher Slate."

Lyla stared at the folded slip in Hope's outstretched hand, its sharp edges lined up exactly. She could see the orb again, the orb Teacher Slate had convinced a baron to donate, half zipped into her coat like a pregnant belly, as she stole it from the Bright. "What does he want?"

"I don't know. It's *yours*. I didn't read it."

Quit being a coward. She reached out, took the slip from Hope, and quickly unfolded it. The block letters formed an address, the next day's date, a time, and two words: *See me.*

———

The address led her to a street she'd never been on, at the southern end of town, almost where Main Street turned into West Road and wound off around the Hill. Rose Street was narrow and crooked, with narrow crooked buildings painted odd colors— purple, sky-blue, orange—all faded and peeling. Out of the corner of her eye, down an alley, she glimpsed a flicker of movement, which she'd also seen once or twice as she snuck down the Hill— maybe Jit or another squattie, but more likely a figment caused by her jitters. If anyone asked why she'd come here, she'd tell them the truth: She'd been summoned by Teacher Slate. For a lecture? An accusation?

Lyla realized she'd stopped, and she started to walk again, past an ox cart clattering up the street, carrying several passengers. Ahead lay an intersection with a street lantern on each corner, one with a broken glass globe. Beyond that, an orange building with the number on Teacher Slate's message: 23A. Instead of steps and a stoop, it had a ramp.

She crossed the street. The trellises that stretched up the building's orange sides were bare, and its windows were dark.

She knocked. No answer. She knocked again, and then she stepped back from the closed door. As she turned toward the street, Teacher Slate was rolling up the sidewalk, spinning the large wheels of his chair. His face wasn't angry, but it wasn't welcoming, either; his wide-set eyes studied her. "Northstrom."

"Hello."

He rolled up the ramp, and he unlocked the door. Every question she thought to ask—*How are you? How is the Bright?*—had an answer he likely didn't want to say, and she didn't want to hear. As he rolled into the house, he said, "Pull the door firmly behind you. Sometimes the latch doesn't click."

After she followed him into the tiny entranceway, she snapped the door shut. Teacher slipped off his gloves and gestured to hooks on the walls. "You can hang your coat."

"I'm all right."

"Are you cold?"

"Yes. Sort of."

He hung his own coat, and then he rolled slowly through an arched doorway barely big enough for his chair. If he had brought her here to shout at her, she wished he'd just shout.

She followed, the sight of the room stopping her. The windowsills were crowded with clay pots, each one overflowing with cooking herbs. Braids of garlic and dried peppers hung from the ceiling, dangling low so Teacher Slate could reach them. The cookstove and sink basin were low too, and the countertops and all the cupboards. A table sat in the center of the kitchen with only one chair. The other side of the room stretched back to window-paneled doors, beyond which lay a small, snowy backyard, mostly filled by a cold frame.

"This is where you live, sir?"

"You sound doubtful, Northstrom."

"No, sir." Her eyes flicked to the low cupboards and counters, then to him. He was watching her, and suddenly her cheeks were hot. "I mean, you had the key to the door."

He gave a sharp laugh. "The door gave it away?"

Her face flamed.

He rolled his wheels a little back and forth. His high wide brow furrowed, but he didn't say anything.

She finally said, "Thank you. For helping out Hope."

"She's earned it." He rolled to the side of the table, but he didn't invite her to sit. He held himself still, like Da when he was trying not to shout.

What? Just say it.

"Are you continuing with the tour?" He spoke so low, he was tough to hear, but his voice had a doubting, slicing-at-her edge.

"Of course, sir."

"Oh, of course. Of course I should assume you're still working to get yourself clean even though you're now expelled from the school."

"I had to get expelled. I had to for my tour. You can ask Riverton, if you don't believe me."

With one hand, Teacher Slate swept her answer away. "The Advanced Studies room attack—you were there?" he asked. "You brought thieves to the Advanced Studies room for the orb."

Lyla felt as if he had just thrown cold water in her face. "Sir, I can't really talk about the tour."

He snorted. "Don't hide behind that, Northstrom."

"I'm not hiding, sir." She glanced at the window-doors. Only the cold frame stood outside; at least, that's all she could see. She lowered her voice. "I have to be careful. So my family isn't hurt."

"I won't do anything to hurt your family, Northstrom. You know I won't. I simply want to know if you helped plan the attack on the Advanced Studies room, if you know what happened to the orb."

She could just say nothing, but he had helped her get her tour. She owed him. "There wasn't a plan—"

"So wrecking the entire room was some whim of yours?" he asked.

"No!" Lyla crossed her arms.

"A lark?"

"No. You don't care if we can stop Red Fist from doing worse things," she accused, and Teacher Slate startled. "You're just mad because the orb's gone."

He was quiet a moment. "That's not the case. The baron who lent the orb to me, Mistress Regin, is a good friend. I'd like to return it to her. And you have 'friends' who know where it is."

"None of my friends know." Not Spinner, not Gill.

"You sound certain."

"I am certain."

"And you?" he asked. "Do you know where it is?"

"No."

He rested an elbow on one of the arms of his chair, and he rested his chin in his hand, studying her the way he studied students during examinations. "Could you find out?"

"If I find out and tell, and if Red Fist starts suspecting me, my tour will be wrecked."

"I see."

He paused and then said, "I'm sorry," not sounding sorry at all. "I won't be able to tutor you once you complete your tour."

Lyla took a step back, and then forward.

"I won't be teaching anymore. Not at the school."

"They can't fire you."

"Surely that's not such a surprise," he said. "The headmaster just found a replacement. I'm speaking to students tomorrow."

"But I thought—they didn't fire you right off. So I thought you'd be all right."

"The headmaster started 'an inquiry' then into my conduct, and I suspect he also started looking for my replacement at the same time."

"They *can't* replace you—the thieving wasn't your fault."

"I agreed to keep the orb in the Advanced Studies room. 'Failure of judgment' is, I believe, the official cause for my dismissal."

"But you're a great teacher!"

"You're the expert on this? You were only in my class for a few weeks."

"Hope says you are, so you must be."

Teacher Slate actually smiled a little. He shook his head. "I thought when I sent the first message to you that if they found the orb right off, they might not replace me."

"What 'first message'?"

"The first message I sent you," he repeated, as if stating the obvious. Then he frowned. "The one I gave Riverton to give to you, asking you to please see me."

"Riverton didn't give me any message."

They stared at each other.

Teacher Slate said, "I thought you ignored my request."

"I wouldn't do that," Lyla said.

He shook his head. "The lying slag."

Teacher Slate had actually called someone—a bluecoat—a *slag*. Riverton was a slag.

Teacher Slate rubbed his wide forehead with his fingers. "He didn't want you to talk to me, apparently. To tell me where the orb went and risk wrecking your tour. It probably wouldn't have mattered anyway." He sounded kind of tired. "I have some things to take care of. You should get on, Northstrom."

"I would've come if I had gotten the message." She wanted to ask him if he would please, please, reconsider, if he would please, please, tutor her anyway. *Don't be a baby. You can't ask him that now.* "I'm sorry, sir. I'm truly, truly sorry."

"I'm sure you are." Still tired, but also angry. "Goodbye."

Lyla hesitated. "What will you do, sir?"

"I won't starve, Northstrom. Cripples make the best beggars."

"Sir—"

"Don't look so stricken. I'm not serious. I can probably tutor baron children privately. The children of friends of friends."

"Oh, good. That's good."

"Yes, as long as I can remember to continually tell the parents how *brilliant* their children are. How *gifted*. No matter what their abilities or behavior." He pressed one temple with the heel of one hand, as if his head ached. "Don't you have other places to be, Northstrom?"

She nodded, not wanting to say the wrong thing. And right now, every single thing she could possibly say was wrong.

—CHAPTER TWENTY-THREE—

LYLA hurtled through alleyway after alleyway on her way to meet Gill. Meet Gill, and then go on to the Red Fist hideaway. She stumbled in the flat gray light of early dusk, barely keeping her balance. She gasped; her chest burned.

Overhead, a roof-leaper whirred—the fourth since she'd left Slate's—and she dropped to a crouch by a back stoop. She covered her mouth with her arm, muffling the sounds of her breathing.

Did Riverton still mean to arrange for a tutor after she got herself clean? Maybe. But he had failed to mention that Teacher Slate wouldn't tutor her. That Teacher Slate had been fired because of her.

You slag, Riverton. You slag.

The roof-leaper's light stared down near her. A ways off, more toward the center of town, hounds bayed. A *crack-crack* sounded: gunshots. Lyla hugged herself smaller.

The roof-leaper light swept on, but Lyla couldn't move. Every direction seemed wrong.

Up. Get up.

She stood, and she began to run fast again—so fast that she might have run out of her own skin, splitting it and sloughing it off and becoming a smoother, sleeker, stronger, smarter person. Someone who could find the right direction.

She ran all the way to the hidden wood. She closed the little door behind her, shutting out the gunshots and the hounds. She leaned back against the door.

The trees stood tall, silent, and secret. They pointed toward the evening's first stars—the Pearls.

Light glinted in the wood too. Across from her, in one corner, stood a single pine tree, with branches that arched downward, the bottom ones hanging like old-fashioned skirts. From within the skirts flickered a lantern.

Gill.

The flickering candlelight pulled Lyla forward. It pulled her across the wood, past smooth trunks and reaching branches, to the pine tree and the yellow-orange glow.

She slipped under the boughs. Gill was sitting in a hollow, the space between two roots. "Hey," he said, though he didn't look at her straight on.

She knelt a bit away from him. "Hey."

He unbuttoned his coat a little, reached in, and brought out an old bag. He smoothed the paper against his knees and splayed his hands, hiding whatever he'd written. "I brought you something." He still didn't really look at her. "Consider it an apology for the other night."

"You're apologizing to *me?*"

He winced. "I'm sorry. I know I'm a surly slag."

"Oh. No," Lyla said faintly. "Really, don't apologize to me."

"Cap." He sounded exasperated, and he began to refold the paper he'd brought.

"Wait," she said quickly. "You're taking back my present?"

He stopped. "Not if you actually want it."

"Of course I want a present," she insisted.

"You do?" he asked, his tone better.

"I do."

"You don't have to say that just to be polite, Cap."

"Since when am I more polite than you?"

"You've got all these Bright-girl manners nowadays."

Lyla rolled her eyes, and she reached for the bag.

Gill drew his hands away quickly, as if to keep from touching her. She avoided touching him, too.

She unfolded the paper and smoothed it out against her legs. On it, he'd sketched their wood. The unfurling leaves almost overran the page, spilling out across her lap.

"I love this."

"It's just a sketch, Ly. You don't have to say that," he told her, but his ears had a dark reddish tinge.

"I wouldn't say I loved it if I didn't. Can I have it?" She held it to her chest.

"Sure. Of course," he said. She slipped the drawing inside her coat.

She smiled at him, or at least one side of him. He still kept his scars partially turned from her.

"What are you looking at?" He smiled, but tilted his head more away.

She wanted to ask if he planned each turn and shift. Or did he simply hide the damage without thinking? "I'm looking at you."

"That's all right. It's not a requirement."

"I know I'm not required," she said, but he raised the shoulder closest to her, as if he was preparing for something painful to hit him. She leaned forward, a little to the side, so she could look at him square on. He stared directly back at her, his eyes pale blue, or gray.

There's something I haven't told you yet.

There's something I need to tell you.

"You have the most incredible eyes," she said.

He went completely still.

He bent toward her, and she drew back. He gave this bitter laugh, as if he was used to people flinching from him, as if she was just everybody else, doing exactly the same stupid, horrible things everybody else did.

She leaned close to him, and her nose bumped his. She kissed the good corner of his mouth, half missing.

He grasped her face, thumb and fingers gripping her jaw-bone. He caressed the side of her nose with his. He kissed her top lip, her bottom lip. She drew his lower lip between her teeth and gently bit.

His fingers tightened on her jaw. She slid her hands under his coat, his sweater, then both his shirts, and she pulled off her gloves. His smooth, warm belly contracted away from her touch.

"Cold," he whispered.

"Oh. Sorry." She started to pull away.

"No, I like it." He kissed her.

She pulled off his gloves and brought his hands under the back of her shirts, flinching at the first cold touch. His fingers slid flat. Then they curved, pressing her spine, and the heels of his palms pressed her sides, gripping her bare skin.

———

After they kissed for a long time, Gill rested his face against the top of Lyla's head, in her hair, and he whispered, "We've gotta go. We can't just bolt off. Not show. I need the credit points they owe me."

She nodded.

"But we gotta try to talk to Preacher or something. Gen'ral and Knife and all—they're no better than bluecoats. They're no good."

Lyla nodded again. She saw her thoughts inside her head, spinning scraps of paper, off-white, with jagged edges and blurred words, smudges she couldn't read.

They left their hollow, their tree, their wood, and they ran through alleyways. WE WILL FIND YOU. Eyes stared at her from every wall. WE WILL FIND YOU.

He led her into a cellar, across its cracked concrete floor, and through a door to a tunnel of rock and dirt—one of the many abandoned mines. He took her hand, his fingers interweaving with hers. They fit together perfectly.

There's something I haven't told you yet.

The papers whirled—smudges, blurred words.

There's something I need to tell you.

The tunnel stretched before them, crisscrossed by other tunnels that sloped downward or split and split again, like roads leading to dozens of underground towns. Gill glanced back over his shoulder. "Bluecoats patrol down here sometimes. Or scout when they're planning a raid. Keep an eye out."

They turned abruptly down another tunnel, and they descended to a little room with rock shelves. Gill stood and listened. Lyla couldn't hear anything.

Against a wall of boards, he tapped a complicated pattern that sounded like a code. The wooden wall swung open, and yellow-green light blinded Lyla. Gill went in, and she followed.

A long, tiled cellar full of chattering, working people stretched ahead of them. Half the cellar was like Da's workshop, all piles of metal, tools, and partially built steamers. Nearby, several guys stood at a narrow table, working on metal scraps and old rubber tires. A woman sanded a long wooden board. The other half of the workshop was a cold frame, the windows so clouded on the inside that the people working within looked like hazy ghosts. Here and there through the windows, vine-looking shapes glowed. "Are the plants in there shining?" Lyla whispered.

"Yeah. Wild, huh? There's a word for it, living things that shine light. What is it? I can't remember. Do you see Preacher?"

"No." Did she want to? Could Preacher help her sort this mess?

Gill led her forward. The entire cellar was thick with smoke and steam, a fog that hovered like mist rising off the river. Near the tiled ceiling floated shining silky globes, and hanging from the globes, suspended from strings, were baskets that carried rounded metal burners. Flames rose from the metal and made the globes glow and flicker.

Above, painted on the ceiling: raised bloody fists; MINES = SLAVERY; HAVOC; IF YOU CAN DREAM, YOU CAN INVENT; SCHOOL = BRAINWASHING; RAGE.

"What is this place?" Lyla whispered.

"One of the workshops," Gill said. "People build steamers to sell in the shadow markets. You'd be surprised how many barons send somebody who works for them to buy steamers—I've heard they keep collections that they show off to one another. Slagging ludicrous. But some of the stuff here just gets used by Red Fist. The moss and vines that glow—those end up in lanterns all over the tunnels."

"But. It just doesn't seem . . ." A group of laughing women worked on a thin metal machine that looked like a hand-crank pump. Behind them stood a bunch of odd steamers, one a narrow boat shaped like a fish. Lyla said softly, "I don't understand how Gen'ral rules here. Why *he's* the leader."

"Shhh," Gill warned, glancing over his shoulder. "Even in the workshops, some Red Fists think he's great. He's the head of the soldiers 'cause he decided he is, and he's meaner than everyone else. Also, he says things that lots of Red Fists agree with. Like he's always saying that barons keep Protean and alchemyks from the rest of us, and they need to be beaten down. Alchemyks and Protean belong to all. We all can be inventors."

Lyla thought of the 572—the 572 killed in the capital city, when Red Fist tried to harness stolen Protean and exploded their hideaway, the school, the hillside. "Do you think he's right?"

"About Protean, yeah. I used to think he really wanted to help people. But now," Gill murmured, "I think he just wants to find a way to get rich off Protean."

"So cynical, Jack." She meant this to be teasing, but she couldn't manage a smile.

Gill stopped a woman carrying a bucket. "Have you seen Preacher?"

"I don't think she's around. Sorry."

"Thanks." Gill didn't start walking again. He simply stood by a table with a half-built tiller lying on it. "Gen'ral's gotta be waiting. We can't—" He shook his head.

A loud *clang, clang, clang* made everyone freeze, laughter dying away.

Gill took Lyla's hand again and gripped it. "That's a summoning. A call for a meeting," Gill said in a hush. "Gen'ral's got something he wants to say. That's never good."

People began to leave the tables and the cold frame. Their murmuring voices rose and fell as they headed for the back of the workshop.

Lyla and Gill followed the crowd. Ahead, Red Fist soldiers

flanked a tiled door, both of them huge with faces as still as masks. People asked them questions, but the soldiers shook their heads and said, "Through the door. Let's move."

Gill whispered, "If this goes bad, follow me."

"How do you think it'll go bad?"

"Don't know."

There's something I haven't told you yet.

There's something I need to tell you.

Beyond the doorway, a fog of candlelight and steam hovered. The room was already full of people, all kneeling. Large Red Fist guards completely surrounded the crowd. Not too far off, Spinner knelt next to Zeb. Spinner held out a hand to Gill and Lyla.

"Get on your knees," ordered one of the Red Fists who'd been standing at the door. He must've come in after them.

Lyla started toward Spinner, but the Red Fist grabbed her shoulder. "I said, on your knees," he ordered, shoving Lyla.

Gill steadied her. "All right, all right. We're just getting out of the way of the door."

"Shut up, Monster," said the guard, but he let them walk to Spinner.

Lyla lowered herself.

"What's going on?" Gill whispered to Spinner.

"I don't know." She took Lyla's other hand, the one Gill wasn't holding. "Some bad crap. Have you seen Nose? Or Jit?"

They both shook their heads. Spinner said, *"Merde."*

Lyla's breath snagged in her chest.

Near the back wall, Gen'ral and Knife walked forward through the still forms of kneeling people. They reached the middle of the room, and Gen'ral stepped up onto something, so he towered above the crowd. He still wore that wide-brimmed hat pulled low, to keep his eyes shadowed. His collar was open, so his tattoo was visible: a fist dripping blood.

Gill held Lyla's hand tight against his thigh.

Gen'ral said, "A soldier's life is tough—you've all been watched. Marked. Knocked around. You've lost brothers.

"We honor our lost brothers. And the brothers that bluecoats have locked away in cells smaller than shit-houses."

"Slagging hell. I see Jit," murmured Spinner as Gen'ral went on and on about bluecoats. "He's behind Knife."

Jit was standing in the back, with a bunch of other Red Fists. His arms were crossed, and he wore that grim Red Fist mask.

"He earned his tattoo?" Lyla murmured.

"Or he's about to?" whispered Spinner.

Zeb shook his head, and Gill whispered, *"Merde."*

"But we got worse enemies, right here," said Gen'ral. "We got traitors in our ranks. Spies. The bluecoats know just what to say to some kid with no guts. They say they'll open the prison door, or maybe they'll even scrape that kid's wrist clean. 'So you can work for a merchant or an inventor,' they say. 'All you gotta do is *squeal.*'"

Lyla's rib cage squeezed her lungs.

Two Red Fists walked toward Gen'ral, and they pushed a

thin squattie guy a step or so ahead of them: Nose. Gill gave a little hiss through his teeth, like he'd been slapped.

"No," Spinner whispered. "No, no."

Nose didn't look directly at Gen'ral; he stared into the crowd, shifting his weight. Everyone stared back at him.

"I didn't do nothing, Gen'ral." Nose slurred his words, as if he was drunk. "I didn't."

"Are you accusing Jit of lying?" Gen'ral smiled a little.

"No, Gen'ral."

"So, he's telling the truth?"

"He's just . . . Jit, come on, man. You know I wouldn't. You know it."

Jit shook his head, and smirked.

"I didn't, Jit," said Nose.

Spinner whispered, "What can we do?"

"I don't know," whispered Gill.

"How will they punish him?" Lyla barely had enough air to say the words.

Before Gill could answer, Gen'ral said, "Explain to everybody why the bluecoats let you go so fast."

"They questioned me, and I didn't say nothing, Gen'ral. Not a thing."

"Jit says you told him they asked about the Project."

"Yeah, they asked, Gen'ral, but I said I didn't know."

"So then they just opened the door for you? Let you walk straight out of the prison?"

"Yeah, yeah."

Jit and the Red Fists next to him started to laugh.

"The mine where we met that night after the Project mission," said Gen'ral, "is crawling with bluecoats. How did they find out about that mine if you didn't tell them?"

They found out from me.

"We have to do something," whispered Lyla. "We have to help Nose."

Zeb asked, "You see a way, Bright?"

"I didn't tell them about the mine." Nose's voice climbed higher. "They questioned me for a while, and I didn't say nothing, and they let me go. That's what happened. That's all that happened, Gen'ral. That's all."

One Red Fist called, "Slagging idiot."

A girl cried, "Just confess, Jacques. Please."

"Listen to your sister, Jacques," sneered Jit. "Confess."

Nose shook his head as if bewildered. "But I didn't do anything."

Lyla could feel Gill's hand shaking.

"Oh, no." Spinner's voice wavered. "No, no."

A woman with long braids stood. "This isn't the way to question some kid."

One of the Red Fist soldiers started toward her. "You're disrupting the tribunal."

"Guilty!" someone in the crowd cried. A Red Fist soldier? Someone else? "Guilty. Guilty!"

The sister started crying.

"Stop this," cried the woman with the braids as the Red Fist soldier grasped her arm.

Gen'ral's voice rang out, "Guilty." He sounded triumphant or amused. "We declare you guilty."

"No, Gen'ral!" Nose shouted. "That's not . . . I mean." He tried to run, but Jit and another Red Fist grabbed his arms.

The crowd stood and surged, and Lyla couldn't see Nose through the trousers and coats. As she and Gill stumbled up, she was bumped from behind, and a Red Fist shoved past her.

"You can't do this!" shouted the woman with the braids, struggling.

Gill tripped, tugging Lyla's arm as he dropped to one knee. Not enough air—the bodies all around stank of smoke and sweat-soaked wool.

A shrieking: "No! No! No!"

Spinner yanked Lyla up. Lyla tugged Gill's hand, and he stood. Another shove from behind—Lyla knocked into the guy ahead of her, who lashed out with one arm, his elbow hitting her jaw. Pain fissured her chin. She staggered back.

"The door," Gill said.

She was able to turn, pain still tremoring. The door was unguarded now, and between her and it, open space, a gap.

The shrieking was Nose. He sounded like some animal, a battered dog yelping and whimpering. Lyla glimpsed Jit striking out at Nose as he curled into a ball on the floor. The crowd shoved forward. "Spy!"

She had to get away, but her chest had squeezed all the air out.

Gill stood staring, like a kid lost and alone on a street.

Spinner shook Lyla's shoulder. "Let's go."

"I can't breathe at all," Lyla gasped.

"You slagging have to." Spinner shook her, and Lyla staggered forward. Spinner and Zeb started for that gap, the door.

As Lyla pulled Gill with her, he said, "They'll tear him to pieces."

A wailing: the sister keening. A triumphant coydog howl: Jit.

"They already have." Lyla's skin felt paper thin, easily torn. "We can't stay. We need to go," she urged. She tugged Gill toward the door. "Come on, Jack."

Gill shuddered like someone trying to wake from a night terror. "We have to get out of here. I've gotta think."

"Where should we go?" she asked as Zeb yanked the door open and then pushed Spinner out.

"I don't know," Gill said as Lyla tugged him out the door. "I don't know."

—CHAPTER TWENTY-FOUR—

LYLA ran with Gill, Spinner, and Zeb through dark tunnels as Nose's animal moans echoed in Lyla's head. Gill, holding a lantern he'd grabbed off a wall, led them inside a tunnel that was all concrete. It stank of sewer. At the end of it, they scrambled up a ladder, and as Lyla followed the others onto a deserted street, a long cry wailed so loud, her ears hurt. A siren.

"An attack?" she asked, dashing with the others to a narrow gap between two abandoned warehouses.

"It can't be," said Spinner. "Red Fist's all back there."

"Maybe not *all* the slagging bastards," said Gill. "Most."

"But they weren't gonna do small attacks anymore," said Spinner. "Just get ready for the big one."

"*Merde,* Spinner. Who cares?" Gill demanded.

In the pale light of Gill's lantern, Spinner's face looked odd, like it might crumple.

"Stop." Zeb halted them at the alley mouth. The street beyond was eerily empty, no people, only the wind skittering a piece of faded ribbon down the icy street. "Where are we slagging going?"

"I don't want to see Jit," said Spinner. "Not ever again."

Gill clutched one of Lyla's hands with both of his.

I'm sorry. I'm so, so sorry.

Gill said, "My room."

"What?" asked Spinner.

"I said, my room. We can go there."

"Really?" asked Zeb.

"Jit doesn't know where it is."

"Yeah, no one does." Spinner gave a brief, shaky smile. "Do you need to blindfold us or something?"

Smiling a little, Gill shook his head.

The sirens wailed again, like needles stabbing Lyla's ears. She said, "Let's get off the street."

They rushed through alleys: broken windows, crumbling walls, WE WILL FIND YOU, dripping red fists. They saw only one other person, and he crossed the street ahead of them. The sirens seemed to be wailing from across town. Everyone was hiding, or creeping to wherever to gawk at the attack.

Gill led them to a bulkhead and through a damp cellar. They started the long climb up a cramped stairway, and all wheezed, even Gill, who had to be used to walking up the flights. They trudged steadily anyway, toward Gill's perch. His refuge.

Gill led them down a long hallway to a door with a padlock,

which he opened, and they stepped into a wide, mostly empty room. Zeb leaned against the wall, hugging Spinner, hiding her face against his shoulder. Gill set his lantern down on a giant spool-table. Graphites and an ink bottle sat on top of it, along with flattened paper bags and paper scraps.

"This is it," he said. He jammed his hands in his pockets. "We should be all right. Besides my ma, no one else knows where it is."

The room didn't have much besides a table for drawing: a small battered iron stove with its stovepipe stuck up inside an old hearth; shelves made of cinderblocks and boards, where his *Pirate Jackman*s were stacked. He'd painted the wall near the hearth. Trees stretched up toward the ceiling, branches reaching, leaves unfurled. At the base of the trees lay his thin pallet. His tangled blanket's rounded curves looked like a shoulder, the bend of an arm. Lyla looked away.

"Thanks, man," said Zeb. "For bringing us."

"I know it's not Spinner's," Gill said.

"It's fine," said Spinner, just as Lyla said, "Oh, yeah. We'd much rather be out in the street than in your room."

Gill smiled at Lyla. "You can sit . . . uh . . ." He went to the bed, smoothed the blanket, and stacked papers in a corner. "You can sit here. Or on the floor."

They all ended up side by side on the bed. Though Spinner sat on one side of Lyla, and Gill, so warm, sat on the other, Lyla was cold.

"I have to admit, Scribbler," Spinner teased, "I always wondered what it'd be like to go to bed with you."

Gill didn't seem able to manage a word, and Zeb said, *"Hey,"* in mock outrage. Lyla laughed with Spinner.

They quickly fell silent. Someone whimpered, and Lyla almost asked, "What's wrong?" Then she realized the whimper was an echo of Nose in her head. His sister had called him Jacques. "Do you think . . ." Lyla said. "They can't have killed Nose."

"They could have done worse," said Zeb. "Crushed his eyes. Broken his back."

Spinner was shaking her head. "He's just dim. Why would anyone tear him apart?"

Lyla hugged her bent legs. Gill put an arm around her, and she pressed her forehead against the boniest part of her knees. She caught a glimpse of her marks, and she shut her eyes tight.

Merde. Merde, merde, merde.

"It's a threat—to scare all of us." Zeb's voice was furious. "The soldiers want to make sure we do what we're told."

"I hate them," said Spinner.

Lyla heard paper shifting. Gill was flipping open the newszine nearest them. She lifted her head: Pirate Jackman and Lady Captain. Then Gill said, "Oh, yeah," and flipped the pages closed.

"That's the next one?" Lyla asked.

"It's no good. Well, part of it is good."

"What do you mean?" She reached for the newszine and opened it.

Lyla reread the last two panels. Lady Captain and Pirate Jackman had returned to the university, where they lived and studied when they weren't in the war. They were university students. With nice clothes and rooms. With books, so many books—and they could read any they wanted.

Their parents had big houses, she now remembered from an old *Pirate Jackman*. Mansions, with huge flower gardens lit in the night by shining orbs.

"Lady Cap is a baron," Lyla said slowly.

"You didn't know that?" Gill sounded surprised.

"I knew it." But she hadn't *known* it. Not like you know that putting your hand in a fire will hurt you badly. "Lady Cap is a baron, and so is Pirate Jackman."

"That's why I never like the first and last pages," said Gill. "You can sort of forget otherwise."

They were barons. Saving Highland for barons.

"When you think about it," said Zeb, "everyone in *Pirate Jackman* is a baron."

"Yeah, they are," Gill said. "A while ago, I went through all the *Pirate Jackman*s I have, looking for diggers. Even merchants." He gave a sharp laugh. "There's almost none. None that are important. Usually none at all. Only sometimes in the background."

"Like we weren't there." Lyla set the zine down and pulled her hands away from it. "Like we don't exist."

"That's why I mostly don't read zines," said Spinner.

"*Pirate Jackman* just seems different," said Gill. "'Cause of the war. The spying."

AN OPEN DOOR FOR ALL WITH TALENT AND DILIGENCE.

AN OPEN DOOR.

"And the universities, the real ones—they aren't open," said Lyla. "They're locked shut."

"You're just figuring that out now?" asked Zeb.

"She was a Bright-room girl." Spinner nudged Lyla gently. "You know they can be kind of stupid."

"'Stupid,'" Lyla repeated. All her life, she had seen the locked-up university fence—the barons' kids going in so easy; the digger kids working, working, working, and a lot still never going in—she'd seen the fence her entire life, but as if it was far off, sort of blurry. The only thing that she had seen clearly was the work *she* had to do to make it through the university gate.

"I actually thought if you worked hard, you'd get into the university," she said, and the words sounded so dimwitted. "But you usually don't. And even if you do, you could still end up shoved out later. Teacher Slate, the teacher in the Bright, had gone to the university, but something went really wrong." Spinner and Zeb were staring at her, and probably Gill, too. But she couldn't seem to stop talking. "So that's why Slate isn't an inventor. He teaches primary alchemyks. I mean, *taught*. He taught at the school. But now he doesn't. We stole the orb, and he got fired.

"He's decent. He didn't do anything to get the orb stolen. The headmaster and the bluecoats knew he didn't. But they wanted someone to blame. So they fired him."

"Tough," said Gill.

"I studied hard, to get into the university." She'd licked barons' boots at the Beacon. She'd licked Riverton's boots. She'd stolen Mistress Regin's orb, and she'd gotten Teacher Slate fired. She'd kept terrible secrets from Hope, from her whole family. She'd lied to Spinner and Zeb. She'd lied to Gill.

"It's lies." She was loud, too loud; she couldn't make herself quiet. "*Pirate Jackman* is full of lies. All through it." She wouldn't ever read it again. "And the barons lie. They're awful. And Red Fist is awful. *Merde. Merde!* Nose is torn to pieces."

"Not because of us." Spinner gave Lyla a one-armed hug. "We didn't hit him. Or squeal to the bluecoats."

Lyla drew her legs closer to her chest and pressed her spine hard against the wall. Her chest was full of something smashed, sharp shards and splinters.

Gill said, "I'm not working for those Red Fist slags anymore."

"But if we don't, how will we eat, Scribbler?" asked Spinner. "Take jobs down the hole? We'll be raving in a day."

"The soldiers don't let you quit working for them," said Zeb.

"I'm not telling them I'm quitting. I'm just quitting."

"You think they won't notice?"

Gill ran one hand over his cropped hair. "You want to help Gen'ral knock everybody around? Tear kids to pieces?"

Zeb was shaking his head.

"No," said Spinner.

Lyla could feel the rise and fall of Gill's ribs, and, on her other side, Spinner's. If Lyla went to Riverton and told him everything that had happened, he wouldn't help Gill, Spinner, and Zeb stay safe. He hadn't even protected Teacher Slate, whom he'd known since he was little. He had let Teacher Slate get fired.

Fired, because of her. Like Red Fist tore Nose apart, because of her. Because of *her*.

"Did you hear that?" asked Zeb.

"What?" asked Spinner.

A sound leaked through the boards nailed over the windows. An alarm, but different than usual: *cree, cree, cree, creeeeeeee*.

"That's—" Lyla had heard the sound before, but she didn't remember when or why.

"The Project," said Gill, and Lyla did remember. Once, while inventors were fixing up the Project building, that *cree-cree* alarm sounded, so loud, you could hear it anywhere in town. The town councilor had announced it was a practice alarm, to see if it worked in case there was a Protean accident. Not that there would be an accident, he had said.

Cree, cree, cree, creeeeeee.

Gill stared at Lyla, his eyes green-brown, his mouth open, as though he were about to ask her a question. She gripped his hand so tightly, her fingers went numb. She could hear Zeb talking about his sisters. She told Gill, "I have to get to Hope, and Ma and Da. I have to get home."

He nodded, not saying what he—they all—had to be thinking: If there was an accident at the Project, she might not have a home anymore. The side of the Hill might be gone.

———

Lyla runs down the stairs in a dream. No, this is real—but it feels like a dream. She is running as fast as she can, and she's too slow, as if the air is dragging at her legs. "Come on," she says to Gill, to Spinner and Zeb, who are even slower. "Come on."

At the bottom of the stairs, she crosses the cellar, but at the metal door, Spinner grabs her arm and stops her. "Remember there was no one on the street?" Spinner asks, breathless. "Something's really wrong. Maybe we shouldn't go out."

Gill shakes his head. "If there was an explosion, we would've heard," he says. "We would have felt the shake."

"We're on the other side of town," Spinner says.

"A big explosion, like when the five hundred seventy-two were killed—we still would've heard. It isn't that."

"They may have just sounded the alarm to get everyone off the streets."

"I gotta find my sisters," Zeb insists.

"We'll find Isla," Spinner says to him. "She'll know where all the rest are."

"I have to get to Hope," says Lyla, and then she asks Gill, "What about your ma?"

"This is her night to sleep over at the baron's where she cleans. 'Cause his huge house takes so long to scrub. For once I'm glad she has that slagging cruddy job." His lips thin, a kind of smile. He says to Lyla, "I'll get you up the Hill."

No one says, *Unless the Hill is gone.*

Zeb wrenches the door open.

There isn't anybody in the alleys. No squatties, no diggers. As if everyone above the ground died while Lyla and the others were in the Red Fist workshop. There is only them, and Red Fist.

At Digger Street, Zeb stops and whispers, "We're going up here." He points to a metal ladder bolted to the side of a building. He clasps Gill's hand. "See you."

Then Zeb steps close to Lyla, and he wraps a clumsy arm around her shoulders. She half hugs him, but he steps back abruptly, a little off balance. Spinner kisses her cheek.

Lyla wants to ask their real names, but instead says, "See you."

Gill's hand clasps hers. That perfect fit.

He leads her through the alleys, as roof-leapers crisscross above. They stop at a turn. Ahead, on Main Street, a bluecoat stands on every corner, each wearing a white facemask and black goggles.

Gill pulls her close. "You all right?" he whispers, his words warm against her ear, melting her skin's chill.

He could've stayed safely in his room, but he came out here to help her, to protect her. He has risked himself for her.

There's something I haven't told you.

She drops his hand and steps back.

"What?" he asks, sounding confused.

There's something I haven't told you.

"What?"

"Nothing."

———

As he leads her up the Hill, over paths she didn't know existed, she doesn't look at him, so she sees only glimpses—his boots crunching into the snow, the slight swing of his arms. He has closed his gloved hands into fists, the way he used to when they were kids and he was upset. She glances away.

The Hill stretches up ahead of them. No crater, no rubble, no ash and dust. The dark green trees sway and creak.

Although the Hill seems fine, Lyla's chest still squeezes tight, as if there's a chance an accident destroyed only her farm, Ma, Da, and Hope.

Not possible. But her rib cage is still too narrow. She runs, almost faster than Gill.

———

When she and Gill reach her farm's half-falling-down barn, that *cree-cree* siren is still screeching. The sight of flickering light in the farmhouse makes Lyla dizzy. Maybe this *is* a dream. Maybe she's imagined everything—especially the light shining from the kitchen window—because she wants so badly for Hope and Ma and Da to be all right. Maybe she will wake up and find out they aren't. They are hurt. They have disappeared.

Gill crouches by a tree. "I guess we could've tried to spot the Project on our way up," he says. "But, man, tonight would not be the night to get caught by bluecoats."

"No."

He reaches for one of her hands, but she hides it behind her back.

"What's up, kid?" His expression is confused, hurt.

"Nothing."

"Well, obviously something. What did I do?" he asks. "Or not do."

She shakes her head.

He stands. "What's that for?"

"What?"

"You rolled your eyes."

"What are you talking about? You aren't even looking at me."

"Yeah, I am." He looks at her straight on, his eyes storm clouds. "Sorry to be stupid, but I don't know what I've done to piss you off."

"You haven't done anything," she snaps.

"What have I not done, then?" he demands.

"It's nothing, I said."

"Fine." He begins to walk away, finally. Finally.

But the sight of his back, his shoulders a little hunched, makes Lyla feel worse. Sick and terrible.

A quick walk, then a run. She passes him and stops. He halts abruptly, only the good side of his face turned toward her, the rest hidden.

"What the slag do you want?" he asks.

"I have to tell you something. Something bad." The words flow out on their own, a stream breaking through a wall. "You remember when I got that first mark?"

He nods, and she says, "Riverton, Dyre's lap dog—he's the one who marked me. After, though, he offered me a deal."

"'A deal.'" Gill says the words strangely, as if they're words of a language he doesn't understand.

"He offered me a tour of service. If I spied on Red Fist—"

Gill laughs suddenly, a sharp bark. "You had me going, kid. I admit it. A tour of service? *Merde*."

"Gill, I'm serious. Riverton knew you were working for Red Fist. And he knew we lived near each other when we were young." Gill has gone so still. "But he didn't know we were really close friends," she adds quickly. "And I didn't tell him."

"You've been squealing," Gill says.

"I never told Riverton much about you, or Spinner, or Zeb. Just Jit and Knife and Gen'ral." The secret is a river breaking its banks and drowning dry land. "I'm the one that told the bluecoats about Jit's mission and the mineshaft where we met Gen'ral after."

Gill stares, his face carved stone.

"Riverton thought Nose was kind of dim, and I said to Riverton that Red Fist didn't tell Nose secrets. I thought it'd help Nose. Get him out of a cell."

"Gen'ral accused Nose of squealing right in front of you."

"I know. I—" The press of all those sweat-smelly wool coats, the elbow striking her chin, and the fissuring pain. "I didn't know what to do."

Gill looks off to the side. One shoulder raises, warding her off, and his stony face alters slightly—disgust. "Riverton the Righteous. Junot Riverton. He's so honest, so hardworking," Gill sneers, and Lyla feels, like she does just as a winter storm blows in, that whatever's coming will be awful. "Such a hero."

"I swear," she says, "I didn't know he was the one who marked you. Not till Spinner talked about it earlier."

"You think he's so upright? Well. A few years back, I was, like, twelve or thirteen? You and I weren't friends, 'cause you had gotten Hill-girl snotty. You actually crossed the halls at school to stay away from Marked." He laughs again, that bitter bark. "Or even just kids from Digger Street."

Her face flames.

"This civics teacher at the school was trying to get me to be a bluecoat," Gill tells her, and she is so stunned, she doesn't know what to say. "'Cause I'm big, and I'm fast. I didn't really want to be a bluecoat, but the money is decent, and Ma had lost her job. We were about to get booted out of our place on Digger Street. And then where the slag would we live? Of course Stan still only sat around all day. He didn't look for work.

"So I let that teacher talk me into going to the officer trials, the huge ones for a bunch of the mountain towns. I was actually too young, but the teacher spoke to the bluecoats, and when they saw me, they let me. I was there with Riverton the Righteous.

We got along pretty good. He was one of the guys who wanted to help people, rather than just knock heads.

"Here's the thing: he isn't all that big, is he?" Gill says, and he sounds as if he's daring her to disagree.

"I guess not. No."

"He isn't. Lots of other guys there were stronger and faster than him, especially after we got to eat some decent food. Some of his scores at the trials—the races and the climbing and the lifting—some of his scores were kind of bad, and mine were great, even though I was young. I saw our score sheets, his and mine, since lots of times we went to look at ours together. A few of his scores were so poor, he was really worried. He stopped sleeping, and then he did even worse in the trials. He wasn't going to make the cut.

"But, see, on the last day, he didn't walk up to the office with me to find out whether or not he passed the trials. The bluecoat in the office said I hadn't passed. When he showed me 'my' score sheet, I knew it was Riverton's. And I saw 'Riverton's' on the desk—it was mine. I don't know how, but Riverton stole my scores, so he made the cut and I didn't. I went to find him after, and couldn't. I only passed him once as I was leaving the trials. He didn't say a word. He pretended he didn't know me. The slagging pile of crap."

"Riverton cheated?"

"You don't believe me." Gill shrugs, as if he doesn't actually care what she thinks anymore. "But it's true."

"Riverton cheated," Lyla repeats.

"He used to avoid me, but now, the few times I've seen him, he talks like he's sure I'll end up dead or in a cell. It's like he wants to kind of prove that I'm no good every time he sees me. Like, even though he cheated, he deserves to be a bluecoat, and I deserve to get locked up."

"But why didn't you tell anyone?"

"Come on, Bright. Who's going to believe me instead of Riverton?"

She shakes her head. No one would believe Gill, except her.

"So that's your *Righteous* Riverton, Bright."

"Quit calling me that, Gill."

"Yes, mistress. Whatever you say."

"Gill—"

He turns, and then he is walking off through the trees. She begins to shake badly. He veers into deep shadows, and he's gone.

—CHAPTER TWENTY-FIVE—

THE next morning, Lyla sat in the Aerie, as far as possible from all those lying *Pirate Jackman*s stacked in the corner. She didn't want to touch them, or the pictures of Pirate Jackman and Lady Captain on the wall. Not at all. Or even look at them. She stared down the hillside at the Project, so dark except for small flashing siren lights. Dark, like the Project was broken or shut down. Which made no sense. Nothing made sense.

Riverton had cheated. He had cheated Gill. And she had betrayed Gill by using him to spy for Riverton.

Lyla's thoughts were circling around, the same ones over and over. Wheels on an overturned cart, spinning fast in the air. Taking her nowhere.

She wanted Hope. But the town councilor had issued a curfew; the entire town had to stay inside until further notice. Hope hadn't returned from meeting the inventor friend of Teacher Slate, Mistress Regin; Hope must be staying at Mistress Regin's mansion. And if Hope were home, would Lyla really tell her everything that had actually happened?

Gill was gone, for good.

Lyla picked up the paper in her lap, which a messenger had delivered with the curfew announcement, and she read the article again.

EMERGENCY UPDATE: RED FIST STRIKES AT PROJECT

Hazard alarms ripped through the dark chill yesterday evening, echoing across Hill's Ridge, due to an apparent Red Fist strike on the Project.

For safety reasons, inventors will not leave the Project at this time, nor will they allow reporters into the building.

However, the young guards, who daily risk life and limb as they watch over the Project, did speak to this reporter. These elite "eyes" for the Project confirmed that Red Fist attempted an attack a few days earlier but was driven off. During the botched attack, peace officers, now stationed at the Project to provide essential aid in dangerous times, captured Jacques Spurwood, age seventeen. Officer Junot Riverton, who was mentioned in these pages last summer for his heroism in the capital during the tragedy that left 572 dead, determined that the Spurwood boy was a decoy and petty thief. After marking the seventeen-year-old, Officer Riverton released him.

According to Captain Samuel Dyre, Red Fist in Hill's Ridge and across Highland has intensified attacks, because it has developed grandiose ambitions.

It aims to capture and control all means of Protean gathering, harnessing, and selling. This goal is, of course, "laughable," as aptly described by Captain Dyre. And yet it has inspired Red Fist cells to collaborate to an unprecedented degree—to plan and execute increasingly sophisticated, bold, and damaging attacks both here in Hill's Ridge and in all of Highland's towns and cities.

How could people not notice that this emergency report didn't really explain what happened? It made the attack last night seem as though it had been by Red Fist. But last night, during the "attack" on the Project, most Red Fists had been in the workshop, tearing Nose—Jacques Spurwood—to pieces.

Lyla pulled back her sleeves, and stared at her wrist: two blue marks. One for stupidity, one for courage.

She didn't want anyone else torn apart because of her. She didn't want to help Riverton get the promotion he wanted so badly. And if she ever actually ended up at a university, what would she say to a bunch of barons' kids who had never been Marked? She couldn't imagine a single thing. But she wasn't spending her life down the mine hole, either—not that Gen'ral and Knife were likely to let her head down the hole or stay on the farm if they found out she was a spy.

Where did that leave her?

Nowhere. She had nowhere to turn.

——

Out of the Aerie, down in her room, Lyla paced, but silently, so Ma and Da wouldn't hear her and ask what was wrong. Her thoughts spun.

Then she heard a rap on the bedroom window. She stared at the quilted sacking that covered it—a messenger would knock on the front door, but Gill wouldn't. Gill knew which window was hers.

Hands trembling, she walked softly to the window and drew the sacking aside. Beyond the cracked glass, snow fell lightly from the afternoon's overcast sky. She didn't see anybody.

A form rose in front of the window. She started to smile, but he wasn't tall and broad and half turned from her. He was ragged, with a wolfish grin—Jit.

Her smile stuck on her face, pasted and fake. Shaking, she gripped the windowsill to calm herself.

Jit gave her a jaunty wave, and he gestured for her to come out. She scanned the snow and the tree line. He was on his own.

He gestured again, eager or impatient. As if he could hurt Nose, or anyone else, and then keep doing exactly what he wanted.

Which he could—because no one had caught him. Lyla's thoughts quit spinning. She didn't have any idea what she was going to do to stop Jit, but she forced one hand into a fist and she held up a steady finger. *One click.*

Jit nodded.

She crept out of her room and down the hall to the sitting-room doorway. Ma and Da sat near each other, Ma in Da's big comfortable chair and Da on the arm of the couch, a little bent toward her. They talked softly, as if they didn't want to be over-heard. Da took Ma's hand, and he clasped it in both of his, turned it over, and brought her palm to his mouth. Lyla felt she should look away but couldn't as Da kissed Ma's palm. Ma smiled like a stranger, like a woman in love with some man, not her mother at all.

Lyla didn't want to explain that she was leaving again, so she slipped past the doorway, left a note in the kitchen as she quietly pulled on her coat, and crept outside. She ran lightly through the snow to the corner of the house, and she peered around it. Jit prowled there, muttering to himself.

As she reached him, she told him she had to talk to him near the trees, not at the house where her parents might see. "Yeah. Good," he said, and he dashed ahead of her, to the tree line, as if she'd tossed a ball and he was chasing it.

Just inside the trees, they both stopped. Jit rocked side to side, too close to her, but Lyla stood her ground. "Well?" she asked.

"What the slag's wrong with Monster and them?" he demanded.

"What do you mean?"

"He told me where to find you, but he and the others won't come. We got a mission, an important mission, and they won't help."

"What kind of mission?"

He grinned at her, his breath as terrible as always. "I'll show you." His grin faded. "But Gen'ral's expecting me to bring the rest, too. The pack. That's my orders, the orders I gotta follow. What the slag's wrong with them?" he asked again.

"You don't think it has to do with Nose?" she demanded.

"Don't cry for Nose. He squealed and he got what he deserved."

"Will he . . . Is he all right?"

Jit shrugged. "A healer took him in." Lyla wanted to shove Jit. "You don't know what's wrong with Monster? *Merde,* Bright. This is a big mission."

"Wait. Is this the big mission at the Project?"

"How do—" Jit smiled. "I'm not telling you. I'm not telling you a thing. You gotta come with me and find out." His smile faded. "But we need to get the pack. Gen'ral said to. They gotta listen to me. And Monster and them could earn a lot of credit points, and if they weren't so slagging stupid, they could earn tattoos. Like I got mine."

Lyla was almost certain this was the big scheme to attack the Project, the one Riverton had talked about. Or it was related to that scheme.

She said to Jit, "Let me talk to Gill."

———

Once Jit and Lyla reached the alley outside Spinner's building, Lyla stopped and told Jit to let her see Spinner, Gill, and Zeb without him. He paced and snapped his teeth at her, but she finally convinced him. "You better be quick. *Quick,*" he warned.

Because she knew Spinner wouldn't let her in the bulkhead

doors, Lyla climbed into the building through one of its broken windows. She slipped down the stairs and through a dark part of the cellar, toward a doorway with candlelight shining through it. She could hear scraping and thumps. Then Spinner. "These should go in that crate."

"You got a lot of crap," observed Zeb.

"I've lived here almost two whole years." Spinner's voice cracked.

A silence.

"We'll find another place," promised Zeb. "A better place."

"I'm sorry," said Gill.

"She played all of us," Spinner said. "It's not your fault."

Lyla walked into the candlelight. The three of them were packing Spinner's discs and other things into crates. Lyla stopped, and Gill saw her first, his expression stark surprise.

Then his face hardened.

"Merde," said Spinner. "Slag it."

"The bulkhead," said Zeb, taking Spinner's arm. "Leave it all. Leave it."

"There's no one else here," Lyla said quickly. "Just me. I didn't bring anyone. Well, Jit. I made him wait outside."

"Jit?" Spinner and Zeb stopped.

"Gen'ral sent him," Lyla said. "Red Fist has a mission they want us for. I think it's the big one — the mission at the Project."

"You came to get us?" Spinner laughed. "You think we've already forgotten what you did."

"No. Of course not."

"Nose won't ever be right. Not with so much broken." Each of Spinner's words hit at Lyla. "He isn't awake much."

"Might be best if he don't wake up again," said Zeb. "Bright, you should see him for yourself."

Lyla heard the echo of Nose's animal whimpers; she tried to shake the sound from her head. "I will."

"Right." Gill laughed. "Sure you will."

Spinner went to Gill and took his arm, intertwining hers with his. She gave Lyla her glittering cat's-eye stare.

"Bright, Gen'ral will figure out you're a squealer," Zeb stated, so toneless it was hard to tell if this troubled or pleased him. "And Knife hits back at girls differently than boys. Knife cuts apart their faces."

Lyla's hand started to rise toward her face; she forced it to drop. "I didn't squeal anything about you," she said. She tried not to plead. That would only make Spinner sneer. "Practically nothing at all. I didn't want you hurt."

"Thanks, Bright," Spinner said, mock-grateful.

"And if I wanted the Coats to haul you in, why did I tell Gill about the tour?" Lyla asked.

No word from Gill, not even a glance.

"You got some good reason, I'm sure," said Spinner. "Bright girls always got good reasons to save their own skins. Get out."

All those crates—they were leaving, and she wouldn't have any way to find them, or Gill, again.

"Look, I want to hit back at the Red Fist soldiers. Stop them from knocking everybody around. Make *them* hurt," Lyla said.

"I have an idea." She took a step toward Gill. "You want to stop them too, I bet. And you also want to make Riverton hurt. If you tell him where to catch Gen'ral and Knife, he'll hate that he needed your help, especially if Captain Dyre sees you helping him. He wouldn't be able to turn you down, 'cause he really wants to catch Gen'ral, but he would hate that he couldn't turn you down. I know it'll help the barons, but wouldn't helping them for just this one thing be worth it? To get rid of Gen'ral?"

Spinner's cat stare glittered. "We're not squealing to any blue-coats," said Zeb.

Gill, though, was completely still. Gill was listening.

Lyla said to Gill, "Jit and Gen'ral and Knife would end up in prison forever. And Riverton would owe you forever."

Gill finally, finally looked up, though his scarred side was still turned away from her. He studied Lyla. Changeable eyes, gray and green. Storm clouds and river. He studied her like he studied something before he drew it, to get the true shape of it.

She fought the urge to hide her face in her hands. "You'd shame Riverton. You'd hurt him bad."

"Slagging *merde*," Gill said. "No more of this slagging crap." He wheeled and headed for the bulkhead doors.

—CHAPTER TWENTY-SIX—

LYLA stood in the dark cellar stairway of Spinner's building, one hand on the wall. She was far enough away that she couldn't hear Spinner or Zeb, and Gill was gone. Gill was gone. *Riverton didn't tell me he cheated you,* she thought toward Gill, toward the street. *And if some bluecoat had offered you a tour, what would you have done? Said no? No to getting yourself scraped clean?*

Gill would've said no.

She smacked the wall with the flat of her hand. Eyes closed, she leaned her head against the stone's chill. She heard the echo of Nose whimpering.

She owed Nose. He had taken her beating, and she had let him. She had stood by while Red Fist hurt him—maybe hurt him permanently.

She had to stop Gen'ral from damaging anyone else. Or anything else. The Project. The Hill.

She climbed the stairs to Jit, who had slipped into the building, and she said that the others wouldn't come. He whirled around the room, kicking the walls. "If you don't stop, I'm going without you."

"You don't know where to go," he sneered.

"Yeah? Then where *do* we go?"

He raged, but then said that he had to take her, he had to take her, he *had* to. Because that was Gen'ral's orders, to bring back squatties before tonight. It was too late to try again with Spinner and them. It was too late to find anybody else.

"Yeah," she agreed. "Let's go."

He led her out of town and into the sewers, then along many dark tunnels she'd never known existed before, inside the stench of ash, of iron, of pond muck and fish, of rat piss and worse—something dead and rotten. Down a ladder into an old mine's cavernous hole, a pool of night. Ahead was an opening in the rock, where a green-white light wavered.

As they neared the opening, Jit swerved close to her. "All right," he whispered. "Just don't talk. I'll talk. Don't slag this up for yourself."

"What do you mean? Don't make you look bad? You do that all on your own."

Jit spun in front of her, shoving his face close to hers. "I could have my brothers hold you down for me."

Her cheeks stung as if he had slapped her.

He smiled and patted her hair. Then he ducked through the opening.

He thought she couldn't stop him, but *he* was the one who couldn't stop her. And Knife couldn't stop her, and Gen'ral couldn't. She would get them hauled in—stopped for good.

She followed Jit through that opening, into a cavern much

larger than any she'd ever been in. Walking through the green-white glow of moss and ivy lanterns, they went past Red Fist soldiers who nodded to Jit, into the steam rising from pipes that jutted straight from the rock floor, past many tables where ragged Red Fists sorted metal and scraps or worked on steamers. One of the steamers was a little cart, like for a kid to ride in, and Lyla remembered Gill saying that sometimes barons sent their servers to shadow markets to pay a lot for steamers they thought funny or lovely. Though barons always accused diggers of giving Red Fist all the credit points they used to survive. Liars.

Jit circled around Lyla. "Quit slagging dragging your feet. If you piss off Gen'ral, he'll make us both hurt."

She was practically jogging, and so was he. "We don't want to look like scurrying rats," she whispered. "Skittering all over."

"I don't," he snapped, but he slowed to a walk.

She steadied her pace as they walked past a girl working on a triangular buggy; past kids sorting metal, and a burly woman working at a forge, the chimney pipe sticking into a rock wall; past a guy hammering metal flat, who looked sideways at Jit, a narrow-eyed stare. A whole town, in a way—a whole town of Red Fist that obeyed Gen'ral and his soldiers. Maybe a lot of the town didn't want to, but they did anyway. They let Gen'ral rule.

Yet Gen'ral didn't seem to be anywhere in the room. Lyla and Jit went by a hillock of glowing moss, which up close was a gleaming filigree of stems. Beyond was the other end of the cavern. Two guards leaned against a wall, flanking a tall, wide fissure. The two guards clasped hands with Jit, eyeing Lyla. Then Jit slipped sideways into the narrow fissure, scooting quickly.

Lyla scooted after Jit, into the opening. She knew it wasn't really closing inward, but it felt as if it were. She laid her hands on the rock in front of her and pushed to keep the curved wall from collapsing. Her lungs squeezed.

And then, as she stepped into a grotto, her lungs released. Ivy trailed up one wall and crossed the entire ceiling, a pale green-white web. The walls were arched and hollowed in the shape of water ripples; the grotto must have once held enough Protean to have exploded the entire mountain and perhaps even the peaks alongside of it. At the far wall, behind a table, towered Gen'ral. His wide-brimmed hat shadowed his face as he studied papers on the table.

"Finally." Knife grinned at them. "You're slow enough. Where are the others?"

Jit licked his lips. "They've crawled into a hole and they don't want to come out." Knife's grin disappeared.

Gen'ral straightened, his eyes still shadowed. Knife said, "You lost them."

"It wasn't me. They're yellow," Jit snapped.

"Are you saying I'm wrong?" Knife took a step toward Jit.

Gen'ral said abruptly, "Jit, you're supposed to be a soldier. We can't surprise the bluecoats if we can't gather our troops to strike fast and hard. The bluecoats are distracted—this is our time."

"I know, I know. I said that to the others."

"You couldn't get them to follow you," Gen'ral said, disgusted.

"No. I told you, it's them. They're yellow."

"Fetching them was your job. You lost them."

Knife started for Jit, and Jit crouched, a fighting stance.

"Not now," Gen'ral ordered. Knife stopped where he was, although he still leaned forward toward Jit. "We're already short. A bunch of our boys got swept up in raids."

Jit held his stance. The air felt thick, like before a storm, heavy with rain and wind.

Gen'ral took two steps to the edge of the table. His fingers closed around its corner, and a woman's bracelet, a delicate chain, fell half over his hand, its small charm dangling and swinging. A token from a ma or a love, though he didn't seem like someone who had either. Without paying the bracelet any attention, Gen'ral smacked the table with his palm.

"We should'a tattooed Bright and made her pack leader," Knife said to Jit.

"Bright tried to get them to come," Jit crowed. "They didn't listen to her."

"She hasn't failed as many times as you."

"Quit," Gen'ral barked at Knife, and Knife went silent, his lip curled, like a hound's just before it bit you.

Gen'ral bowed his head, thinking.

Lyla had to go on this mission *now*, tonight. She needed revenge for Nose tonight. She needed to stop whatever it was Red Fist had planned—for it had to be bad. And to finally, finally be done.

"I'm ready," Lyla told Gen'ral.

He looked at her.

"I don't want to end up down the hole the rest of my life. I don't want to be earning gold for someone else." This was all entirely true. "I don't want to *hate every single thing I have to do.*"

Gen'ral smiled a little at her anger. "You're not yellow."

She shook her head.

"Hey. I'm ready to go," said Jit. "I'm ready right now."

"A few eager soldiers are better than a bunch of yellow ones," remarked Knife.

"What do you need us to do?" Lyla asked.

"All right. All right." Gen'ral sounded a bit calmer. "Every great mission has its setbacks to overcome. I'll recompute, see who we have, where each group will go." Gen'ral said to Lyla, "Bright, you could have a chance to earn your tattoo tonight at the Project."

She felt she had been heading down this road to the Project all along, to the Project with Red Fist, where Riverton and Captain Dyre waited. And there was no way to step off the path. No way to take another path. No way to turn and go back the way she had come. She had to keep going straight forward, right into it. "I'm ready."

―――

That night, as other packs of squatties crept through the trees toward the Project fence, Lyla and Jit climbed into a hole in the ground, a narrow abandoned mine near the Project. Its rickety ladder creaked. Lyla counted the length of her breaths to keep herself from panting. In, two, three. Out, two, three.

She climbed down the rungs faster. The mission was simple: to attack the Project and take it over, now that its guards and bluecoats were weak. The town councilor's emergency report had made it seem as though Red Fist had attacked the Project, but Gen'ral had said Red Fist hadn't—which meant something else had gone so badly or shamefully wrong at the Project that the bluecoats or inventors or whoever had tried to make the problem sound like a Red Fist attack. They had lied so they wouldn't get blamed.

In, two, three. Out, two, three. Down into the small dirt tunnel. Once Red Fist had the Project, Gen'ral would say to the town councilor that he was holding the Project hostage, and he would make a bunch of impossible demands. Free entry to the university for all. Free power from the Project. He would threaten to explode the Protean if his demands weren't met. And yet secretly, carefully, Red Fist would thieve all the food and supplies out of the Project to sell cheap in the shadow market. They would thieve the Protean, keeping some in Hill's Ridge and sending some to other Red Fist workshops in other towns. From how Gen'ral talked, it seemed Red Fist soldiers in all of Highland's towns and cities had plans to do the same whenever they could—attack their Projects, thieve the Protean, give it out to Highland's many Red Fist workshops. They planned to hit university libraries as well, wherever they could. And they planned to start "free schools." Gen'ral had mentioned slogans that he wanted painted all over Hill's Ridge: JOIN RED FIST. LEARN ALCHEMYKS. TAKE BACK THE BOOKS. TAKE BACK ALCHEMYKS. TAKE BACK THE POWER.

As Lyla had listened to the general spout all this, she had kept thinking of the 572 blown to pieces in the capital when Red Fist experimented with Protean. Also, how free could any "free school" be if it was overseen by someone like Gen'ral? Or Knife?

After Gen'ral had finished the explanation, Lyla had volunteered to help snatch Riverton and Dyre. She had said, more brazen than she ever thought she could be, that she could find Riverton and Dyre in the Project and pretend to turn coats. She could tell them she would lead them to Gen'ral, but instead she'd lead them to a ravine, where some Red Fists would be waiting with an ambush to snatch them. "Grabbing Dyre would be a real triumph," Gen'ral had said, and she'd barely hidden her relief that he'd approved of the scheme. "Without him, the rest of the bluecoats at the Project might even turn tail." Lyla had tried to convince him to let her go without Jit, but Gen'ral hadn't allowed it. "I'd send more of you if I could spare more from the main attack. Don't fail."

Gen'ral thought this was his big chance, but he was wrong. It was hers. Lyla's one big chance. *And, Gill, if you had come, you could've hurt Riverton at the same time.*

The pale light of Jit's lantern shone on a wall of dirt and rock ahead of them, a cave-in. Lyla's lungs squeezed empty. "Slag it! Slag it!" shouted Jit.

"Shhh. We're close. They'll hear you," she said in a thin, airless whisper. "There was a side tunnel, remember? A little bit back."

"Oh, yeah." Jit swooped over and kissed her cheek. Then he held up the lantern and stared into her eyes like they were in a romance zine, like he was hungry for her and hated her all at once. She suppressed a shudder.

"Come on." She grabbed the lantern from him and turned away.

In, two, three. Out, two, three. Grit filled her nose and mouth. Her chest ached, and her head felt as if it were going to float off. She wished Hope were beside her, but at the same time was so glad Hope was somewhere safe.

They reached a door that led to a little root cellar, and they climbed up its stairs into the Project. At the top, they crouched at another door. Through it, they heard the wail of an alarm. Voices shouted. Quick footsteps thudded nearby. They had to go out there—but they couldn't let themselves be seen.

Jit bounced a little, his hand on the doorknob. "Come on. Come on."

"Shhh," said Lyla. Though this *was* taking too long. They didn't have time.

Her job, hers and Jit's, was to lure Dyre and Riverton out of the Project. Right now, while she and he were stuck at this door, several Red Fist packs outside were attacking the Project fence. To drive off these packs, the bluecoats and guards would have to "spread out," Gen'ral had said, "which would weaken them." After Lyla found Dyre and Riverton, they would follow her far from the Project, leaving it "thinly guarded." So later, during the "battle," Gen'ral would send a pack of Red Fists up through the root cellar. They would overwhelm the Project guards and take over the Project.

Which meant she and Jit had to get to Dyre and Riverton as soon as possible. So she could warn them. So they could grab Gen'ral, instead of Gen'ral grabbing them.

"All right," said Jit, leaping up. "Come on." He reached for her arm.

She stood abruptly, before he could touch her. "Shhh," she hushed him again, but he was right; beyond the door, the footsteps had gone. The voices had gone. Only the siren kept on, wailing, wailing.

Jit yanked the door open. They peered into a passageway, all paneled walls and thick oak doors. Something was wrong with the parquet floor. It slanted down. Lyla had the feeling that she was in one of those stories that always made her want to shout at the characters, *"Don't! Go back!"*

She glanced down the hallway. No one.

"We should split up to look for Dyre," she whispered.

"You just want to catch him by yourself," Jit accused. "So you'll earn your tattoo."

"You think I'll find him before you do?" she goaded. "You're right. I will."

He laughed so loudly she drew back into the stairway, listening hard for footsteps. Nothing.

"Oh, yeah?" he said. "I'll find them before you, Bright." He rocked back and forth. "How about a deal? If I find them before you, you have to show me something good," he said with a leer. "And if you find them before me, I have to show you something good."

"Great," she said, so he'd go. "I can't wait."

He grabbed the lantern from her and rushed down the passageway, finally leaving.

The alarm kept shrieking, as though the building were shouting. She slipped down the hallway, peering ahead of her, peering behind.

The passageway seemed to form an outer square around a huge central room that was walled off. In a few places, there were windows, but these were boarded up. A couple of signs hung on the wall with cords hanging near them: PULL CORD IN CASE OF EMERGENCY. The lights above the signs were dark. The entire floor tilted inward, as if the center of the building had sunk. She went to the closest door and gently took hold of the handle. Leaning forward, she listened.

A sudden pounding. Many feet running.

She pulled back with a jerk.

She realized that the sound was above her, the next floor up. Not through the door.

Again, she gently took a hold of the doorknob. It turned a tiny bit and then stopped. Locked shut.

She tried the next door: locked shut. The next: locked shut.

So many doors, but no slagging way in?

She reached the end of the hallway, where the wall rounded; this must be one of the turrets. Beyond her, around the corner, voices barked at one another. She stopped and pressed herself against the wall.

A voice shouted, "Out! Out!"

Lyla's fingers gripped the walls' cracks and seams. There was nowhere to hide. The doors were all locked.

Suddenly the voices drifted away.

She looked around the corner. The hallway was empty.

She had to go. Rounding the curve, she was struck by an acid stench.

Gagging, covering her nose, she kept walking. There were more doors, a long line. In front of one, thick at the doorjamb because of the floor's slope, puddled yellow vomit. It was streaked with blood. Next to the puddle lay an abandoned rifle and blanket.

She was tempted to pound on the door and demand what the slag had happened here. What the slag was wrong?

Riverton the Cheat would know, if she could find him.

She began to jog, soft cat's feet, quick, quick; moments were clicking past. Down a long passageway to the next turret corner, where a large stairway circled upward. She crept under it, into its shadows.

Voices drifted down. Shouts. Barked instructions. From outside sounded muffled thunderclaps. No, they weren't thunderclaps — they were gunshots.

She couldn't think about that.

Lyla eased around the staircase and crouched. Ahead, down the wide main passageway, stood a much larger staircase with sweeping banisters. A ways in front of the staircase, near an immense entrance door, stood a stocky man in bulky clothes. Grime smudged the mask and goggles he wore. His coat had some kind of badge, as if to mark that he was boss.

She was almost certain it was Captain Dyre, because behind him stood a taller, gawkier guy, also wearing goggles and a mask: Riverton.

She felt something inside, like a bright color underneath a haze.

She crouched and waited. Moments clicked by. Her legs cramped. She wanted to scream.

Then Dyre said something to Riverton and took off up the stairs. She picked up a pebble from the grit at her feet, and she pinged Riverton with it. He didn't seem to notice.

She hurled another, larger pebble, as hard as she could. He turned, and she leaned out of the shadows a little.

He walked over quickly, murmured, "Northstrom," and tried to take her arm, but she stepped away.

"Just lead," she whispered. "I'll follow." She went with him back underneath the stairs, to a small bare room with boarded-over windows.

Once they were safely inside, he thrust a white mask at her. "Northstrom, why are you here?" His hushed voice was rough, as if he'd been shouting, or maybe he hadn't slept in ages. "How long have you been in this building without a mask?"

As she tied it on, she demanded, "Why do I need a mask?"

Riverton shook his head. "Never mind. Wait. The Red Fist attack. Are you here because of the attack?"

"Tell me what's happened. Why everybody needs to wear masks. Why?"

"There'll be an official announcement later."

The haze inside her burned away—sharp, hot heat. "What do you mean? Why won't you just tell me? Do people on the Hill need to be warned about this place?"

"There's nothing to warn about. We don't want a stupid panic. The inventors will tell everyone once everything is completely taken care of."

"What's taken care of?"

"They said it's nothing to worry about, and the masks are just a precaution. Is Gen'ral here? And Waterhouse?" Riverton's mismatched eyes bulged because of his goggles. "Where is he?"

"Would you stop asking me about Waterhouse? He's not here. He's not the problem. How do we know we don't need to worry, when the inventors have lied about what happened here? They said Red Fist did it."

"Red Fist has slagging messed up your head," Riverton snapped. "They've got you thinking like them."

"I'm not messed up in the head."

"There's all kinds of squatties out there, and Red Fist. This is a big attack. The biggest I've ever seen. Is Gen'ral here? Where is he?"

Lyla was blazing light, hot fury. He was a cheat. He was a liar. Why should he get to capture Gen'ral? Why should he get to impress Dyre and win a promotion?

This attack is a lark, she almost said. *It's just us kids.*

She heard the echo of Nose crying out like an animal.

"Gen'ral thinks I'm going to lead you and Dyre into a ravine for a snatch," she said. "He wants Dyre, and he wants to take over the Project. I can show you where he's waiting."

"Yeah." Riverton raised a triumphant fist.

Lyla wished she could slap him.

—CHAPTER TWENTY-SEVEN—

IN a top tower room, Dyre went still at the sight of Lyla, like she was a ghost. And he was some kind of monster that had crawled out of the ground, stocky and grime-streaked. His goggles and mask were a blank.

He sent the other bluecoats in the room away, except for Riverton. "Well?" Dyre demanded.

Ignoring Riverton, Lyla told Dyre that Jit was in the building, and Dyre had Riverton slip out for a moment to order one of the bluecoats to find Jit. Then Dyre asked, exasperated, "That's all?"

"I've got a lot more."

Riverton returned as she told Dyre Gen'ral's plan to take over the Project tonight. His plan to hold the Project hostage, to threaten to explode it all. And yet to steal Protean and send it around to Red Fist workshops, where Red Fists would try to harness it. As she spoke, Lyla heard a whispering inside her: *the 572, the 572*. She told him that Red Fist in other towns and cities also planned to attack Projects there and steal Protean.

But she found that she wasn't saying a word about Red Fist's plans to also attack universities and to steal books. To start a free school.

AN OPEN DOOR FOR ALL WITH TALENT AND DILIGENCE. What if they truly were able to open the door?

She wasn't going to be the person who helped keep it slammed shut.

"So," she said, "I know where Gen'ral is."

"Finally. We've finally caught a chance," Dyre said to Riverton, and he sounded as though he was smiling. Riverton grinned, and Lyla ignored him. "Where is he?"

Lyla said to Dyre, "He thinks I'm bringing you both to an ambush. But I can take you to where he is, so you can snag him. We should go quick."

"Nice," said Riverton. "Nice work."

Slag off, cheat.

"I didn't expect you'd do so well," Dyre said. Pleased? Suspicious? Both. "I wonder, are you leading *us* into a trap?"

"No!"

"I'm not a bleeding-heart, Northstrom. A lot of talk isn't going to dupe me. You just need to give me proof." He said to Riverton, "Cuffs."

She didn't know what he meant. Riverton said, "Sir?"

"She'll wear cuffs, so if this is a trap or she tries to bolt, she'll be easy to grab. You stay right with her."

Lyla shook her head. "Sir—"

"Yes, sir." Riverton unhooked metal wrist cuffs from his belt.

She took a step back. "I'm not leading you into a trap."

"If you aren't," Dyre said very quietly, "why so jumpy?"

"I'm not—"

"What's the matter with you, Northstrom?" Riverton asked, exasperated. He walked close and snapped a cuff around one wrist and then the other, chilly metal locking against her skin. The cuffs covered her marks, but they were so much worse than blue ink.

She pulled away from Riverton. With her wrists locked together, her elbows stuck out awkwardly to the sides. "Sir, these will make it tough for me to stay hidden," Lyla said. "We don't want Gen'ral to see us. He'll know something's wrong, because I'm supposed to lead you to the ravine, not to him. He'll bolt."

"You saying you can't do this?" Dyre demanded.

"No. I want Gen'ral caught. We have to catch him. Lock him away forever."

Riverton grabbed her arm. "This is it. Your last test," he murmured quickly to her. He held her arm tightly. "We catch Gen'ral, and you'll have proven yourself. You'll get your marks off. You'll be clean."

"Then I'll start working with Teacher Slate one-to-one right away?" she asked softly, as if she really believed this would happen.

"Oh. Oh, yeah," he said, looking off to Dyre, the door, the stairs down the tower.

"Great." *Cheat. Liar.* "I can't wait to see him again."

Riverton didn't even bother to answer.

I won't let you end up with everything you want. I swear.

Dyre sent out an order for several bluecoats to join him, a pack to hunt Gen'ral. She would lead them like a hunting hound.

Once the bluecoats arrived, Dyre brought them all down the back stairway to the Project's small rear entrance, Riverton still gripping Lyla's arm tightly.

At the Project's back door, they stopped and listened. Through the woods, they could hear shots echoing like thunderclaps. Only outside, though; Lyla didn't hear any hint that the Red Fist soldiers had come up through the cellar yet. Also, now bluecoats were ready and waiting at the top of the cellar steps. The Red Fist soldiers would have to fight to take over the Protean. Once they saw that, they'd suspect there was a traitor. Her. Or possibly Jit. But more likely her. Even if she didn't help catch Gen'ral today, her tour would be done. If she failed, her tour failed.

Dyre kept on listening at the door as if something had caught his attention. Lyla tugged her arm away from Riverton. He glanced at her, and she pretended not to notice. Still, Dyre listened and waited.

Open the door. Let's go, let's go.

And then he opened it. Outside — smoke, shouting, shots. Nearby, three Red Fists lay face-down in the snow, their hands cuffed behind their backs. A guard in black stood over them, his rifle aimed at their heads.

Far off, toward the front of the Project, bluecoats stood on a platform so they could shoot down over the fence. A smoking chunk of metal came sailing up over the fence and hit one of the bluecoats. He collapsed on the platform, shrieking.

The crack of gunshots. Screams. Drifting smoke, acrid and thick.

Riverton grabbed Lyla again, his fingers digging into her arm. "Come on."

"I am," she said, but he still held on like he didn't mean to let go of her.

They slipped through the back gate, up a winding route into the woods, to avoid the battle and to try to stay out of the sightline of the cave where Gen'ral was overseeing it all. Or where he said he'd oversee it all. What if they got to the cave and it was empty?

Gen'ral would be there. He had to be there.

They swerved into a long stand of trees so they'd be difficult to see. Dyre sent a bluecoat ahead of them to scout for packs of prowling Red Fists, and he sent another one to scout behind them.

Battle sounds echoed strangely on the hillside: gunshots, shouts, screams. A huge, hollow boom. They all flinched.

Lyla looked back—only trees. "Do you think that was the actual Project or something?"

"No," Riverton said, just as a couple of other bluecoats also said, "No."

They sounded certain. Because something had already happened to the Project, but Riverton had refused to tell her what. *Liar. Cheat.*

"I bet they've broken the fence," Riverton said, yanking Lyla forward toward Dyre. As if she were actually a hound and he was her master.

She wished she were a hound. She'd bite his hand.

"Sir?" Riverton said.

Speaking fast, Dyre told them that half of their pack would create a diversion on the hillside. The other half would follow Northstrom to the cave. "This is the right direction, Northstrom?" he asked her. He sounded grim, as if he doubted her.

She nodded.

"It'll be all right," Riverton murmured to her. He gave her arm a squeeze, which if they were friends would've been reassuring.

Dyre sent off the diversion. They waited.

Lyla kept imagining the cave, its small, dark entrance; the short, narrow passageway; the wide opening; a room of rock and shadow. And emptiness — it was empty. Gen'ral had escaped.

She shook her head.

"What?" whispered Riverton.

"Nothing."

Shouts on the hillside. Three long whistles.

"That's it," said Riverton as Dyre stood.

Lyla started off, and Riverton held on tight to her arm, which made running difficult. They went through the stand of pines, then through a fall of boulders, a narrow gap between two rocks. She could barely breathe.

The hillside echoed with gunshots, a larger bang. A woman shouted orders somewhere — to the side of them? Behind them?

They slipped out of the gap. Lyla gulped air. Riverton whispered, "You all right?"

She didn't bother to answer. She dropped to a crouch. Riverton dropped with her, still holding on.

Ahead, on a narrow ridge, stood the cave opening. There wasn't any light. No sign of anybody. She told them, "There it is."

A long silence. Riverton asked, "Are you sure?"

"Of course," she snapped. "This is where he said he'd be."

"Stay here," Dyre commanded her quietly. "If you need to move, get to another stand of trees. Once we see he's really here, you'll have earned those off." He gestured to the cuffs. Then he stared at her a moment, as if he were giving her a chance to confess that she'd accidentally or purposefully led them astray. That she was wrong.

She couldn't be.

Then he turned from her and said, "Let's go."

Drawing his pistol, he started away, and the other bluecoats followed. Except Riverton. He grinned at Lyla, that little-boy excitement, so eager to get what he wanted. Then he left.

This was her hunt. She wasn't going to sit around waiting.

What if Gen'ral isn't there?

He had to be there. But as she snuck after Riverton, hiding behind trees, she couldn't see any lights at the cave mouth. There was fighting somewhere on the hillside. She could hear the *crack, crack* of guns. The wind carried smoke.

Ahead of her, Dyre, Riverton, and the other bluecoats crept up to the cave. As they stood to the side of the opening, a ragged

Red Fist hurtled down from the hillside above. He struggled with them, a knot of lashing arms.

Then the bluecoats knocked him to the ground and held him there, cuffing him and covering his head with a bag. One guard hauled him up and away while the rest streamed into the cave.

Lyla was on her feet. She was running up the hillside to the cave mouth.

He's there. He has to be there.

At the cave mouth she stopped and dropped low, crawling awkwardly into the dark, narrow opening. A green-white light shone ahead. Voices shouted. She could make out only "Halt!" "Bolt!"

He's there.

She stopped at the end of the narrow passageway. In the lantern light she saw a jumble of men and shadows struggling. They punched and wrestled and grappled with guns. A few lay bleeding on the floor, so still. Knife had knocked a bluecoat down and was pummeling him. Dyre had a Red Fist pinned to the wall, his pistol aimed at the back of the guy's head. Dyre seemed to be whispering in the Red Fist soldier's ear. Jit stood at the side, shifting from one foot to the other, as if he didn't know what direction to head in; the bluecoats must not have found him at the Project and he must not have looked very long for Dyre, just returned to Gen'ral. Riverton was aiming his pistol at a Red Fist, whose hands were raised in the air, and Riverton shouted: "Where is he? I said, where is he?"

Lyla scanned the room a second time.

Gen'ral wasn't one of the fighting men. He wasn't near Knife, who began to stand, leaving the beaten bluecoat on the ground. He wasn't the Red Fist that Riverton had now shoved to his knees. He wasn't the Red Fist that Dyre held against the wall, a gun to the back of his head.

He wasn't here.

Lyla pushed her wrists and their cuffs against her belly so the metal bit into her skin. Her whole tour, the lies and the stealing, Nose's beating, Teacher Slate getting booted, Gill hating her—all of it was for nothing.

And how could she ever, ever tell Hope?

Dyre hit the Red Fist in the back of the head, and the man crumpled. "Where is he?" shouted Riverton to the Red Fist with his hands raised. Jit started toward Riverton, who didn't see him.

And then the bluecoats and Red Fists fighting toward the back of the cave suddenly dropped their hands, looking into the cave's shadows. They each took a step back, as though they had caught sight of something surprising.

Walking forward into the green-white light was Gen'ral. Beside him was a bulky Red Fist soldier Lyla didn't recognize. Some kind of machinery, metal tubes and wires, was strapped to his chest. He wore a crazed smile.

Knife grinned. Riverton called: "Captain!"

"Yeah, I see." Dyre aimed at Gen'ral. "Halt. Or I'll shoot."

Gen'ral pointed to the bulky Red Fist. "He's got enough burners strapped to his chest that if he lights them, we'll all explode. And if you shoot him, that'll explode the burners too."

He's here.

Dyre didn't lower his pistol, but he couldn't shoot.

Gen'ral and the Red Fist soldier began walking in Lyla's direction, though they couldn't possibly see her; they meant to walk straight out of the cave. Knife swerved to join them. Dyre kept aiming at Gen'ral, tracing his path.

He's going to get away.

Lyla stood and walked forward, out of the shadows, into the lantern glow.

Gen'ral stopped at the sight of her, cocking his head so the wide brim of his hat tilted. The Red Fist soldier beside him halted, still grinning. All the rest, all of them, were looking at her, startled—Dyre, Riverton, the few other bluecoats and Red Fist soldiers, Knife, Jit.

"See?" yelled Jit, pointing at Lyla. "I told you she wasn't leading them to the ravine."

Don't just stand there, Riverton. Grab the crazy.

Riverton seemed to realize this was his chance, and he started quietly forward.

"Northstrom, don't be an idiot! Out!" shouted Dyre. Because he was truly worried? No, because he wanted everybody to keep focusing on her, not on Riverton. "I told you to stay outside."

"Traitor," Jit snarled, launching toward her.

She said, "You don't know a thing about me."

Gen'ral caught sight of Riverton and pulled the crazed Red Fist with the burners close. "Stop," he commanded Riverton.

As Jit reached Lyla, she raised her hands to fight him off. He caught ahold of the chain that linked the cuffs on her wrists, and he dragged her toward him, to the side of the cave. She could hear the others fighting too, and they sounded far, far off. She tried to wrench away from Jit and couldn't.

"Traitor," Jit snarled again, shoving her into the wall. Pain ricocheted through her back. "Monster will hate you."

"He already does!"

"I'll bet he does."

She kicked out at Jit.

"Quit," he commanded. "Or I'll hurt you worse."

No.

Jit's fist slammed into her belly. His fingers dug into her arm, gouging her.

No.

She shouted, "No!"

She drew her knee up between his legs as hard as she could. He shrieked and crumpled against her, his stinking breath moist on her neck.

He was heavy, like that guard had been, crushing the air out of her. She shoved him away, and he fell to the ground.

She was suddenly so light. Like feathers.

She looked around the cave. Riverton was pinning Knife, who spat in his face. The other bluecoats were still fighting Red Fist soldiers. She didn't see Gen'ral or the crazed Red Fist with the burners, or Dyre. Not anywhere in the cave.

Still, Riverton spotted her and gave her a wide boyish grin, as if everything in the world had shifted from wrong to right. Gen'ral must be caught.

For a moment, she felt the world *had* shifted from wrong to right. She felt like she did after a sip of lager: bubbles popping on her tongue.

A couple of bluecoats grabbed Jit and Knife; they cuffed Jit and he spat at Lyla; the bluecoats dragged him away. The rest of the fighting ended quickly, with the bluecoats beating the Red Fists.

Riverton, bleeding a bit from a cut over his eye, limped over to her.

"Where's Gen'ral?" she asked.

"He and the one with the burners strapped to him left the cave. Captain Dyre went after him. The others on the hillside, the diversion, are supposed to circle back. Dyre and them'll grab him." He sounded mostly certain, a touch worried.

"Oh." Her bubbly glow dimmed.

She let Riverton unlock the cuffs at her wrists. He turned over the right one, so they could both see the two blue lines. Her marks.

He ran a finger gently over them, and the feeling of the world shifting, the glow, winked entirely out. "You did your part. I can scrape you clean. Dyre will agree to it. There'll be a scar," he said apologetically. "But that'll be easy to hide."

Lyla drew her wrist away from him.

"You don't seem happy."

"Just kind of . . . shocked. Gen'ral's not caught yet. Plus there's still the Project. Whatever's wrong there."

"Captain Dyre will catch him," said Riverton, smiling. "The Project's not your problem to worry over."

"I need some fresh air."

"I'll be right out."

She made her way outside the cave, into the cold. Snow was drifting from the sky in large flakes.

The hillside was quiet, as though most of the fighting was done. Dyre most likely had stopped Gen'ral. Even if the Red Fist soldiers had grabbed the Project, they wouldn't hold it long without Gen'ral. And whatever had broken at the Project wasn't her problem.

Ahead was the path home. Next to it was the path to the Project.

She started for the path to the Project.

A TRUE ACCOUNT
BY LADY CAPTAIN

WITH PICTURES BY

PIRATE JACKMAN

Of course, I'm not really Lady Captain, but I can't give you my name. What I can say is that I'm Marked, and for a while now I've been serving a tour for the bluecoats so I can get scraped clean. This, what you're going to read, is what I saw, and telling you about it will ruin my tour with the bluecoats. Think on that, if you don't believe what you read here. I'm wrecking my chance to get scraped clean, to maybe go to a university. But I'm telling you what I saw anyway.

I knew the inventors and all were lying about the Project. The reports said Red Fist had attacked the Project but Red Fist was in its lair when the alarm screamed—I knew because I was in the lair, too. Red Fist didn't attack the Project. Because of my tour, I had learned a secret way in, so I went to find what actually happened. What really was wrong.

They brought that guy back in. Or maybe it wasn't him but was a bunch of other guys.

I swear, this is the absolute truth.

—CHAPTER TWENTY-EIGHT—

LYLA sat in a windowless stone cell, at a rickety table, staring at the zine Gill had made from words she'd written—the account of what she had seen a few nights ago, after she left Riverton and snuck back into the Project. Shrouded bodies. A gaping hole.

Apparently Gill had read the note she had stuck to the stairway door of his building. And though he hated her, he had actually gone to the message rock as she'd asked him to, and he had found her true account there. Words and words and words that he'd turned into pictures and titled *The Absolute Truth*. Preacher or someone must have a machine Gill had used to make a bunch of copies really quickly. Then he had handed *The Absolute Truth* around quite a lot in only a couple of days, despite the curfew, enough so the bluecoats had found a copy. The other morning, before she'd been hauled in, she'd seen this family of barons standing outside the Project fence, demanding to be let in. Their son, she'd heard them say, was an inventor in the Project, and they hadn't heard from him. Maybe they'd seen *The Absolute Truth*, and it had made them worry?

Gill had done what she had asked. He could've just ignored her but he hadn't. Because he forgave her?

There was no way to know now, maybe not ever. Riverton wanted her to rot behind bars; this was one of the few things he'd said to her when he came to the farm to haul her off to prison. He'd said that because she'd been working for the bluecoats, she wouldn't have a regular tribunal; she'd have a tribunal of bluecoats who would sentence her. As soon as he had seen *The Absolute Truth,* he had known she had helped make it. Who else, apart from guards and bluecoats, had entered the Project? Jit, but he was already in prison. Riverton hadn't asked who had helped her. He hadn't seemed to care. He had cuffed her wrists and pulled a bag over her head, as Ma and Da had asked frantic questions that another bluecoat had answered. Out in the cold, Riverton had dragged her down the steps so fast, she hadn't been able to ask what he thought of the truth, now that he'd seen it. She hadn't been able to tell him she knew he was a cheat. She hadn't even asked if he and Dyre had caught Gen'ral. He was so furious, she had feared he would throw her down and beat her.

When he put her in the cell, he'd also tossed in the copy of *The Absolute Truth* that he'd been carrying. She had been locked in this cell for more than a day, but not a lot more. She had sat at this table, she had slept on a pallet in the corner, and she had pissed in a bucket, so the room stank. Sometimes the walls had closed in, and she had counted to keep her breathing slow. In, two, three. Out, two, three.

She stared down at her right wrist. Two blue marks—stupidity and courage. Fear and anger. Secrets that were no longer secrets.

Then she opened *The Absolute Truth* again. It was . . . startling, like a bird suddenly flying right before your face, wings beating fast. Startling and frightening and beautiful.

———

Finally, finally, the door to the cell opened, and Riverton walked in. His face was blank.

Behind him walked Ma, who stared at Lyla like she was an accident, a boat sinking through the ice. And then, back from the inventor's mansion—Hope.

Hope was cleaner. Her clothes, her hair. Her face and lips seemed softer, no sign of the roughness caused by the wind and cold. As she sat in the chair opposite Lyla, a scent of roses drifted from her. As if she weren't a digger's kid at all, but instead a baron's kid who had needed the grime scrubbed off to uncover the true Hope.

"Lyla?" Hope asked, a little uncertain, as though Lyla were the one who looked different, instead of her.

"Yeah," said Lyla. She wanted to take Hope's hand, but it was so clean, the nails so even and rounded.

"Mistress Regin arranged for us to visit." Hope said.

Riverton crossed his arms, staring over of their heads. Lyla bet he hadn't wanted to allow the visit. He wanted to shut her into a tiny cell and forget she existed. Like he wanted to shut Gill away, so Riverton could forget he had ever cheated.

"Where's Da?" Lyla asked.

"He went to the northernmost mines." Ma wheezed. She shoved a folded paper bag across the table. "Here's a letter for you from him."

Lyla nodded. She turned the letter over, but she didn't unfold it.

"Officer Riverton told us you'd earned your marks off." Ma's voice cracked. "He told us he was going to scrape you clean."

Lyla nodded. "He was," she admitted.

Hope looked from Lyla to Riverton, her lovely face troubled. "What happened?"

"She chose Red Fist," he said.

Lyla said, "I haven't."

"You're the one who sent her off to run with them," Ma burst out, turning to Riverton. Hope put a hand on Ma's arm, but Ma said, "You should've known she was too young."

"He's not even that much older than me," Lyla said to Ma. "And I'm old enough to know what's right and what's wrong."

Riverton said distinctly, "You all agreed to it. But then she let Red Fist mess with her head."

Lyla pointed at *The Absolute Truth*. "This has nothing to do with Red Fist. You really think people shouldn't know about the Project?"

"Lyla, stop," Hope pleaded.

"They're already going to shut me away forever." Lyla laughed. All her life, she'd always had to watch what she said, to earn a job at the Beacon, to get into the Bright, to impress Riverton.

It was like she had always worn a collar squeezing against her throat. But now that she was shut away, she could say whatever she wanted—the collar was gone. "If you weren't troubled about the Project," she said to Riverton, "why were you wearing a mask and goggles there? You must've been worried about getting sick."

He pressed his lips together, a thin line, and he shook his head.

"And the roof is broken. Don't you think that might mean something's leaking out into the air?"

"The masks are a precaution," he said in a low voice, speaking like he thought she was an idiot. "The air is fine. Inside the Project, and outside. All you're doing is spreading panic, which the Project inventors were trying to avoid. That's why they were taking care of everything before they gave an official announcement."

"The air is fine? Guys were coughing up bloody snot. Like they had some terrible Mine Cough. The inventors are making it seem like the Project was ruined by a Red Fist attack, but that's not what ruined the Project. The inventors are liars. And there're people dying. Did you know that? Did you know they're tossing bodies into that hole at the Project?"

As Ma said, "Lyla, that's enough," her voice high, Riverton suddenly strode to the table, leaned on it, and thrust his face close to Lyla's.

His mouth was lopsided, an uneven sneer. "The guys near the hole got sick, yeah, but just those ones. And nobody's tossing bodies into the hole."

"I saw it," she insisted. "They are. Tossing them down."

"Why do you keep saying that?" asked Ma.

"She's saying it for Red Fist," said Riverton. "To stir up people in the town, so they'll agitate and distract the peace officers. Then Red Fist can try to attack again."

"I don't want Red Fist to attack," Lyla insisted.

"Lyla," Ma said, her voice rising.

Lyla ignored Ma. "Why would I help them?" she asked Riverton. "I led you to Gen'ral."

"But he got away. You didn't tell us about his bodyguard, with all the burners strapped to his body. He got away."

"I didn't know about the burners. I can't believe you and Dyre let Gen'ral escape! Do you know what he's done?"

"We didn't *let* him escape." Riverton slammed his palm against the table. "He escaped because you've been playing both sides."

"I haven't."

His hand raised, palm open. Hope cried, "Officer Riverton!" which made his raised hand stop. It trembled a little, as if his muscles, about to strike and holding back from striking, were at war.

His face was so close to Lyla's, like he was about to kiss her. Except that his mismatched eyes were wounded and furious, like the eyes of a hurt animal.

Lyla asked, "You're going to hit me because I won't lie? Or *cheat.*"

He jerked back, his hand dropping. "What?"

"Cheat, I said. I won't cheat to get what I want. Not like some people I've heard about."

Riverton's face was stricken. His mouth opened and closed, as if he were struggling to find what to say.

"Slag off, Northstrom." He spun away from her. He strode to the door, went through it, and slammed it shut behind him.

Ma was staring at Lyla like she was a stranger. "Why were you taunting him?"

"I wasn't. I was just . . . He knows what I meant."

"Your da and I never should have agreed to let you work with him," Ma cried. "Look how you ended up."

"I'm all right," Lyla tried to reassure her. "I'm fine."

Hope touched Ma's arm. "I'll talk to Mistress Regin. She can find out what we can do to try and get Lyla out."

Ma nodded a tiny bit, but then she sniffed and wiped her nose with the back of her hand. "I can't—" She turned to the door and pounded on it.

"Ma—" Lyla called, but what could she say? She couldn't untell what she'd told or undo what she'd done.

A bluecoat opened the door. Hugging herself, Ma left. Though the bluecoat kept holding the door open, Ma didn't return.

Hope said to the bluecoat quietly, "I'll stay a little longer."

He frowned, but nodded and shut the door to the cell, leaving them alone.

Hope folded her hands, and she sat very upright, as if her skin were made of some polished smooth substance. Lyla said, "Sorry. Sorry Ma's so upset."

"I'll go after her. We have to leave soon anyway. They don't really want us here. They let us in because of Mistress Regin, because she insisted."

"She did?"

"She hires a lot of Marked. She says people deserve second chances. She doesn't like the Marks Law, or a bunch of the safety laws. Too many people get stuck for life without any opportunities, she says. There are actually barons trying to change the safety laws. She's one of them."

Lyla had a hard time believing that if some barons truly wanted laws changed, they couldn't get the town councilor to change them. "Sounds like you and she talked a lot."

Hope smiled. "Yeah. She doesn't talk to you like you're a digger or a server. She talks like you're anyone, a baron's kid or something. And she's so generous. While I was there, I had a room to stay in, with a tub that had hot and cold running water. She lives on her own in this huge old house, with this huge workshop. She invents flying machines—all these amazing roof-leapers. Except she likes to leap mountain peaks instead of roofs. Teacher Slate was there while I was, when we all had to stay in after the alarms. I think she and he used to be together, or maybe they wanted to be and weren't? I don't know. They aren't together now, but they so obviously like each other." Hope's smile faded away. "I wanted to see if you would work for her, just give up the tour. But then I found out you were in here. Officer Riverton wouldn't even speak to Ma and me at first. Mistress Regin had to talk to Captain Dyre. You're in terrible trouble."

"I know."

"Do you? Terrible, terrible trouble. That zine—the peace officers have declared it a 'threat to public safety.' They say it 'provokes agitators.' A bunch of copies are being passed all around. Diggers and squatties, this crowd, is filling Main Street. They're holding up signs that say things like 'What's down the hole?' and 'Who did the hole swallow?'

"And people are also worried about breathing, like you were talking about—what might be in the air. They're demanding the town councilor give everybody soothers—the whole town. Ma seemed to be getting better until the Project broke, and now she's been wheezy again. I mean, she's all right. Not truly sick, only wheezy. Those diggers on the street have signs about soothers, too. 'What's in the air? Soothers—now!' It's crazed. You can barely walk anywhere. The school's still closed, and so are lots of other places."

"Really?" Lyla touched *The Absolute Truth* with the tips of her fingers. "That's kind of great."

"You don't understand. There are officers with rifles and helmets. All kinds of scuffles, and people shouting. You walk down the street feeling like you might get shoved to the ground at any moment. The town councilor announced that peace officers from the capital are coming to quiet the town."

"Would you rather people didn't know what really happened?"

"No," Hope said. "But a lot of people could get hurt, and you're shut in here. Ma and Da are so upset."

Lyla turned over Da's letter again. She noticed he hadn't written "Little Girl" on it. Instead he'd written "Lyla." She pulled her hand away. "I didn't want to upset them."

Hope leaned toward her. "Lyla, is all this actually what *you* want? Truly? Because those pictures in that zine—I know those are Gillis's. You don't have to help him out of trouble."

"I'm not—"

"You don't have to protect him, just because we were friends when we were little."

"The hole, the bodies, are what *I* saw. I saw them," Lyla declared. "Gill wasn't even there. And the zine was my idea."

Hope drew upright again. Lyla stared down at the table between them. It suddenly seemed miles and miles wide. Too wide to ever cross.

She and Hope would rush in entirely different directions, like leaves swept along by different currents of a river. Spinning so far apart, they would soon lose sight of each other.

"You'll come visit?" Lyla asked suddenly. She forced a smile. "Even if I'm locked in here until I'm an old lady?"

"You won't be here that long," Hope insisted. Then she smiled a little, her chin quivering. "Of course I'll visit. Goose." She reached one hand across the wide, wide miles and took Lyla's hand. They held on tight.

—

Lyla woke. Concrete walls on all sides, concrete ceiling near.

She listened to the sound of her own breaths, the slow deep rise and slow deep fall, rise, fall, rise. Though the cell wasn't much wider than the pallet that was her bed, she had learned to chase her night terrors away on her own.

She sat up, pulling her thin blanket around her. Above was a barred window, and through it, she could see the sky turn from black to pearly blue: dawn. The bluecoat tribunal had sentenced her to ten years in prison, though Captain Dyre had requested longer for her "traitorous agitation." He'd been mad when they read the sentence; he'd actually argued with the panel of bluecoats, while Ma and Hope cried. Then Captain Dyre had marked her a third time and put her in a cell. She hadn't seen him since. Hope, with help from Mistress Regin, was trying to get her a new tribunal with a panel of barons. Mistress Regin thought that kind of tribunal would let her out sooner because Lyla was a kid— and because she'd uncovered what the broadsheets now called a "cover-up" and a "tragedy" at the Project. Maybe a new tribunal would let Lyla out, but maybe not. She tried not to wish she were outside the cell, because the days went better if she didn't wonder every moment if she could leave soon. She was here, and dawn was beautiful, even when seen through bars.

Hope visited every few days, and told her what was going on outside the bars. The town councilor had sent around a statement about the accident at the Project. It said that this winter, as part of a competition among inventors across Highland, the inventors in Hill's Ridge had invented alchemyk equations to fix a very large amount of Protean in a solid state, and they had worked to invent small, cheap chargers they could attach to the Protean and charge with power. Each household, they thought, could own several chargers, and these chargers would power things like lights and pumps, so people wouldn't need steamers and smokers. When the chargers lost charge, people could bring them back to the Project to be recharged, for a fee. But the inventors had messed up. The large amount of Protean had apparently stayed so hot that its center had actually shifted back and forth between solid and liquid, which had made the Protean hotter, which had made more of it shift back and forth between solid and liquid, which had made it even hotter. The inventors couldn't cool it, and the Protean eventually melted through several hundred feet of rock, pooling at the bottom of a hole, part liquid, part solid. A molten mess. The town councilor claimed that it wasn't dangerous, and that bluecoats had capped the hole as an "extra precaution." He claimed that no bodies had been tossed down the hole. Also, that nothing had risen from the Project into the air, nothing was causing breathing problems or coughing like Mine Cough. Anyone who said it was was passing rumors sent around by Red Fist.

Hope had said Mistress Regin didn't agree with the town councilor about the air, and then Hope had offered Lyla soothers from Mistress Regin, which had helped Lyla's breathing. Mistress Regin, in fact, and a number of other inventors were fighting with the town councilor because, in Hope's words, he was a liar and a bully. They were demanding that the prime councilor come from the capital city to investigate the cover-up, though he hadn't said he would. Also, Marked in the street kept marching and holding up signs, and others had joined them, even some barons. They were demanding an end to safety laws. The marchers kept getting dragged into the prison, Hope said. But the bluecoats had to let a lot of them out of prison, because there weren't enough cells to keep them in. Hope talked of better things too, of food and music and Mistress Regin's piano. She played every day for at least an hour and, Hope confessed, was writing her own song. "I'll play it for you," she said, "when you're free."

Ma's visits were more difficult than Hope's, though Ma wasn't so sick anymore. Mistress Regin's soothers had helped her get better, as had staying out of the mines. But Ma didn't say much, just studied Lyla as if she were a locked door that shouldn't be locked or a tree that had mysteriously grown all wrong. As if Ma wondered if there was a way to fix her. Lyla wanted to tell Ma, *I don't need fixing.*

Da hadn't sent any more letters. The one that he had left for her didn't say much of anything — that he was leaving, that he'd be back in the spring. It didn't say "love" at the end, only "Da." Like they barely knew each other. Lyla thought of things she might tell him when she saw him again, but everything she came up with seemed wrong. Hope said that he was just really sad and mad, but that he'd calm down. Lyla wanted Hope to be right.

Lyla never saw any other prisoners, though she assumed Jit was locked away close by. Hope had told her Gen'ral was still free, and no one knew where he was. Red Fist hadn't attacked anyone or anything much since the night the Red Fist soldiers had tried and failed to take over the Project. So maybe Gen'ral and his soldiers had bolted off. Or maybe Preacher and the Red Fists in the workshop had driven them off. Junot Riverton had requested, and had received, a transfer to one of the cities downriver. He hadn't come to the cell to see Lyla before he left. She supposed he was trying to forget her like he was trying to forget Gill. Lyla once asked Hope if she had seen Gill at all. "Quit worrying about Gillis," Hope had said sharply. "He always lands on his feet."

On her pallet, Lyla shifted her head against the stone wall. The same thoughts, around and around. Shut in a tiny cell, you don't make a lot of new memories, so you just keep seeing the old ones over and over.

She thought of what she might write, when someday she left the cell and had paper and ink. Things about Hill's Ridge, Red Fist, bluecoats, barons, and Marked. True things that would keep getting her into trouble. She smiled.

And she thought of the dreams she had most nights of Gill. Of going with Gill to the wood that grew up through cracks in the old warehouse floor. Spinner was in the dreams sometimes, and Zeb. They drank lager and danced, whirling and laughing. In other dreams, she was alone in the wood with Gill. They shouted at each other. They kissed, their hands inside each other's clothes. They lay on the ground together, and they looked up at the sky and the stars as night turned from black to indigo to pearly blue: dawn.

AFTER

BY LYLA & GILL

G.W. & L.N.

His hand rose and his fingers sketched pointed noses and long, streaming tails.

Where are the otters?

Lynx, half-hidden, running among the treetops.

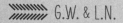 G.W. & L.N.

Heron, feathers
fanned, taking wing.

G.W. & L.N.

ACKNOWLEDGMENTS

MANY thanks to Cerridwyn, Magdalene, and Colin for their endless patience and their fierce support. To my colleagues and students at Pacem School and the Solstice MFA in Creative Writing Program—thank you for the inspiration, as well as the many laughs. Thank you to Nancy Gallt for her perseverance during this process. Thank you to Jennifer Greene for the insight, for the hours of hard work, and for the risk-taking. Thank you to Kerry Martin and to Sally Cantirino for their vision. To Leda Schubert and Tod Olson: The phone calls and the dinners are more important to me than I can possibly express here. Perhaps I could have completed this project without them, but I doubt it. And to Tod, who has read every page in this story and the hundreds of pages that no longer are—thank you for staying on the ship even during my worst Ahab moments.